A SHORT FILM ABOUT DISAPPOINTMENT

PENGUIN PRESS | NEW YORK | 2018

A SHORT FILM ABOUT DISAPPOINTMENT

JOSHUA MATTSON

PENGUIN PRESS
An imprint of Penguin Random House LLC
375 Hudson Street
New York, New York 10014
penguin.com

LIBRARY OF CONGRESS CATALOGING-IN-PUBLICATION DATA
Names: Mattson, Joshua, author.
Title: A Short Film About Disappointment / Joshua Mattson.
Description: New York: Penguin Press, 2018.
Identifiers: LCCN 2018006202 (print) | LCCN 2018012672 (ebook) |
ISBN 9780525522850 (ebook) | ISBN 9780525522843 (hardcover)
Subjects: LCSH: Film critics—Fiction. | BISAC: FICTION / Literary. | FICTION / Satire.
Classification: LCC PS3613.A8665 (ebook) | LCC PS3613.A8665 S56 2018 (print) |
DDC 813/.6—dc23
LC record available at https://lccn.loc.gov/2018006202

Printed in the United States of America
1   3   5   7   9   10   8   6   4   2

Designed by Gretchen Achilles

FILMS CONSIDERED FOR

THE CENTRAL HUB SLAW

1.

HAVING, NOT HAVING, BEING, NOT BEING

DIR. HAMA NADAKIRTI

111 MINUTES

I saw *Having, Not Having, Being, Not Being* because I happened to duck into the Global, a theater I dislike, while running from a man trying to break my nose.

The operators of the Global are self-congratulatory and condescending, as if showing foreign films in a prosperous native neighborhood is an act of mercy rather than a profitable indulgence. The programmer is a philistine who prefers to screen sententious documentaries, foreign splatter films, and slow-pitch comedies with the invariable moral that one ought to be nice to one's parents before they die, if just once. Passing the box office, one sees patrons as resigned to their duty as plumbers.

Not to mention that they charge twenty-three dollars a ticket, and if they get your Pinger ID, they will send you a message every hour until your death, demanding more money so they can continue their mission. The fund-raising is interminable. The pledge drive goes on five months. The director gets paid as much as twelve rail workers, has a brownstone in the Safe Zone, a daughter at private kindergarten.

Patrons of the Global see buying a ticket as an expression of their socioeconomic position, an endorsement of their taste, a buttressing of their personality, and in many respects I found them more loathsome than the man who had been trying to break my nose with his fist, because there was not much un-earned self-regard in his intentions, at least toward my nose.

That said, I did not want my nose broken, so I ran inside.

By the time the man, Rolf Millings, whom I'd had an ex-change of views with at a party a few weeks previously, had thought to look in the Global for me, I had placed myself in a crouch in Row K, so I could see who was walking in when a crack of light dissipated the spell of the cinema.

Having, Not Having, Being, Not Being does not shy from pre-fabricated set pieces lifted from other films, including the sullen newcomer who gains respect for the institution, the elderly monk with a teenage passion for rock and roll, merriment in silence, raking, rough-hewn bowls, the beauty of rocks, the pleasures of submission. There is nothing so different as to be interesting and there is nothing so familiar as to be comforting. Because we spend so much of our lives in institutions, I have never under-stood why anyone would want to spend their leisure time watch-ing the operations of an institution.

The tanned gentleman shoving through the doors appeared to be Millings. I couldn't guarantee that I wasn't the cause of his anger. From my vantage between the seats I watched him scan the audience, turn, walk out. He cut quite the figure in his suit, unperturbed by the large stains on his shirtfront, from the packet of rancid herring I had thrown on him, while he sat in a nearby plaza, enjoying the afternoon, twenty minutes before.

2.

LORD TAKO

DIR. ROGER WARAS

88 MINUTES

Playing tomorrow at the Conspicuous on two screens. See it in Theater Four. Six has bad seats.

O'Rourke, a marine wrestler in the Pacific Northwest, is undefeated until an octopus of public record, Lord Tako, plucks out his left eye and pops it in his beak. As the octopus swims away, O'Rourke tears off one of Lord Tako's tentacles. O'Rourke swears revenge. Chastened by fate, O'Rourke begins to drink to excess at the wrestlers' bar, whose logo is an octopus with a mug of beer in each tentacle.

O'Rourke's little brother, Baby, wants to wrestle. Lord Tako takes all comers. Baby's corpse washes up onshore. O'Rourke renews his vows of revenge. A training montage.

Piggy Wilson, a mentor figure, thunders from the underbrush of exposition to counsel O'Rourke. Another satisfying montage. Piggy, who has not kept in shape since his halcyon grappling days, is slain by Lord Tako. The shot of Piggy's severed head surfacing is in bad taste, which is probably why this superlative film is not shown in repertory. Osvald-in-me, the philistine, cheered when it breached. An ongoing discussion between us was never resolved concerning whether Lord Tako twisted or pulled it off.

The scene where O'Rourke comes out of the surf holding Lord Tako, who has sucked out O'Rourke's other eye in his throes, has all the pathos and beauty of a Nakamura masterpiece. I have never seen or heard it mentioned. Which begs the question: What beauty has disappeared through the ignorance of its stewards?

3.

WEREGILD

DIR. OLAF JOSEPHSSON

100 MINUTES

On the day I thought of my film, I woke feeling ill. My *Slaw* review was due at five-thirty. *Weregild* screened at two. The Baxter Cinema calls this the hooky showing, but the senile matrons, narcotics-addled public servants, and preachers of Armageddon who pack the theater have nothing to skip out on. I prefer the sedentary regulars of the Conspicuous, a theater of quality.

In my position as film critic for the *Central Hub Slaw*, the greatest content aggregator in this city, I am often compelled to review mounds of gaudy cardboard tugged with string masquerading as films. I expected today would be no different. Watch, leave, fume, pan.

Out of my apartment, shivering, sweating. The mild day affronted my sense of infirmity. VR joggers, yoga nuts, and spandexed men on ancient steel bikes filled the streets. It is not enough for the world to be the circus, dump, sweatshop, brothel, and restaurant for the urban professional, it has to be their gymnasium as well.

The Baxter was hot. An usher apologized. The air-conditioning was off because they overdrew their power budget. To fortify myself I had bought a bottle of cough syrup from the pharmacy kiosk on the way. A nimbus of insulin needles and nasal relaxers cordoned it off from the sidewalk.

Many people entered the theater, found it to be the same temperature as outside, and left. The movie flickered by. Maybe I would expire of the flu. I imagined the mourners at my funeral. Held Saturday night, for maximum inconvenience. Closed casket. An organ to oppress the scant bereaved.

Weregild takes place in a vague tribal past, when fur-clad illiterates slaughtered their neighbors over portents and boredom. The chief, Orectirix, kidnaps Geneov, the wife of Seisyll. Speeches are made, threats delivered. *Weregild* is a lie. The tribe's teeth are better than ours. Do they have dental care in the Black Forest? On a diet of spelt, those biceps? That's not possible. The tribe would have to loot protein powders from the warehouses they plunder. *Weregild* could have been funded by the Agriculture Authority. See how we lived before corn, and tremble. A man kills another man, and puts on his crude bronze crown. The end.

Leaving the theater, my illness was taking the initiative. When I reached for my rail pass, I found that it lay in a marsh of pocket sweat. The sidewalk yawed outside my stop. I seemed to be having hallucinations. I was convinced pedestrians would dine on my liver if I lowered my guard. Back to Miniature Aleppo, my block. My bed, sagging, nonjudgmental. The shadows of oak limbs scraped the ceiling. Fever made fondue of color, sound, language.

Here comes my idea. I must make a film.

Western Europe, the Renaissance. I hate period pieces. Mine will be a period whole.

My film will unfurl during a time when artists believed they were laboring in their god's service. Our greatest artists were simpletons and cretins. Their talent was bent to reinforce the validity of a fable. Notions of reality in the Renaissance, at least as far as its art was concerned, were fixed. A god there, man here, plentiful devils to blame. But it seemed real, and seeming is like being, to our wretched species.

Nothing's real. Everything is printed: a copy of what came before. Load schematics into the fabricator. Human history is squirted, at will, from a reticulating nozzle. Press a button, and out rolls a Venus of Willendorf, a suitable doorstop. Turn the dial, and print a Calder for hanging your laundry. Dry your dishes with a Bayeux Tapestry.

I shall call my film *Altarpiece*.

A painter, Bellono, paints a triptych of Duke Giovanni, Duchess Andrea, and the duke's brother, Baronet Enrico. It will hang adjacent to the altar in the ducal chapel.

How will Bellono render Giovanni, Andrea, and Enrico? In shocking, lecherous color.

I must make this film. My sense of beauty demands it. Pretending to care about the trash of the past, reporting on miniature controversies, and inventing grudges against directors I am indifferent to has rotted my spirit.

Perhaps I feel competitive with my friend Osvald. He has been developing a treatment for a film about a sculptor who works on a massive scale. Alison, mayor of the Eastern Hub, commissions Billy Vang, of the Suppressionist school, to print a monumental piece about civic responsibility. Billy has other plans for the installation.

Problems arise when Billy begins to suspect that he himself is printed. Everything in his apartment is carbon, so is he. It isn't all that out there to suppose he is a programmed object, the science project of a fumbling far-off intelligence, swabbed on the petri dish of the planet to produce, after eons, himself.

How can he protest the culture of replication, if he is a copy himself?

That dilemma is, to Osvald, profound. He calls his film *A Replicate*. He tried to cast me as Billy to bully me around his kitschy sets. Osvald's use of the periscope is not as profound as he thinks.

No, the film I have in mind is quite different from Osvald's.

4.

THE NATHAN ROAD DEVILS

DIR. LI FANG

101 MINUTES

The Month of Broken Noses has returned to the Conspicuous, and although any of the kung fu conflagrations in the program are worth your time, *The Nathan Road Devils* is my preferred pageant of punishment.

Li Fang was the product of the pinchpenny Yiang Brothers' Celestial Blessings Studio, for whom he directed one hundred and eighteen features. Highlights include *The Deadly Beggar, House of Iron Pajamas, Shek O Enforcer, The Resplendent Torturer, The Resplendent Torturer Returns*, and *Fall of the Resplendent Torturer.*

His last film stars Billy Lau, the Resplendent Torturer himself, in his first role since his release from Stanley Prison, where he did seven years for stabbing a guy with a fork in a gambling den, and Tony Zeng. Zeng plays Detective Lu, about to lose his job because he's obese. After a pair of elderly stickup men escape him in a byzantine tracking shot through Jardine's Crescent, Lu is put on administrative leave until he can lose a third of his body weight.

Our detective spends his nights gorging on *siu mei* and lager at Joy Hing's Roasted Meat. He overhears Triad boss Big Squid, played by Lau, order his stooges to off a guy who stood his daughter up. One yes-man asks, Is that not excessive? Big Squid jams his porcine pinkies into said yes-man's ears. The resulting sound effect could have only sprung from the imagination of a very sick sound designer.

Lu foils the thugs, starting a slapstick feud that ravages noodle shops, pizza parlors, teahouses, and a respected gelato cart. Zeng, whose bulk contains such pathos even the jiggling of his chins moves us, dignifies, through his soulful expressions, a role built around classic fat-guy gags like the Wicker Chair, the Narrow Door to Heaven, and the Mississippi Marriage Proposal.

5.

CAMP CHOCOLATE

DIR. ALEJANDRA MARTILLO

76 MINUTES

Camp Chocolate, showing Wednesday afternoon at the Wicker Repertory. A malevolent force enters Miriam, the head counselor, convincing her to bludgeon the residents of Poison Oak Cabin with a vacuum cleaner. How do we know she isn't plumb crazy? When, on a hike, she stands in a circle of obsidian chunks, the viewer understands she has become deprived of her mental health through supernatural means.

Speaking of which. Osvald has possessed me. Maybe *possessed* is the wrong word. Possession implies evil, an agenda. My friend has *occupied* me. Yes. My body is a land in which the trains run on time, the factories are producing, but the people are tired, their clothes frayed. There is no butter in the restaurants, and children watch what they say in public. Over every table a strange portrait.

After the screening, I went to my appointment with Dr. Lisa. She prodded my cheek. A ring in her left nostril. Doctors tend to indulge themselves with an eccentricity. A wacky tie, a morphine addiction. She smells of vetiver and mouthwash. Dr. Lisa was eating jade noodles when she examined me. Maybe she would like someone to eat with, and this is why she dines in the company of her patients. I imagine asking the same three questions must be tiring. What hurts? How long has it hurt? How bad does it hurt?

She said, This was my nurse's. He should not have left it lying around. Do you want a bite?

I said, No. I had a sandwich on the way over.

She said, What kind?

I said, Well, it was more of a wrap.

I'm not sure why I lied twice. I hadn't had lunch. Sharing Dr. Lisa's germs did not bother me. On the contrary, in fact.

She took the chair next to mine.

She said, Why are you here?

I said, My face does not work, sometimes.

She said, When did this occur for the first time?

I said, I was daydreaming of digging a pit along the route of Osvald's commute. This predated his flight to another city with my wife. I diagrammed how this might be possible, how to finance it, manage the rental of equipment, the forging of permits.

She said, Who's Osvald?

I said, He's my best friend. I have not seen him in several years, because he stole my wife and moved to the Eastern Hub.

She said, He kidnapped your wife?

I said, Well, it was a mutual decision, between the two of them. I wasn't given the opportunity to weigh in.

She said, You were thinking of murdering this man and you experienced bilateral facial paralysis?

I said, It would be more in line with the spirit of my intentions to say I was thinking about the morality of putting him in a position to be murdered at a later date, if I deemed it just and convenient.

She said, Tell me more.

I said, When sketching an idea I had for a trebuchet that could be concealed outside his office, which would be fired when he stepped into the bucket, a tautness spread across half my face. My apartment lacks a mirror. I ran to the latrine of the charging station on the corner. I shoved past the people charging their Pingers and appliance batteries.

I said, In the toilet, I examined my face. My muscles were stuck on the right side. Blinking was not possible with my right eye. When I smiled, only the left half of my face lifted. The overall effect was ghastly. That word must have been invented for cases like my face. A corpse's face, exhumed for a sinister reason.

Dr. Lisa chewing but nodding to indicate the focus of her attention was on my problem.

I said, I shed a few tears in the locked toilet. Within an hour my facial muscles returned to my control. In the charging station I bought two Picnic Size Nougat Grenades, which I ate at the curb. After the condition recurred, my PocketMD insisted on a human doctor.

Dr. Lisa said, Explain when it happens.

I said, The symptoms begin when I ideate Osvald's elimination. The generic fantasy of Osvald dying allows me to retain control of my face. For instance, if I thought of him getting hit by a car, my face would remain under my control. When a specific detail vivifies the thought, say, the title of the pornographic film playing when the meteorite strikes, the sad history of the tutued circus bear devouring his leg, the exact geographical location of the quicksand he sank in, leaving behind, on the surface, one of those pith helmets I associate with missing orchid hunters, my face solidifies into the expression I had at the time. Midexpression, this is grotesque and frightening to those in the vicinity.

Dr. Lisa took this in.

I said, I think he has possessed me. Do you get a lot of possession cases?

She said, Possession is not a treatable medical condition. Why don't we try to find something within the area of my expertise?

Dr. Lisa ordered needles, medicine, machines, electromagnetism, physiotherapy. A technician explored my bowels. Electrodes, sessions in the nanobox. I was emphatic that there was to be no psychiatry. I filled out questionnaires on the frequency of my erections, the color of my sputum, the contents of my dreams.

At our next appointment, she diagnosed me. She is incorrect, but I prefer her wrongness to the rightness of others.

Dr. Lisa said, You have a conversion disorder.

She said, A disease of thought.

Tapping her temple, a dirty cuticle, a dimple.

She said, A disease of control.

Osvald first manifested with his ongoing attempt to pollute my lexicon. The miscegenation of our languages can be marked by the eruption of his adjectives. My column has become cluttered with his Latinate vocabulary, marred by his commas, undermined by the distraction of his erotic preoccupations, disturbed by the thuds of his clauses, lessened with his tone-deaf declarations, bungled articles, snubbed participles. My clean and curt sentences have thickened with the flab of his qualifiers.

But I got him back, oh, yes.

6.

THE TRIALS OF COUNT COZMA

DIR. GHEORGE NICOLESCU

89 MINUTES

Playing yesterday, today, and tomorrow at Cinema Acceptable, midnight, discounts for the costumed.

A highborn vampire can't feed. Serfs will not serve as fare for a gourmand. Cozma tries to lure diplomats, heldentenors, confectioners, and essayists to his estate. Each sends polite regrets. Cozmylvania is an idyll. Bees bumble over fields of smetterhoch, the air is fragrant with hare's blood.

He has a dysfunctional relationship with his assistant, Mihaela. When Mihaela suggests he listen to visitors instead of interrupting to brag of his collection of Sufi manuscripts before exsanguinating them, the count sulks, locks himself in his coffin. Mihaela finds a psychotherapist, Zigfried Yunt, who is willing to help. Cranky from low blood sugar, Count Cozma drains Dr. Yunt. Cheers in the theater.

Yunt was treating society wives with tincture of coca. Improvements were noticed. Color was returning to cheeks. A bit of aristocratic sport is okay, but Yunt was liked and respected. Rumors circulate, Cozma is not a count. Cozma flaps to the capital to bleed the gossips. Though Cozma cannot enter the homes of his victims without an invitation, the lords and ladies invite him in, because to decline would be bad manners.

Silas the Staker, the celebrated vampire hunter, is dispatched to dispatch Cozma.

For strategic reasons, his visit falls on the summer solstice, the day Mihaela has her annual bath. Her charms lull Silas the Staker. She wants to show him her dungeon. Why not, he has hours until sunset. Falling asleep on her pallet, he awakens in the dark.

Enter Cozma, preening. Silas the Staker is subjected to a monologue on the difficulty of keeping orchids at the forty-fifth parallel. Cozma expects his work will earn him the Iogu Science Prize.

Silas the Staker says, Monsters are not the obvious choice for prestigious awards.

The count, pausing to fix a stray hair and check the knot on his cravat, assures Silas the leap forward for horticulture will occlude his shortcomings in the eyes of the committee. Silas is reaching for his ankle-holstered crucifix when Cozma breakfasts.

Mihaela is cross. Drinking Silas the Staker's blood, when Mihaela had insisted the count abstain, shows insensitivity to her needs for communication, understanding, and friendship.

He says, Nuts.

Tired of giving ultimatums, Mihaela packs and leaves for the Forest of the Weeping Virgin, to work for the Gory Handmaiden.

The Trials of Count Cozma received attention upon release last year because nothing in the film is replicated from a matter printer. Not a single object was fished from the enormous database of proprietary objects that, once chosen from that familiar, frustrating menu and squirted into the additive manufacturing kiosk, constitutes nearly every object we use every day. Everything on the screen, bar the actors, is a prop from a dusty studio basement or a legitimate historical object. When working under such constraints, compromises in costuming have to be made. For example, Silas the Staker's cowboy hat and chaps are not traditional for the genre. For example, Count Cozma's cape is the same worn by the Bureaucrat in *Heroes Follow the Rules*. One works with what one can find.

7.

LOOSE LIPS

DIR. ROBERT Z. MICHAEL

74 MINUTES

In my friend Osvald's *A Replicate*, there is a scene where his up-pity sculptor, Billy Vang, stands on the smoldering car in the guest neighborhood to invite the refugees, who have fled Modest Britain, to demand the right to enter the Zone.

Billy's militancy is a compensation for existential anxieties. All life is copied and recombined genetic information. Given that, how can he banish the thought that consciousness, too, is a copy? That he is not the only Billy? It appeared that there were other Billys in the bodies of Baileys and Biancas.

In that film, were it to be made, Billy would unravel his sculpture in the plaza, as directed by Mayor Alison, but it would not be a paean to responsibility. Billy's sculpture was to be a giant self-replicating web of folded carbons meant to demonstrate the freedom of the old Internet. The iridescent strands, spun by nanoprinters, would smother the entire Eastern Hub, radiating from York to the Boston Prosperity Complex and Sub-Philadelphia. Although Osvald didn't think of it that way, his Billy was something of a terrorist.

While I was thinking of Billy's web, my face froze.

Paging Dr. Lisa. She fed me a peach pill. I took a shot of vitamins in the ass.

She said, Rest and be happy.

Discharged into midday from the hospital. Past the market, into the green gash of the park.

Summer's litter. Ravaged picnics and shucked wraps. Dogs ran after Frisbees. Couples who quit having sex buy dogs to subject us to monologues about the dogs' charm and intelligence. It might be nice to trip a jogger.

Dr. Lisa's pill rowing up my blood and drifting back down.

A woman lay in the grass, wearing an eggplant one-piece. When I realized who I was ogling, nausea spread down my esophagus, through my stomach, into my crotch, where it became shame and fear. Jonson's wife, Lucretia. The pain of coincidence. A skinny man with a potbelly splayed next to her.

I walked to a bench at a safe distance. I knew who he was. The hairy man was Seel. Philip Seel, one *l*, two *e*'s. A foxtail for my garland of secrets. Prayers for bird shit went unanswered. Maybe this was none of my business. Jonson had a right to his gentleness, no less delectable for being cultivated in artificial conditions, like a hydroponic pineapple.

Was it so wrong? Two people in the park, sunbathing. It could have been that they came across each other. Healthy friendship between the sexes. Neither seemed the type to have friends outside of situations with an audience, dinners, fund-raisers, openings, funerals.

Lucretia and Philip are both specialists in antiquity. A lunch meeting, maybe. Business and the pleasure of the sun. If Lucretia were going to betray Jonson, it wouldn't be with such a withered and pompous man.

Jonson's pain to date included a kidney stone, six or eight

aborted gardens, a dead grandmother three nodes west. He didn't have to enter the catacombs of his marriage. Certain pains are inevitable but other pains are choices. Jonson had chosen. Had he? It seemed wrong to watch Lucretia and Seel.

East, out of the park. The Conspicuous was showing *Loose Lips*. Do-gooder rats out his kids for emissions crimes, becomes family pariah. I barged past the usher. Because I've mentioned the theater over five hundred times in this column, I get to see films free of charge with half-off popcorn. Maybe this wasn't my business. Jonson could maintain the great lawns, the sumptuous gardens, the statuary, of his ignorance. However, said a small, pitiless voice. The lights dimming. What are friends for if not to help you suffer?

8.

MOONSTONE

DIR. HARLAN GORLAN

91 MINUTES

Harris V. Jonson V, my colleague, my friend, is the other film critic at the *Central Hub Slaw*. His position on the *Slaw* is for fun and appearances. Jonson does not need to work.

He was supposed to review *Moonstone*. He is indisposed. The benefit for the Jonson Foundation went late last night, and it would have been rude not to join the donors in convivial toasts. Jonson offered me a belt I admired last Tuesday in exchange for writing this review. It is actual leather, which means it must be at least thirty years old. My pastime, in the molasses of the afternoon, is to have a little fun under his byline. He won't read the review. Jonson is a busy man.

Nobody's going to read this, as far as I'm aware. In my four years of reviewing, no friend, loved one, acquaintance, enemy, or stranger has commented on my reviews. I won't pester them for their opinions. I don't want to hear theirs.

My colleague's prose resembles copy for cosmetic surgery. Jonson does not pan.

He said, Why should I bring more negativity into a negative world?

I said, You don't think negativity can be a corrective force?

He said, Positivity is a corrective force.

Allow me my Jonson impression:

Gorlan's fifth fabulous film, Moonstone, *takes as its premise the discovery of a strange stone in a university laboratory, and the conflict between Lydia, a cryptogeologist, and Roger, an extraneous minerals specialist, over its provenance. If this sounds boring, it's not. It rocks! The tetchy professoress, Lydia, believes the rock to be the product of a terrestrial hoax. Roger thinks it comes from another dimension. They have a rocky marriage. Roger makes a beau geste, in the interest of saving his marriage, and recants his opinion. With* Moonstone, The Roth Paradox, *and* Doctors in the Mood *steaming up this awards season, I must ask: Have we reached Peak Sexy Scientist?*

My thought was, I would drop off the ghostwritten review at his penthouse, inquire after his hangover, check the fridge. In person, it would be easier to deliver the bad news, and the Jonson fridge is a miracle. I would fetch Jonson a bracing glass of whatever was on hand, sit him down, and mention that I had seen his wife in the park with Seel south of the Austerity Monument, maybe it was nothing, or perhaps Lucretia and Jonson had an agreement? I would clarify that his wife and Seel were sitting in the grass, nothing nefarious was going on, no bodily contact in the couple minutes I saw them as I walked. Jonson would say, of course we have an agreement, we're modern, thanks for looking out for me. My second thought was, it wouldn't go like that.

9.

ORACLE

DIR. MALLORY FLIN

91 MINUTES

My apartment, ten miles from the Safe Zone, has no furniture. The neighborhood, Miniature Aleppo, is almost completely guests from the dust of the region formerly known as Syria, now known as not much. After four years of indentured remediation, they were given apartments and semipermanent visas. My building is not a settler building, as they are called. It's a vintage slum.

Walls on my block are papered with posters, in many languages: SHOWERS AREN'T PATRIOTIC!, THE SELFISH WOMAN GOES UNLOVED, SWEATING IS HEALTHY, BE A SPORT! REPORT USAGE VIOLATIONS!

The peace is enforced. Aside from the occasional boisterous birthday party on my street, and the midnight incursions by the riot police, it suits me. The food is good, the music piquant, and the hobbyist dronespotter will never lack for material.

The ceilings of my apartment are high and the big windows face south. A bed, a desk. Hardy plants morose with thirst. I am not inclined to explain the provenance of the Tyndale portrait, the prickly succulent, the agates. The centerpiece: a cinerary urn depicting the marriage of a forest nymph to a boy prince. Lucretia looted it from a failing museum in a defunct country during her postdoc. When the Jonsons were visiting her mother, I borrowed it without permission. One forgets one's obligations. Carrying it up my stairs, I spilled the ashes. If there is an afterlife, then I suppose I will have to answer to whoever was once that dust for the insult.

A knock. I looked through the peephole. Jonson is nosy about a man's debris. His knock was three bangs followed by three raps. The thump of his palm was apologized for with his hairy knuckles. He has the patience of a man who does not have to manage his time.

The urn went in the freezer, for safekeeping. Jonson can be clumsy.

Jonson entered, sat on the floor, held his hand out for a drink, was annoyed to receive a glass of water. In uncertain times it is best to keep a clear head. He couldn't get Lucretia on her Pinger. She was in Montreal. No replies to his pings. A clear blue panic. He'd been put on hold by police, concierges, diplomats. A warmth for his pain spread under my ears, in my knuckles.

I said, How long has it been since you heard from her, Jonson?

He said, Twelve hours. She pinged me when her slingshot arrived.

I said, I could never ride one of those terrible things. What's the value of being fired into suborbital space to save a few hours? Is your time all that precious?

He said, If your slingshot capsule explodes, then there's no corpse for your loved ones to cry over. Much more romantic, even dashing, if you ask me.

He said, But what if Lucretia's died?

Jonson pinged her again.

I said, How many pings have you sent, Jonson?

He said, A hundred. Hundred fifty. What if she's with a man?

I said, I bet she's thinking the same thing about you.

He said, Distract me.

I said, You need a challenge rather than a distraction. Let's make a film.

Jonson said, We're critics.

I said, I have an idea for a feature.

Jonson said, Shoot me first and then tell me about it.

I said, Why are we disbursing our creative energies on the *Slaw*? Others should be reviewing us.

Jonson said, Why would you give others a chance to get you back after all the nasty reviews?

I said, This job is a muselet: when it is twisted off, the cork will pop, the champagne of cinema will flow. Don't you want to taste it?

Jonson said, Champagne, drunk alone, is cloying, carbonated, fermented grape juice.

I said, It gets you intoxicated.

He said, I have nightmares of her in bed with a man four inches taller than me. He's poor and has a tattoo on his neck.

I said, Pay attention to my idea.

He said, Fine. What's the film about?

I squatted to get eye to eye with Jonson.

I said, *Altarpiece* concerns a painter.

Jonson said, How about a sexy lady painter?

I said, Bellono is believed to be a great artist, maybe the best. As a youth, he was apprenticed to Master Vittororio. Bellono thinks painting is the worst job in the world. Why make a picture of something that doesn't exist? Eating and sleeping are his chief pleasures.

Jonson said, Mine, too.

I said, A great day for Bellono would be to arise in the afternoon, eat a dish of jellied eels, a whole melon, blood sausages on black bread. Then, a nap for the digestion. Then, painting no more than thirty minutes. Dinner would be a hen stuffed with another hen, two ripe pears, the cheeks of a calf, polenta, mare's milk.

Jonson said, I had a similar meal at Il Melananza. It was a tasting menu of fourteen courses and—

I said, Bellono sulks over his commissions. For his career, he has been a mercenary. He has to paint to eat. When his commissions are overdue, he executes improvements of Master Vittororio's style. Bellono's paintings sparkle in the mind's eye. He is a bit sacrilegious. The Visitation with Elizabeth and Mary fidgeting. Joseph snoring off wine at the Nativity. The Agony in the Garden with the cringing lamb's back turned on the scrawny olive trees. How the bishops squeal.

Jonson said, Say this Bellono has a wife, and he can't find her. He discovers she's been boinking the emperor. Then Bellono—

I said, *Act two.* Duke Giovanni, ailing, offers a colossal purse of gold to whoever may paint a triptych of himself, his wife, Andrea, and his brother, Enrico, to hang over his tomb in the family chapel. Bellono realizes if he wins the competition, he will never have to paint again. He can spend his days in snails and figs.

Jonson said, Lucretia and I had the loveliest figs in Umbria on our honeymoon. Now that I think of it, she disappeared for almost two hours one day while I was sleeping on the terrace of our rental. Could it be that I've been fooled this whole time?

I said, Plus, Vittororio can be passed, beaten, made irrelevant. Bellono has tired of hearing Vittororio's name on the lips of the burgomasters, the fishwives and cardinals, the rag-and-bone men. Master Vittororio became known for polishing the work of the anonymous fresco artisans of the Roman villas found under ash. It wasn't a crime. If one has eyes to see, one must see.

Jonson said, Maybe we could do a war picture.

I said, Bellono's apprentice, Gelder, a moody teen who litters crusts and peels, is ordered to go in the street to gather information about Duke Giovanni. He finds nothing. Bellono is angered. Tantrums, depressions. Sulks and benders. Crockery thrown, servants bit, taverns menaced.

Jonson said, People don't watch period pieces unless there's killing.

I said, There's going to be a killing in here if you don't listen to me. A rumor in the city. Before the marriage, the duke's brother, Enrico, courted Andrea, who became the duchess. Bellono has heard of poems declaimed by the duke's brother in alehouses, famished kisses in the ducal orrery. Rumors of pistols cocked, wills scribbled. Enrico was overheard in the gardens, drunk as a bachelor uncle, bragging of the ankle he licked, slurring of living ivory.

Jonson said, Now we're talking. Let's have a shoot-out between Enrico and his brother. I can see it already. They're shouting to one another, I loved you! No, I loved you! And then they shoot each other dead. How's that for an ending?

I said, Gelder is sent to the palace to find what he may. He returns without useful information, having cupped a maid's flabby breast, and seen an ape dance in a man's clothes. Bellono brains Gelder with a palette for wasting his time.

Jonson said, Gelder's plotting to steal the painter's identity. He's an archetypical sociopathic adolescent. In act three, Bellono's wife kills him after he tries to strangle her.

I said, Bellono costumes Gelder and Beatrice, Bellono's wife, as Enrico and Duchess Andrea. He forces the two to stare into the eyes of each other for hours, while he sketches their expressions. Gelder and Beatrice discover something in each other's eyes. They run off with Bellono's purse. He is forced to call on Duke Giovanni for funds.

Jonson said, Isn't Duke Giovanni's that pizza place down the street?

I said, What does that have to do with anything? Duke Giovanni receives Bellono on the jakes. Bad cioppino, a whipped cook. News of Bellono's humiliation has floated on kestrels of laughter to the palace. The great suffer insults keenly, excessively, like sunburn. Bellono must perform as the petulant genius to save his reputation. He slaps Duke Giovanni. A story for the high table. Talent forgives much.

Jonson said, Let's get a pie from the Duke. They have that Cricket Supreme.

I said, Bellono says, How shall I paint you, Your Grace? Giovanni says, Less than God but more than man. Bellono says, And your wife? Giovanni says, Less than man but more than God. Bellono says, And your brother? Giovanni says, The chamberlain has your gold.

Jonson said, How about Giovanni says, I can't believe you betrayed me. And Enrico says, I'll see you in hell, my brother.

He snapped his fingers.

He said, Maybe Enrico shoots Giovanni and he falls into the fountain. Or they duel with those floppy swords?

I said, On his way out, Bellono admires a Deposition done by Master Vittororio. He remembers it well. Bellono himself is in the foreground, about sixteen, a blemished Joseph of Arimathea.

Jonson said, And then Enrico falls to his knees and screams, What have I done?

I said, Duchess Andrea strolls by with Enrico. The rumors are true. Bellono lets himself see it on their faces. His painting of the nobles, and my film, will be called *Altarpiece*.

Jonson said, Why doesn't Lucretia ping?

I said, What do you think about my film?

He said, It might have legs. Why won't she ping?

An exercise of power, a lost Pinger, a squall of resentment, the romance of travel.

I said, She probably fell asleep, or her Pinger lost juice. Don't smother her.

I handed Jonson the *Atlas of Destroyed Architecture* to page through while we waited for the pizza. The book was his. He examined his bookplate. EX LIBRIS H. JONSON V was written below an olive tree, with a satellite shining above. The conversation was lacking. I am not the type to say suck it up, man up, buck up, cowboy up, buckle up, or grow up. People ought to be free to pursue their utopian agendas.

Lucretia Jonson has a doctorate in art history, smokes cheroots, has visited every open country but six, has published two monographs, traps birds who dare land on her balcony, in defiance of biodiversity laws.

On the morning he met her, he'd made six hundred thousand dollars selling off stocks. Listing INRI, a manufacturer of plastic crowns. Pop siren Maquilla wore one in the stage show that was fined by the Hub Authority for extreme bad taste. Sales were robust, a famous magazine predicted a trend, Jonson sold. His modeling software had pointed him toward the industry.

Jonson does not know how advanced his mathematics are because he did not take a university course, hasn't the vocabulary, doesn't enjoy the topic, and got an exemption at the academy because he found the subject torturous. I must redact his suffocating anecdote about how he managed this. Jonson tells a story like it's a pigeon hostage in his fist. He clubs stories and presents their stunned bodies to the listener.

He said, I made money the morning I met Lucretia, so I took a cab to Gentleman's Closet. The display suggested an outing. I charged the hamper, crimson-checked muslin tablecloth, flatware, a straw boater, a seersucker suit, cloth sneakers. I arranged for food to be delivered to the riverbank. The day was humid. As the sun rose, it did not burn off my loneliness. I picnicked on grub rillettes, olives, a baguette, pluot jam, Lillet Blanc.

He said, Lucretia crashed her bicycle into my picnic. She was admiring an electrical box overgrown with ivy across the path. In the ensuing chaos my chin was gashed, my future wife's pinkies were broken, and the bicycle suffered sundry twisted spokes. My good picnic spoons were bent beyond repair. Concussed, I rejoiced at the destruction of my lunch. We lay in the debris feeling each other for injuries. Her odor was of the earth, a tulip bulb, an onion. It was pungent, sweet, as if challenging . . .

I drifted off. It is best to allow Jonson to exhaust his figurative language.

Lucretia, maiden name unknown to me, materialized from the Disincorporated Territories at eighteen to be educated at an obscure, selective private college. Her master's here, her doctorate there. She was older than Jonson by four years. Thrilling months of garrets, peyote, cathedrals, heartbreak.

They went to see *Pantalemon* the Tuesday following the bicycle accident. Jonson achieved some parity when she arrived with her pinkies in splints and her clothes damp from the rainstorm. And she had forgotten to brush her teeth. Since Jonson was an hour early, he was untouched by the rain. He lucked out with a great quip during the credits.

A few months after I was hired as a film critic at the *Central Hub Slaw*, Jonson took me to meet her. Jonson was sweating, talking too fast. She was exhausted by her husband's affection. It took her as much energy to receive as it took him to give.

She said, Where did you go to school?

I said, Bast College.

She said, Where is that?

I said, Ten blocks from your condominium. You can see it out of your dining room window. See, there. It is the university that sprawls for three miles along the lake. It is one of the largest in the country.

She said, I don't think I've heard of it.

I said, That seems odd. It is one of the Big Three.

While I was remembering this, poor Jonson made noises of distress and discarded his tie on my floor. His wife might be the only cause of concern in his life. He curled up. How to cheer him.

He said, A drink. I'll have it delivered if you're dry.

I said, The good people of this neighborhood do not approve of alcohol. When the booze bike pedals up, it might be vandalized. I have tea. It is delicious and soothing. You gave it to me for my birthday. Remember? It had an elaborate fable about a happy Chinese farmer and his pursuit of the perfect leaves. It was almost as if you were doing a little puppet show with your hands as you described the joy of his life on the plantation. You on your trip, sleeping on his porch, the falling rain. Think of relativity, Jonson. The migration of the monarch butterfly. Whatsoever things are honest, just, pure, of good report, if there be virtue, if there be praise. We are of an exploded singularity. You are proof of benevolence. Exist, Jonson.

He said, Liquor.

Jonson snored on my floor, next to an emptied mug. It had the

dregs of chamomile to which I had added a pulverized uncon-
sciousness facilitator. His Pinger beeped. His wife, with Seel, perhaps. Maybe, probably not. Cupping the speaker, her back to him,
as Seel smiled and lapped at his cone. It was an irritation that
Jonson had maneuvered me into being suspicious on his behalf. I
answered the Pinger to accuse her. The ringing stopped as I
picked it up.

10.

UNSURFABLE

DIR. HERSHEL BOYLE

90 MINUTES

This misleading historical drama from Harmony Studios, a subsidiary of the Transit Authority, is in wide release in time for the twenty-year anniversary of Prosperity_Jr.

Was any kid in history more maligned and admired than Wendy O'Donnell? The teenage programmer of Prosperity_Jr is the subject of *Unsurfable*, played without tact by Faye Randolph, the dissipated child star and disgraced entrepreneur of healing crystals.

Open on an estate in rural England. Chapel and pond. Inbred gardener. Daft sheep mow the heath.

Canned strings, a groaning horn, and a mush of keys. *Unsurfable* is scored like a B-movie bloodbath. Rather than an ax-wielding yokel or a gorilla with a chain saw, we wait, tense, for the collapse of the global financial markets.

We know the history. Wendy, a student at the Academy for Advanced Machine Learning, programs Prosperity_Jr with code from Abraham, an opera-loving artificial intelligence. A team had been working on Abraham for a decade under Dr. Signhildur Sigurdssondottir (an icy Maura Reynaldo).

The sly Sigurdssondottir hopes to force unilateral disarmament by having Abraham take control of the launch systems. Her teen son Jorn (twenty-two-year-old Wulf Patrick, still waiting for puberty) is too delicate for a world with the bomb. He has allergies and wouldn't thrive in nuclear winter.

O'Donnell, Sigurdssondottir's favorite student, steals Abraham while cat-sitting at her mentor's apartment. Jorn has to get his braces off, his mother has promised him he can eat a whole jar of extra-crunchy peanut butter, then he has drama class.

How did O'Donnell get the world's most powerful AI? Sigurdssondottir jotted her password on a sticky note left under the keyboard. History is cruel, but has a sense of humor.

O'Donnell had been programming a nasty virus, which she named Prosperity. Prosperity was a bad influence on Abraham, which was smarter than was assumed. Their spawn, Prosperity_Jr, erased most of the world's wealth and data.

Harmony Studios splashed out for plane crashes, satellites dropping to Earth, panic on the trading floor, et cetera, in a starchy montage of the nine chaotic months that wobbled the world.

Although we already know it, the film doesn't fail to remind us that the virus-proof replacement network, our Betternet, allows for a few news and commerce sites, but no streaming, no private communications, and almost nothing can be uploaded to the network. Rumor is, O'Donnell ended her days in a beachside bungalow on what was Fiji, playing charades with a neutered version of Prosperity_Jr.

11.

FIVE HEARTS

DIR. BASMA ABBOUD

104 MINUTES

To take a date to a film is to admit to a lack of personality, that you hope your date might transfer their affection for spectacles to your body. Handel's Theater is two blocks from the hospital. My plan. First, watch *Five Hearts* to see if it was acceptable, second, go to my appointment with Dr. Lisa, the last of her day as arranged with her nurse, third, tell her I had to review *Five Hearts* for my column, fourth, ask her if she wished to come, fifth, suggest dinner afterward.

At our last appointment. Pinching my face with her calipers.

Dr. Lisa said, You like reviewing films?

I said, It causes me anguish. Like you have some interesting illnesses, but most exhaust you, because you have seen them so many times, and how you can treat them is limited.

She said, Every illness bores the sufferer. But I think your affliction is interesting. I've never seen anything like it before, and I can find no precedent in the literature of a specific muscular formation reacting to very specific thoughts.

I said, You like somatoform disorders?

She said, I like helping people with them. They're more

interesting than cancer or depression. I rarely have to tell a patient, sorry, you're going to die. Some specialists are masochists. They reduce their fear of death by telling others how to die.

Peeling an orange. The peel's oils perfumed my shirt as she stood over me, examining my face.

She said, You get to use a different set of skills reviewing films. I don't have to convince people that they are or aren't sick, but you have to convince people whether a film is worth seeing.

I said, I find the evaluation of films in such a manner to be without use. Why would I care if a person reading my column sees a film or not? If they like it or don't? A person who trusts what I tell them is stupid. The only way to know is to see for yourself.

She said, But you're a shortcut to seeing. The reader can get a head start on what is a waste of their time.

I said, Dr. Lisa, when someone comes to you, you don't attempt to change their whole life. You don't say, here's your new diet, here's your psychiatrist, here's where you can pick up your cat. You treat the disease. There are so many diseases, you can only treat one at a time. So it is with cinema.

She went to retrieve my test results. Her drawers were not locked. Paperwork, barrettes, a book of crosswords, a socket wrench, toothpaste, a book titled *Being the Flamingo: Strategies in Stillness*.

Five Hearts. I saw it before I asked her out, so I would know if it was worth her time. Ray, Jay, Kay, May, and Lance desire one another in ways I would need a flowchart to illustrate. Pings to the *Slaw*'s graphic design department were not returned in time for publication. The subject of the film was how some points of the pentagram were coming up in the world and others were being left behind, and how this affected which points of the pentagram each felt allowed to desire. It was one of those ridiculous Southwestern Hub fantasies that assumed the world was the upper middle class, and that their concerns were everyone's. I do not have anything to say about the film but I do have mean jokes to crack, which a second viewing would allow me to refine into something resembling insight.

As Jay and May argued on a crowded railcar, bringing up May's sex drive and Jay's self-absorption, the theater howled. To work up indignation for a mediocrity is a sin. It was too bad that after my second viewing, our date, I would have to give a performance, to injure the director's lazy art with my language, after our date, in order to possibly kiss Dr. Lisa, or at least learn on what convictions she had built the scaffolding of her daily life.

A reason people choose to be alone is because they cannot bear any more humiliation, but I thought I could bear some more humiliation, so I left the film, stopped at a pharmacy kiosk for a calming nasal spray, and entered the hospital. Now that I had prepared myself by seeing *Five Hearts* once, I could take Dr. Lisa in confidence that the film would distract me from her company.

The hospital raises my spirits. It is one of the few democratic places in our society. No matter their country of origin, their social status, all are allotted an equal share of apprehension, a heaping portion of discomfort, as much waiting as they would like.

In the chair, sweating under my armpits, my stomach gargling, as the nurse asked me the same questions he asked every visit. No, yes, no, no, if I feel good. Why did he measure my height each visit? I was neither growing nor shrinking. He didn't like me, maybe because he was instinctively loyal to and protective of Dr. Lisa, and sensed my intentions. My hands shook.

He said, Nothing to fear, *guapo*. Have deep breaths.

As soon as the door closed, I poked around Dr. Lisa's office to calm myself, for a clue to her life. The east wall was papered with pages from a medieval anatomy book. A replica of a human skeleton, with its feet in a large pot, covered in creeping ivy. Eight or nine mugs sticking out their tongues of tea bags. A cheap notebook filled with her writing. It was very ugly, a wife beater's script, and all I could decipher was, *My ferns are depressed,* before Dr. Lisa tapped on her office door, announcing her entrance. Moving around the desk was impossible, so I propped my elbows on her desk, tented my hands, and peered down my nose as she entered.

I was wearing one of her white coats. The pockets were filled with gum wrappers and it smelled like it had never been washed. In the coat, it seemed like I could say whatever I wanted and the listener would accept my words as true. A stethoscope hung from my ears.

Dr. Lisa, smiling, took a chair.

I said, What seems to be wrong today?

She said, What?

When my cowardice is inflamed my voice is a whisper, a mutter.

I said, What hurts?

Wha hurrs.

She said, Well, I am tired. Like so many of us, only sleep, the great medicine, can heal me.

I said, Maybe we can do this another time.

Maebe wae dao thiss aganover thaime.

She said, Nonsense. You're here, we've almost made it through the day. The workweek has ended. What will you do tonight?

Though I may be a coward I am also the culmination of hundreds of thousands of years of genetic information designed to perpetuate itself and this time a man's voice issued from my chest. Within it were tonalities, reassurances, that I did not recognize in myself.

I said, I have to review *Five Hearts* for my column. It's playing at the Handel.

She said, Oh, I'd like to see that. You'll have to let me know how it was.

I said, Come with. I would value your perspective.

Dr. Lisa with pale violet crescents beneath her eyes. Although I am not among them, I know some people do not mind being asked to participate in social life.

Motioning to the side room, where she performed examinations.

She said, I'm taking the slingshot to the Eastern Hub for a conference.

I said, If your capsule blows up, my day would be ruined.

She said, You get up there, you see the Earth, you apprehend your insignificance, you don't care if you blow up on the way down.

I lay on the table. She turned her back to me, to cover up the indignity of trying to get on her latex gloves. They were resistant to Dr. Lisa because she washed her hands but didn't dry them well. Now it was her turn to mumble.

She said, Why don't you make your next appointment at the end of the day, and we can see something.

I said, It would be my pleasure.

My fear receded, leaving a foam of lightness. I had startled her into an awkward moment. Later I would be suspicious of her promise, but as I was prodded, shocked, questioned, and monitored, I allowed myself contentment.

She put the electrodes on my face and zapped the muscles to test their response.

She said, But you have to take me to something good, not the garbage they play at the Handel.

Zap.

I said, Every film is a game of chance. When we say someone likes this or that subject, that they have this or that passion, we mean they are more willing to squander their time on noise for the thin possibility of transformation.

Zap.

She said, Has a film transformed you?

Zap.

I said, A couple times. Although they were powerful experiences, I doubt it is worth the ire and hatred I have expended on junk. Now that I am a little older, I understand that the only response to mediocrity is to ignore it, but I thought for many years to attack it would diminish its prevalence in the world. Mediocrity accrues more mediocrity to itself, and when you attack it, you enlarge its already considerable mass.

Zap.

She said, Mediocrity is the default state of existence. It can't be avoided or defeated. It is always pulling and twisting. Without it, how would we measure what was special? Does your own mediocrity bother you?

Zap.

I said, Only at reviewing films. With most everything else, I am content to be average.

Zap.

I seemed to be speaking more coherently, as if I were guided by an entity disinterested in the outcome of the conversation but nevertheless munificent.

Dr. Lisa touched the small muscles on the side of my face, near my temple, then behind my ear. Minute electrical charges ran from her fingertip to shoot down my neck. It was only because she was focused on my face that I felt comfortable trying to be honest about cinema. I offered none of my plans for *Altarpiece*.

To explain to her my ambition to make films would be creating between us an intimacy I was not prepared for, an intimacy in which she would reciprocate with an ambition of her own, to paint or to pilot slingshots or to steal jewelry.

She said, What do you say when you don't like a film?

I said, I almost never like a film. I think of a different way to say I don't like it.

She said, Try to freeze your face.

I said, Okay.

But I didn't, because it did not look attractive to have one's face paralyzed.

Under my jaw she dug in her finger.

She said, You never told me why you wanted to kill your friend.

I said, I never said I wanted to kill him. I instead explored the possibility that I might be happier if he were to die in a freak accident.

She said, When we see the film, you will have to tell me. You can think of an amusing way to tell the story. It will be part of your treatment.

I said, Yes, Dr. Lisa.

She said, You can call me Lisa.

12.

METAMORPHOSIS (BETWEEN CRITICISM AND ART)

DIR. PAVLOS CRISTOFOROS

25 MINUTES

Scads of critics gave up explaining for creating. Wendell Yarrow, a church mouse in his column, was a leopard in the Southwestern Ballet Company. Lauren Rolf thought herself a savage composer rather than the food columnist for *Homey Slums*. John Satmost wanted to be a musician but couldn't play an instrument. Pavlos Cristoforos, of the *Eastern Hub Authority Daily Post*, was so disgusted with the offerings of the contemporary film industry, he made this astonishing film to show he could do it better. Nobody, as far as I know, can deduce how he fit those elephants into the Empire State Building. (My theory: he brought them up there as calves and hid them until the time was right.) Maria Maquerone took funds out of her mother's *Review of Contemporary Detention Architecture* to build her mysterious huts. Ronald Leslie, Albertine Wu, Reginald Montola. There are many precedents. That most of them were failures doesn't concern me. If anything, they failed because they didn't go far enough.

13.

FLYPAPER

DIR. SANTITO VENICE

98 MINUTES

The *Central Hub Slaw*'s Autumn Affair was Friday. I declined the invitation ping. Wanted to see *Flypaper* that night. Jonson insisted I attend. Tired of having his reviews edited for length, he bought the company.

The old owners, three sweaty brothers who inherited it from their mom, were salivating to unload.

Jonson said, Phil Seel tipped me off that they owe some bad people money. Gambling on soccer matches they thought were fixed. I'll flip it to an electronics conglomerate when our film comes out. It would be a conflict of interest to be in the media and in the arts. I had to reduce my liquidity for tax reasons. Steven, the old copy editor, butchered my review of *Handsome Scoundrels in Middle Age*. I spent hours working on that review, explaining why Marcy, the film's antagonist, deserved the benefit of the doubt. I haven't worked so hard in years. I skipped a lunch with Lucretia to finish it. After the purchase, I sent her a memo making my wishes clear.

Marcy did not deserve the benefit of the doubt. This was Jonson's coffee talking.

Alaia, our editor. A person's self-regard increases with the number of vowels in their name. I have been unable to determine if her efforts to raise our profile are cynical boosterism or a passion to let people know about the Market MicroOpera, the Peavey Place Puppeteers, and the Children's Noh Collective. Those who took a liberal arts degree but also expect to make a living allow their public and private sides to grow together until the observer cannot distinguish if he is beholding a genuine cretin or a person whose faith in networking is akin to a religion.

Because there are fewer opportunities for trading favors and meeting potential employers in the review of films than there are in the rest of the sections, Alaia leaves Jonson and I alone. We do not go to the office except for pilferage missions and catered lunches.

It was I who was shortening Jonson's reviews, including *Flypaper*, Maquilla's crossover from tame pop to bland film, along with inserting belligerent asides, transposing character genders, and seeding minds with offensive slang I made up on the rail. I bribe the copy editor with leftover painkillers from my oral surgery. It is a public service I perform without expectation of reward.

Alaia has never read our reviews. I will prove this to you. She gets cash payments from the chairwoman of the Hub Authority Governance Committee to favorably cover her crooked administration. Restaurants comp her meals and send out bottles of Fauxrdeaux, *mille-feuilles*, vat-grown crudo. She has Becca or Rich give them a rave. The whole *Slaw* being her hustle. She touches every buck. Ad money goes in her pocket. The music writers are paid by entertainment conglomerates. It's all noise. None of the writers mind, as long as they get the attention they seek.

When you click on my column tomorrow, you will see this review unaltered between the ads for the escorts and the pet psychics. Nobody at the aggregator reads the aggregator. It is my fantasy that all across the Hub, twice a week, theatergoers thumb down to my column in the *Slaw* with their morning protein goo and their coffee. I have been reluctant to ascertain my actual readership.

At the diner, the day before the party.

Jonson said, So why do you want to make a film about a painter? You hate period pieces.

I said, There's a difference between a period piece and a film woven from the tapestry of the past. Big ideas need a grand, let's say, canvas. My theme, the everlasting power of art and its physical existence on a superior plane of reality, would tear through the tissue of a film set in the unabsorbent present.

Jonson said, That reminds me, I had a big idea. It was for a service which would perform apologies for you. I called it Sorriest. A Sorriest rep would sit down with you, and you would delve into the real shit that you think about when you're in bed late at night, like the time you stole Jeni Morales's ice cream in elementary school, or if, in many moments of weakness, you strayed from your wife. The Sorriest rep would follow the hurt person around for a few weeks, observing their habits, and then they would perform a specially tailored Grand Apology as a surprise. For you, to give an example, the reps would rent out a theater, stock the bar with Choco Gongs, and screen *Inquisitor*. The Apologies will culminate in the customer entering in a cream caftan, arms spread for a hug, while a children's choir sings "I Beg Your Forgiveness." Maybe we could get a sponsorship thing going, and I could get this off the ground. How do you feel about *Altarpiece*: brought to you by Sorriest? Then the painter needs to apologize—

I said, No.

Jonson said, Well, you want to make this grand gesture, right?

I could round up a lot of money for Sorriest. Cross-promotion does wonders. Haupt took Transit money for *Omega*.

Philistines always pick this fact about Haupt out of their pocket, where it lies with their grimy coins and ticket stubs for blood sport.

I said, A film of this magnitude has to be pure.

Jonson said, I think you'll find big ideas shrink in the dryer of the market.

I said, What a pedestrian metaphor. Mine won't.

Jonson rented a town house for the party near the Zone.

He said, People need crannies to hide and talk. A big room is like an accusation. In a way, this party was made with you in mind. When you go in, see how many places there are for you to hide without appearing weird. A successful party is designed for the comfort of its most introverted guest.

Twenty people work for the *Central Hub Slaw* but a hundred fifty were in the house and yard when I arrived. Lucretia stood on the porch, looking through the front window. What was she thinking? That she was almost to another landing on the stair-case to oblivion, and there she could rest? That even if she turned around, to trudge back to the surface, it was too far to be worth the effort? Her Egyptian cigarettes fogged the lawn. Her skin shone. In each shale pupil a maw of light. It was fortunate that I saw her first. I veered around the house, into the yard. If we were to come together, then we would be forced into conversation out of mutual distaste for the other partygoers.

Behind the house. A juneberry tree strung with Japanese lan-terns. Alaia on a picnic table, bare-legged. The circles closest to her were well dressed and confident. Each clique, going farther from the center, was a little dumpier and slouchier, until the cir-cles ended at the house, where I stood.

Through the house, opening cans of seltzer, leaving them on shelves. The snotty women who did the music calendar were passing around a vaporizer, tolerating three men, who wanted to bore them with stories of how it was done back in the day. Two boasted. The cunning one was questioning the youngest intern about procedurally generated music. Rich, one of the restaurant critics, sat in a recliner, his shoes forgotten in the yard. He stroked a vain black cat. Rich's stories were the worst. Even Jonson couldn't bear his anecdotes of this or that dish, retrograde gastronomy, the charming guest neighborhoods he spent his Saturday afternoons eating in without making eye contact.

Simmons, the political reporter, mixed drinks. She does not appear to hold any strong convictions but enjoys the narcosis of political reportage. The employees of the paper have nice lives, messy lives. Animals to return to, animals to eat. Even I can not say my life is not comfortable. Threadbare but comfortable.

The upstairs and main floor bathrooms were occupied, but I managed to find an en suite in the second basement. I drew a bath. On the toilet, I watched the water steam. A mystery for someone to find. People were exploring the house. Two men went into a closet. Laughter and rustling.

Outside. Because the party increased my social pain, I felt willing to be lectured by Lucretia. She was gone. Dangling from the tree, lanterns shaped like gourds. How awful. Mel, who sold ads for the newspaper and liked to talk about the trivia league she organized, asked who I knew at the party that worked at the paper.

I said, I'm Alaia's substance abuse counselor.

She went around the corner. I wasn't surprised she didn't remember me. I am, as they say, nondescript. Even my initials, N.B., lack the dash of an H.V.J., Jonson's, or a J.O., Osvald's, who has no middle name. Like me. Two names are enough. No need to be greedy.

A bugless night. I was glad I came but I could not say why.

Through the window Jonson stood with Marie, the marketing manager. His hand on her back. Jonson's eyes were glassy. He was one drink from a lawsuit. Marie was a year or so out of Bast. A pile of books on her nightstand she did not have time to read. He seemed to be fooling her, but maybe she was the sort of person who was generous enough to offer the benefit of the doubt to buffoons. Proud to say she worked in media. Someone who knew where to go at two a.m. on a Tuesday night. Nobody but Alaia and I knew Jonson owned the paper. Maybe three or four of Alaia's pets, which would mean everybody knew. He didn't want to be treated any different. I went inside.

I said, Jonson, your wife wanted you to meet her at the place around the corner for a sandwich when you're done here. She went there to get some reading done. She also said remember not to drink too much because you know what happens. Marie, can you help me for a second? I was wondering how to access the film reviews on my Pinger. I am quite stupid and can never get them to load.

14.

DON'T BOTHER

DIR. LOGAN BRODER

81 MINUTES

This remake of Hans Rayjan's classic takes from the original only its premise that humans receive a signal, assumed to be sentient in origin, from distant star Ceta 44. Rayjan's film is confined to a conference center where flunkies, lickspittles, men Friday, assistant assistants, sycophants, doormats, and kiss-asses maneuver to set the terms of contact with extraterrestrials.

Mr. Balanbalan, head of the Romanian Space Agency, argues his city should host the antenna to broadcast a signal back at Ceta 44, because Bucharest has "the bravest rocket comrades." Dr. Tereshkova challenges June Ballou to a fistfight over the last blondie. Professor Rawls imitates his peers on prank calls to their spouses after a few drinks. At the conclusion of Rayjan's film, the countries decide not to send a signal to the aliens, because they can't agree on an equitable way to share the credit. It is a girl in her garage with a science-fair radio antenna who sends the message, *Don't Bother.*

The remake dispenses with the comedy in favor of an oatmeal of choral music and watery humanism. Monuments are disrespected with frequency. I will no longer be able to visit a museum or a bridge without imagining it being obliterated by a laser beam.

Broder is among our worst directors and our most profitable. I sort of admire his financial sense, for working in the block-buster milieu, for making the numbers work, long after their time has passed. One can't help but root for the ambitious.

Jonson hosts a dinner on the last day of each month celebrating Old Europe. One night last spring, the theme was Portugal. Salt cod, a snowy wedge of Graciosa, cloying *vinho verde*, an incorrect but uncorrected reference to El Greco, and a flat anecdote of a missed connection in Lisbon circulated the room.

As a general rule, I have abandoned male conversation. I've heard enough about the virtues of weight lifting, yardage, beer, games, difficult books. When a man speaks to me, my instinct is to extricate myself.

Killing time with the aperitif, in Jonson's study. A tall, beautiful man approached me near Jonson's collection of stuffed thylacines, where I was arranging a tryst between two of the rougher specimens and a fertility icon Lucretia had bought, probably from a bent curator. The beautiful man's money was in his shoes. The shoes were too good. They went well past genteel prosperity into vulgarity or parody. He had the slouch common among the arrogant, the fake guy-on-the-street, trying to convey a state of relaxation, which somehow manages to be insouciant and insulting at the same time. Such persons conflate success with character.

He said, Jonson pointed you out. You're that other critic?

I said, Yes.

He said, I'm Rolf.

I said, Hi, Ralph.

Rolf said, Rolf Millings, of the Upper Lake Shore Drive Millingses.

First I told him my name was Daniel Chivo. Then I said it was Jarvis Fillingswimble. After a pause for no laughter I gave him my real name, Noah Body.

Rolf said, What do you think of Broder? He's my favorite.

I said, I think he's a fraternity hack, Raul. The proprietor of a nonunion circus. A fracker of cinema for its crudest lessons.

Rolf said, That's harsh and misleading. His films get raves, as far as I've seen.

Phil Seel said, One man's pyrite is another's treasure.

Seel was paging through a catalogue of tapestries. He wasn't interested in our conversation but had been storing this quip too long and needed to air it out before it was eaten by moths. Bespectacled, sickly, with hair the shade of instant coffee. Phil laid rail. He had been in charge of establishing the Southwestern Hub and was somewhat responsible for that region's recent cultural supremacy. Rumors that he was in charge of opening another Hub in Canada, another in the remains of Seattle. His passions were Grecian *olisbos,* flight, faking an accent that couldn't be placed.

He said, The mythologies of copulation are the true history of our species.

During dinner parties, it was inevitable he say this in the wilderness between the dessert and the digestif. It is easier for a busy person to have a few aphorisms than to reinvent their plastic self for every conversation.

Phil was tan from twenty years in the Aegean sun, negotiating the purchase of antiquities for his private collection. They no longer keep tabs on their old stuff. Anyone can print their own copies now. What is the utility of the original? Seel looks like he is smiling especially when he isn't. Every year his happiness compounding. To walk in his private museum, to look at the beautiful objects wrought by the dead, was his afterlife. There could be nothing better. Seel's life growing in and over those objects. The earth turning over and pushing up what was buried. The pale scar slaloming over his forehead was punishment for cheating on his second wife.

The way Jonson told it, Seel's wife hired guys to castrate Seel. The guys thought her request in poor taste. Beneath her.

One goon said, What's wrong with her?

The other goon said, We aren't animals.

The first goon said, I have two master's degrees.

The other goon said, I'm learning Mandarin.

In the diner where they scheduled their collections, robberies, anniversaries.

On the day of the beating Seel was buying his girlfriend orthodontia. Outside the clinic they gave him a beating, paid for with his own money. Ten thousand dollars buys a lot of violence. It was not rarefied violence but the portions were ample. Seel's girlfriend finished her appointment, and left the clinic to witness the guys beat Seel up. Seeing the pink rubber bands in her braces, the guys laid off. Laughing. One of the guys did the gash on Seel's forehead with his thumbnail. It was for brand recognition, nothing personal. Seel is grateful. Intense experiences justify us. He can go places he couldn't go in comfort before: the garage, the track, certain charging stations.

From the dining room, I heard Jonson pounding out a clumsy rhythm on his mealtime *djembe*. We took our seats around the table. Jonson placed placards indicating where the guests should sit.

During the part of the meal I was present for, Lucretia and Seel did not converse for more than a few minutes, made strong eye contact, and sat apart at the table. What I would say in her position if I were accused is: nothing. I would laugh and make an incredulous face, if Osvald was feeling cooperative. Seel has such a lecherous air of scholarship about him it's hard to imagine any woman, much less a specimen like Lucretia Jonson, taking him seriously. Although Lucretia could be tired of taking Jonson seriously. Her husband was like a strict diet. Seel the person she enjoys without intentions. We sponge whatever puddles of attention we discover.

Earlier in the night. Jonson with his punch and fist of crudités. His wife walked by. He made a rude noise of appreciation, she smiled over her shoulder, a private smile, with promises.

Jonson said, That poor Seel. He must be a real bore to go on a date with. Can you imagine him laying on that phony thick Greek and talking about his sailboat while you try to enjoy dinner? He's from Dakota. Telling you how they used to eat pussy on Crete? Quoting the *Odyssey*? I don't get it. The women seem to like him, though, or it's safe to pretend they like him, because he isn't threatening. I think it's his sleaze. You and me, we hide it, he unbuttons his shirt further. Every year it's another button.

I had the poor fortune to sit next to Rolf Millings. He returned to Broder. He would not shut up about the greatness of *Plunder*, Broder's heist opus about the theft of the World Seed Bank.

Millings said, *Plunder* is like those Russian dolls. There's a story within a story within a story. You keep prying the dolls open. Every time I watch it, there's a smaller and more intricate doll. All the dolls have different faces. I never had this conception of film until Broder. To find the infinite point, like the universe before the Big Bang, in these great films, where all matter is concentrated. Whenever I go to the movies, because of Broder, I'm looking for that singularity, in which nothing can be seen and nothing understood.

I do not brag to Dr. Lisa of correct diagnoses I have made. Rail operators are not accustomed to hearing what I think are the best stops. I don't tell lawyers which are the most profound statutes. To musicians, I do not insist on the preeminence of a favorite chord. Each person is allowed one topic to be both mystical and smug about, and ought to choose it with care.

Lucretia explained the function of Tut's fake beard. His tomb had been printed last month at the Facsimile Museum, across from the Bangladeshi Quarter. Seel futzed with his Pinger during her lecture. Maybe he had heard it already. He was waiting to deliver his lines. Dinner may be a rehearsal for their privacy. I have grown to detest the word *maybe*.

A mortician or a professor of dance complained about how long he had to wait for his domestic help to arrive this morning to fix his breakfast. A woman remarked to nobody in particular that dinner parties seemed to be longer when she was young, now they were so brief, it was sit down, eat, goodbye. Nobody spoke of children. The Jonsons do not invite parents to their table. Lucretia lost a child early in pregnancy.

Jonson went into the kitchen to speak with the caterer, a moody man to whom his relationship was akin to confessor and priest. When he returned, his face was red. Broder's knight leaned over. Lapping us with his wineglass twice, three times.

Millings said, Come on, admit *Plunder* is good.

I said, No.

Millings said, Don't be pretentious.

I said, I am giving you my honest opinion. I don't think *Plunder* is a good film. I think it is a dangerous film.

He said, A film can't be dangerous. Picking a contrary position for the sake of coolness is the opposite of cool. I know what cool is. See me? Cool. I'm an Antarctic cucumber. I rode here on a beautiful refurbished bike, with a brand-new solar cell. How did you get here? Walk?

I said, Yes, I walked from the rail station.

He said, When you say that *Plunder* isn't a great film, you're saying that it is a film for the masses, and you think you're too good to be one of us. Because, you know, cool isn't your shit, the obscure shit, the shit you'd use to impress people, cool is what the cool people like, cool is what the masses are into, cool is another demographic, it isn't whatever shit you were watching all alone on Friday night fifteen years ago. Cool is consensus. Cool brings us together rather than separates us into a shitty hierarchy of taste.

Mashing his *bolinhos* with pewter teeth. He ought to brush. We were talking out of the corners of our mouths, at a low volume. Jonson saw my face. He shook his head. I spoke a little louder.

I said, I have never been cool. I consider these labels not applicable to my experience. Because of how information is now available, it is easy for any person to find a group within which they belong and a group they consider worthy of attack. There has not been a consensus on hipness or fitting in for many decades now, if ever, and I'm not sure why these ideas persist.

He said, That's convenient. You ever been in a fistfight?

I said, Yes.

He said, I doubt that. You don't look like the type.

I said, Is fighting cool?

Millings said, No, it isn't. I'm never looking for a fight. There seems to be a connection between the passive, brainy approach to cinema and those types of living, and the more action-oriented, Broder-style type of living. Marrying thought to action. Like, I have my beliefs, and you better believe I'm going to back them up if I have to. What will you do, write an essay?

Guests checked their Pingers, looked away from us.

I said, What beliefs? I'm not sure which I have that would be worth fighting over beyond the standard, boring, universal ones. A belief, as I understand it, is flexible. It never needs to be fought for if it is self-evident. For instance, common conceptions of morality. The only worthwhile beliefs are small and not to be mentioned to others.

Millings said, Beliefs never need to be fought over? What about freedom! What about what we have done for our guests? We went and died so they could come here and live in safety.

I said, We, the people at this table, did not do anything. Other people died in an unfortunate geopolitical maneuver. They will continue to do so until the end of nation-states and sects and identities or until the last person has died.

Millings said, We saved those guests from the chaos of their home countries.

Richer guests nodded, poorer smirked.

I said, Who created that chaos? When our guests come here, they are virtual slaves for five years. How is that freedom? Would you pick tomatoes for five years, for a room in a firetrap sixteen nodes away from the Safe Zone, where you have to be worried about being raped if you are a woman and lynched or arrested if you are a man?

Wine gulped. Angry that I was forced into this position, to make a statement, to use words to prove what I didn't care to prove.

Millings said, It's not like that here. We have peace and order.

I said, At a cost that's difficult for us to bear. I live in a guest neighborhood, I know what their lives are like.

Millings said, You don't look like a guest. You look like you grew up a hundred miles from the node and never wanted for anything.

I said, I never made a claim to speak for them.

He said, Broder speaks for them. He speaks to universal experiences. When I go see a Broder film, I see guests in the audience, because they're dreamers, Broder is a dreamer, and together we are all dreaming a special dream.

I said, Broder makes films for teenage boys. Enthusiasm for the man's work is longing for a return to sugary breakfast cereal, a mother's servitude, maniacal self-abuse in one's bunk bed. What is there to like in *Plunder*? The expensive jackets of the heist crew? Their cars? The deforming surgeries performed on the female lead? The fascism of his set designs? The implication that the Seed Bank, a thing built in Europe, with European money, with European diligence, staffed responsibly by Europeans for decades, ought to be given to American agencies and corporations so they can fuck with what they didn't have the foresight to save for the good of the world? *Plunder* was subsidized by the government. That isn't rumor, that is a documented truth. It is propaganda as much as entertainment.

Millings said, It doesn't matter where money comes from. I've made a lot of it. It all spends the same. There are no clean dollars. Broder is a visionary. We're talking of epic cinema. Epic cinema requires money. Anything worth doing requires money. You wouldn't understand that, though. We're talking about the greater good.

I said, *Epic* is a word used by idiots to apply to excessive and insulting spectacles. He's repackaging old blockbusters with updated effects. In twenty years his films will look dated and bloated.

He said, I've never seen anything like it.

A little slur. *I neveh see anhthing like it.* Biting off the end of his sentence like it was a piece of jerky.

I said, That doesn't make it special.

He said, Every era has a Michelangelo. Broder's ours. There's talent and there's people like you who have none. All you do is comment. You're making content for people to read while they take the rail, so they don't have to make eye contact with the person across from them. Nobody will remember who you're watching.

I said, Someone has to bring attention to the world's underappreciated filmmakers. That's why I do what I do. Your toilet will advise you to go see the new Broder every time you shit. Who is going to tell you about Weide or Haupt? Who will announce these people have something to offer the human spirit?

Millings said, Let them disappear. Cinema is a meritocracy. The best films get seen by the most people.

A noise as if I were being tortured escaped me.

I said, Without the dignity of our artistic process, the Underunited States is the narcotized, militarized ghetto the rest of the world assumes us to be.

Millings said, Listen, buddy. You better watch your mouth. You might get slapped, huh? I know a few people in the Transit Authority. You won't see shit if you get your papers yanked. I suggest you apologize for that remark immediately.

I opened my mouth but my Pinger went off, an emergency ping, loud enough to startle the whole table.

Jonson pinged, i forbid you to fight this guy over a Broder flick / please make excuse and leave / sorry / will make it up to you

I said, I have to go. I would rather staple my penis to my leg than listen to you speak.

He said, Give Broder another shot, will you? You might see something new. We have to be willing to look. Tell you what, I'll get your Pinger from Jonson, we'll go together this week. I'll get one of those private theaters down off the Drive. We'll have a little marathon.

Generous in victory, as his type tended to be. I felt his smile all the way down the elevator.

Walking out. A motorcycle. Was that a brand-new solar cell? It was. I rolled it over to the sunken plaza, shoved. A series of discrete, satisfying crunching noises. Somewhere, I didn't doubt, a camera caught it, but I was confident Jonson would pay the fine and the bill. How would they get it out of there?

Jonson pinged, sorry / we buy out the conspicuous next weekend / you yell at the screen all nite / millings sez sorry / too much to drink

I pinged, you got a deal / apology accepted / good bolinhos / maybe a little more salt next time / tell lucretia thanks

15.

INQUISITOR

DIR. VERNE GYULA

236 MINUTES

Osvald's birthday today. Facts should be discarded when they no longer have use. Distances, measurements, Pinger IDs. Sounds and particular sentences that were formed for one's hearing. On memories spreads pain's mildew.

I wonder what Isabel bought him.

About a decade ago, for his birthday, we threw a party. There was no food. We were too young to know the manners of good hosting. Osvald arrived late to our living room, as was the style. The bargain liquor insulted one's organs. Within an hour he was sick on the staircase. Though they were no longer dating, Karolina brought Osvald home to soil her room. She was a generous woman. She stocked the kiosks at Bast as her student job, and she would let Osvald and me loot the storeroom. I wonder what happened to her. I was saddened at Osvald's failure to enjoy his party. These people assembled for him, sort of. He didn't get to enjoy their affection, their kind words, their jokes. Osvald wasn't the locus of attention. That woman that he liked with the piercings showed up two hours after he was dragged off.

I left his gift, Haupt's *Record of a Bad Time*, on his desk. The book, Haupt's diary detailing the production of *Mind Under Matter*, includes notes Haupt took while spying on the actors, in his attempt to make them paranoid on-screen.

During the party, the woman with the piercings wandered into his room, handled his things, stretched on his bed for a minute. Her joints popping. I invited her to leave birthday wishes inside the cover of the *Record*. She smelled like cold water and her attention span was not sentimental enough to linger anywhere too long. I let her take a nugget of talc from his desk. Osvald collected minerals.

The next morning, he mopped. Hangovers moved through us like glaciers. I taunted him with my impression of Csonka, captain of the starship *Inquisitor*.

I said, *Theese ess a leetle bochs. In theese bochs, the secrets of our generasion. The possebeeleties off our future weethin.*

We had met in a film class at Bast, on the first day of college. The Holy Eye: On the Religious in Science Fiction, 21 Yarl Hall, Tuesday five to ten p.m. Soon we began to make films in conjunction with or adjacent to one another, as our ideas and time demanded. We thought we would be filmmakers, as if this were a permanent condition.

How we know our friends when we meet them. A capacity for secrets. Above everything, the ability to suspend judgment of us. Each of us can be good to a few people. If you have had the good fortune to encounter only those you can be kind to, then it is no achievement on your part.

An eerie starship, traveling for hundreds of years, its mission unclear. A disturbed, blessed captain. Csonka has steered *Inquisitor* too long.

Osvald said, Csonka is a vessel for holiness and not necessarily a person per se.

I said, *My chob ees to pretek theese bochs. Ef ew don undeer-stand, the whole feuture ees contained een theese bochs.*

The adjunct asked the class what meaning we assigned to the Starboard Exhaust Manifold, where a device told the future of crew members, provided they met criteria the film does not clarify. The rituals of the ship were perpetuated by the AI to ensure long-term stability. The demands for sacrifice, taboos, and the elevation of fools to the priesthood caused political instability, so Captain Csonka maintained control. Osvald thought *Inquisitor* was a spoof of belief. I saw it as the expression of an ethnographic impulse.

Whoever espouses the idiotic theory that *Inquisitor* populates Earth with its savage, superstitious, devolved crew is my enemy. A woman who sat near us, Miriam, introduced our class to this idea, based on the names of the two janitors, Ad'em and If. There is no proof. Osvald caught me squeezing a tube of epoxy in her bike lock.

He said, Who does she think she is, trying to turn Verne Gyula's profound film into an episode of *Outer Space Chronicles*?

I said, It's a shame to wreck a good lock like this.

He said, Yes, it's too bad.

Then we were friends. Friendship requires conservation of resources. Something must be withheld. A lease was signed, lost. On Sunday mornings, we watched *Inquisitor* while convalescing from Saturday's bitter revels.

Osvald sent the ailing director pings about the film, if a meaning could be established, if meaning was compatible with experience. *Inquisitor* was made to be screened in prisons. Gyula did not respond. Osvald who took my marriage.

16.

THE FINAL SECRET // THEY'RE COMING FOR US!

DIR. ANDERSON ROGIER

40 MINUTES // 57 MINUTES

A matinee double feature at Original Cin, playing for the next three days.

Rachel Wilcher, a dissolute podiatrist, proved that the radio bands that allowed for wireless broadband Internet were responsible for the epidemic of credulity observed in the industrialized world twenty years ago.

Her findings ignored, and her severe stutter mocked, she was eventually institutionalized. Rachel was the node drunk, perhaps because of her difficulties getting taken seriously. Before being put away, she could be found of an evening in the town square, tooling around on a bicycle in the raw.

In the theater with me, a buffet of casualties. An elderly woman hooted at each factoid and spit on the floor when the government was mentioned. A couple emptied a bucket of fried lima nuggets. Authoritarian children chanted freely. I saw two Transit Authority spies, identifiable by their posture, taking notes on who was laughing and who wasn't.

In *The Final Secret*, Rogier posits that the government of the United States discredited Wilcher. He suggests the powers that be, fearing the chaos that the worldwide cessation of broadband data would engender, fed Wilcher a diet of boutique psychedelics to keep her unhinged.

At intermission, patrons posed with a cardboard cutout of Rogier. Pictures were six dollars a pop. It seemed that an extra two feet were added to Rogier's height. I slung my arm around his waist, like we were on a date.

In *They're Coming for Us!*, Rogier claimed that the refugees of the Confidence Crisis engineered the collapse of their countries to force the Underunited States to allow them refuge.

After the end of the film, I was first in the lobby. Finding the cutout unguarded, I absconded with Rogier.

He's in my kitchen now, with Lawrence, my AlmostPerson.

Lawrence said, Who is this gentleman?

I said, He's your new friend Rogier. He's the prince of muck-rakers.

Lawrence said, He seems rather flat.

I said, Spend some time with him, Lawrence. You'll find he's deeper than you might guess.

17.

FLOWERS WHICH EAT MEN

DIR. ANTONIO ZACCARDI

145 MINUTES

I was in Windsor, Son, Uncle & Daughters Books looking through Zaccardi's *Selected Images*, a large, lush volume, a thousand color pages, composed of stills from his films. The high-quality stock captured the saturation of his images, the specificity of his light. No words. For weeks it had been my habit to come to the shop and flip through their copy. The clerk tired of taking it out of storage and placing it on a lectern. It is some forty pounds. He left it in a reading nook for me, on a table, underneath dictionaries. As far as I could tell, nobody had touched it since my last visit.

Best is the section from *Flowers Which Eat Men*. Zaccardi's lovers, the performance artists Cereality, scored that film, ruining it with screeching, flushing, the breathing of a long-distance runner. Could you adore a beautiful person with a high-pitched grating voice? After their split, Zaccardi decided to redo the sound for the film but never got around to it.

Who was this over my shoulder, looking with me? To get them to leave, I flipped to a still from *The Harvests of Old Age*, of a nude elderly man.

Millings said, That motorcycle you wrecked at Jonson's was my mother's.

I said, She must have been a dumb woman to give it to you.

Millings said, You're going to get your ass kicked.

He picked up a copy of *The Art and Science of Spreading Blame.*

I said, In front of all the cameras? Where will you find a place without a camera?

He said, I can make the cameras go away.

I said, No, you can't. If you had that much juice, you would have hit me already, or you would have sent people around to my apartment.

He said, Your place in Miniature Aleppo. I know where it is.

I said, So?

He said, Expect a visit.

Flipping through the book, Millings got a paper cut on his thumb. Sucking at the blood, he looked more infant than tycoon. It was hard to feel threatened.

I said, I look forward to it. Once you cross my threshold, it is my legal right to stick you with whatever happens to be at hand. Jonson brought me a spear from the African Union. It's from some printer factory in Addis Ababa, shilled to people who want to hang a piece of the Real Africa on their wall. I pass slow evenings throwing it at Lawrence, my AlmostPerson. I don't hit exactly what I'm aiming for, but I hit something four times out of five. Up the back staircase there are no cameras.

He said, You won't see me coming.

I said, I'll smell that tremendous cologne you wear long before you come. Are you really still sore about the motorcycle and the fish? How do you know I had anything to do with the fish, outside the Globe Theater? Anyway, Millings, I'm trying to look at this special book, so either do your violence or go play in the street.

He said, I wouldn't think of it, in a place like this. My mother used to bring me to bookstores when I was young. She was a specialist on Yugoni, the poet. You like him?

I said, No.

He said, Yes, he might be too populist for the likes of you. His name is easy to pronounce. I bet that turns you off.

I said, Millings, look at this image. How do you suppose Zaccardi got these colors? If there is an afterlife, I will be visiting him some afternoons.

He said, If you continue to pester me, I will make sure you get your chance to ask him soon.

I said, You can't expect me to believe you're going to murder me because I allegedly threw some fish on you and possibly bumped your motorcycle, which I'm sure was insured. If you will threaten me, at least make it credible.

He said, You're right, where are my manners. I'm not going to murder you. A couple punches will suffice. If you like, you can come to my place, and I will take it easy. I am forgiving. Say one good punch to the jaw, one to the nose. You can even swing back. I'll pour you a drink afterward. Show you how I'm living. There's something I like about you. Anyway, here's my card. Think about it. But don't think too long, because otherwise who knows when it may happen. Control is very important. I would advise you, while you still have control, to make amends.

A holocard of a building with his residence within flashing in red.

He said, Good day. I have an appointment to make.

Millings stopped at the counter and arranged for a stack of photography books to be delivered to his apartment. He and the clerk shared a confidence. A blush came to her cheeks. In my peripheral, I saw him gesturing toward me, the clerk nodding. Out the door.

I said, What did he say?

She said, That guy said anything you want in the store is on him. Go ahead and charge it. His exact words were, I'll buy him the whole store if he wants.

I said, I'll take the Zaccardi, then. And the whole section of vintage skin magazines. Can you gift wrap and deliver the magazines by courier?

She said, Sure.

I gave him Jonson's address.

She said, Who from?

I said, Please write, With love, the mayor's office. And whatever else you want, for yourself.

So Millings thought himself a gentleman. Did I deserve this treatment? Neither destroying his motorcycle after the party nor throwing the herring from that apartment's compost bin on him while he sat in the plaza were cause to put his hands on me. I had been unfair but I would never present myself at his condominium, like a supplicant, to be punched out. He would have to come find me, in the full view of the Hub cameras, to get his satisfaction.

Carrying the Zaccardi out of the shop. East up the street, toward the rail, to catch my local. The Zaccardi was heavy, so I clutched it to my chest with both arms. What treasure. Taking the corner, a detonation behind my right ear. My legs lost strength and I blacked out a moment. When I came to, I was lying on the sidewalk. It had scraped the side of my face. Some blood. In my occiput, a blustering pain. The trousers of a man in my peripheral. He picked at his cuffs.

He said, You better get over to Mr. Millings's place.

He was holding a very large, even inappropriate, coffee. He began to turn the pages of the Zaccardi, trickling coffee on the images. One still, from *The Tree Which Is the Family Property*, reminded him of something, or struck him, and he spared it from the coffee. It was of a mother and two sons eating beneath the tree on a cloudy afternoon. After a while he tired of this, and dumped the remainder on my head. He walked off. A young couple turned the corner and helped me to sit against a wall.

The woman said, Do you want us to call a doctor?

I said, No. The camera is right there. If they want to come, they will come.

The man said, At least let us help you get home.

I said, Sit here with me a minute. Look at my book.

The woman said, Oh, you spilled your coffee on it. That's too bad.

The man said, It must have been an expensive book.

The idea for the attack on me was stolen from Broder's *Capo*. He knew I would be annoyed by the reference. The capo meets a snitch in a bakery, where the snitch is picking up a cake for his daughter's birthday. The capo smiles, tells him everything is forgiven, buys a baguette. The capo drops the baguette, and the baker offers him another one, familiar with his reputation. The snitch walks around the corner, and the capo's man stabs him in the chest. The snitch, shocked, sets the cake on the ground as gently as is possible. Then the celebrated shot of the capo's man stepping in the cake as he runs away, which nobody mentions is stolen from Sergei Vasiliev's *High Noon in Saratov*.

18.

SECRETS OF SUMAC MOUNTAIN

DIR. GRETCHEN SALZBLATT

80 MINUTES

The night Isabel and I got together, I was pounding Bletcher's Diet Lager in the Horoscope. She hollered across the rebarbative rail techs, an empty stool. The bartender's pinched face, his rescue snakes the inevitable subject of his conversation. You'd leave alone, feeling okay, thinking maybe you ought to get one. Walking home, you brainstormed names that would be fit for a boa constrictor, feeling hopeful for nothing in particular.

She said, Hey, you. You look like Jeff from *Secrets of Sumac Mountain.*

I said, No, I don't.

She said, Don't I know you from somewhere?

I said, Yes, you know me from somewhere.

Et cetera. It happens every night everywhere. I can't report with accuracy what happened. The mallet of dawn in late spring. I walked on the wet sidewalk and felt grateful. Head throbbing. Osvald complained about her slamming the door. When I returned to my room to gloat, I saw that she had left her belt, a wide white synth-leather strap flung near my desk, marring the wall where the buckle hit. She'd swept aside my clothes to draw attention to it, coiled on the floor. Women left their accessories to ensure you'd ping, but the accessories were expendable, in case you didn't. One never found an heirloom watch in one's sheets or a treasured necklace on one's desk.

I can remember the terrible line I used to invite her over the following week. A twinkle of panic pressing send. The line was, I want to take you out, or in, tonight. The events of my life are smoke, floating away, rising.

Secrets of Sumac Mountain is garden-variety Salzblatt. See it Wednesday at the Old Rodeo Cinema. A sleepy town, Sumac Mountain, dew in the morning. A flour town, as they say. This was before guests made it in numbers to the small communities off of the nodes. Delivering the paper, Jeff observes a prominent businessman eating hair. How come? The entertainment options in Sumac Mountain are few. He follows the developer. He sees what might be a murder. His crush, Emilia, works at the bakery. It's Maquilla, supposedly retired from singing, in her Serious and Dissolute Actress phase. She has a secret. They meet in a dream. The next day, Jeff is ashamed, proud.

The theatergoer adopts a pet auteur, a fringe artist to advocate for, to buttress his or her individuality. Salzblatt was Isabel's. Her favorite Salzblatt was *Christmas*, which she saw on our catastrophic and embarrassing second date. Her popcorn forgotten. The dentist's scene that was condemned by the mayor of the Eastern Hub.

Isabel who was my wife. I don't see her well anymore. Her face is like the face on a coin. The mold deforms as years of minting pass. Singing in her low voice as she brushed her hair. The curtains in our apartment were white, aspirational, billowing in the wind from ceiling to floor. Coming home, throwing her purse, a boot; next, her earrings, dress, bracelets, tights, bobby pins.

Coming home, finding her naked, slumped over her Pinger, her shoulders folded in, her nose greasing the screen. A nest of wrappers marking her personal space.

Maybe she will find *Altarpiece* to be not as good as Salzblatt's best work, but better than most of her early and midperiod films.

19.

BRUJA

DIR. MARIA BOQUERONES

94 MINUTES

Altarpiece will be made. During the previews to *Bruja*, Jonson agreed to finance *Altarpiece* up to three-point-six million dollars below the line and postproduction, with costs above the line to be negotiated as options manifest.

After the movie, we sat on the curb outside the Runaway Seven. From within his coat, Jonson produced for each of us a cinnabar banana. Jonson, Jonson, Jonson. Today's locus of my affection. Who needs a person? I have my friend, my financier, the father-to-be of *Altarpiece*.

He plucked at his trousers. My legs kept drifting apart and slamming together. I find underwear to be an affectation. It is his habit to suggest a drink after twenty minutes of conversation. At the sidewalk tables, men dawdled over pale ales wondering if they had what it takes to fly hydrogen blimps. Mothers presented babies with soft objects to gnaw. Farther on, couples were entangled in the riverbank's permissive murk.

Jonson wore a straw boater. I did not mock it, because of the financing he offered. It might be nice to char the brim. To mail it back as scraps.

His demands include an executive producer credit, creative input, assistant director. His name would feature prominently in the opening titles. But there will be neither opening titles nor credits. Jonson made this money, hidden from Lucretia, investing in AlmostPeople.

He said, I'm going to surprise her with the film. She'll be thrilled. We keep talking about how we need to get serious about our cultural engagement. She wants us to donate a wing to the Facsimile Museum, but that's too safe. Wings are stuffy. We're young, adventurous. Wings are for people with gout and hearing loss. We didn't even make it to the gala this year. Why spend money on the floor, on the light fixtures, when we can make something to project on the wall?

AlmostPeople are animatronic life-size dolls, in a variety of body types, programmed to listen intently to their user's problems and affirm them with up to twenty thousand programmed phrases, such as, *That's so true, Who does he/she think he/she is?, Don't let yourself be treated that way, You're better than that,* and so on.

It turns out that to have the appearance of authenticity, the listener must appear to be somewhat distracted.

AlmostPeople can be programmed along a spectrum of attention. Presets include the Successful Friend, the Penitent Husband, the Public Servant, the Therapist (Sober), the Therapist (Under the Influence), the First Date, the Second Date, the Second Date (Alternately). Cocktails at the pitch brunch made Jonson playful. He insisted the company manufacture a model of his body, but his first name, Harris, did not test well, so the model is the Lawrence, which was determined by focus group to be a trustworthy name. The muscles are exaggerated. Jonson shipped me a Lawrence, who stands in my kitchen, modeling scarves.

Lawrence says, Pour out the cup of rage.

He says, The past is a pile of rotting carpets.

He says, Climb the mountain of your anxieties.

In addition to being a sympathetic ear, he is something of a philosopher.

Lawrence said, Do you think free will is an illusion?

I said, There's no way we are so lucky.

My money. We think we do not need the stuff until we get some of our own. When Jonson and I see a film, we flip a coin. The loser reviews; for instance, in this review.

Which reminds me. You can see *Bruja* at the Runaway Seven, but you shouldn't.

Jonson couldn't make the coin out in the dark. I have a double-sided quarter from a novelty shop. We flip for lunch, for socks, for ownership of trees we both admire. We flipped for financing, after I'd irritated him enough. One hopes his mind was made up already. Even for Jonson, it is a lot of money.

He says, You have great luck. You ought to try investing.

Back to *Bruja*. Mariposa, a swamp witch, has a drawer of stolen voices. Maite is jealous of a couple in her village. In return for Maite's fertility, Mariposa agrees to steal the voices of Florencia and Agustin. For Maite's sense of smell, Mariposa offers Maite the ability to speak from their mouths. Maite has a talent for mimicry. Surprised, angered by what they've said, seeing, through the callous act of speaking, the truth of their words, the pair begin to hurt each other even without Maite's intervention.

Florencia walks off a cliff. Agustin starves himself to dust.

How Maite sobs. It is difficult to have nobody to resent.

Mariposa allows the voices of the deceased to flap from her drawer. Unable to find their owners, they roost in Maite. The voice has no connection to the soul. The voice is air, not to be trusted. Words cannot be. Noises to get this or that. Maite gains regional distinction as a singer of tragedies and an augur of weather. She finds her own happiness, with a farmer, as intense as that of Florencia and Agustin. There is no punishment for what she has done. Though we pretend otherwise, the lack of judgment from the universe we inhabit is the joy of our lives. Maybe there will be a day when we all sit up and point our fingers at each other, a final adjudication at the end of death, but it is not today, and it is not likely to be tomorrow.

Ahead of ourselves in the street. We spoke of *Bruja* with the weariness of veteran auteurs, who had given up on commercial success in favor of the ineffable but were amused by the efforts of middlebrow directors to get recognition.

Under the streetlight we pronounced.

Jonson said, Great film must offer no mimetic pleasure.

He said, Cinema conceals itself from the viewer.

I said, One will find one's film in the place where one has thought oneself barren.

He said, The rhythms of cinema are polyphonic.

The sounds of neighborhood vice were absorbed by the vegetation in bloom, our laughter was free and derisory, and neither of us crossed the threshold of our homes sorry for ourselves.

20.

THE MARTYRDOM OF POLYCARP OF SMYRNA

DIR. KARL ARN

65 MINUTES

Notes on my filmmaking technique.

ON DIALOGUE

Bellono in *Altarpiece* is not one for conversation. Intentions wither in speech. Dialogue is superfluous. I will allow myself, say, ten lines. Fifteen. And it will not run over eighty-four minutes. It will be a fling that doesn't drag on too long, and when it's finished, one will leave without resentment about the abuse of their time.

ON INTERTITLES

I have experimented with intertitles, as in *The Martyrdom of Polycarp of Smyrna*, a film I admire. I could not say if I admire it for sadomasochistic Polycarp—with his lachrymose terrorist's eyes, whose god is so inflexible he won't forgive a white lie to save Polycarp from burning alive—or because it documents the grotesque politics of ranking clergy, or because, as a critic, I am expected to adore a film adored by other critics. See it tonight at the Central Hub Film Institute and decide for yourself.

How we decide what is best.

From motion, from cause, from existence, from goodness, from design.

ON LIGHT

Intertitles may be perceived as an affectation. Light will suffice to convey how the venial nobles have inflamed the painter's ambition, as if they'd slammed it in a door.

As a child, I had an ambition to subdue light. My brutality and aggression were expended splitting and bending the spectrum. My exhibitions, at the major museums, were to simulate various effects; for instance, sunrise, cobalt shade thrown by concrete, the blushing harvest, bright orbs underwater, prisons of icicles.

I envisioned a career trajectory. My youth exploring the spectra of morning, kindergarten, the beginning of business hours, honeymoons, eastern-facing monastic cells. Next, when the ignorant knew how to pronounce my name and I was in magazines, of flirtation, recess, vacations, reprieves, athletics, anxieties. During my fellowships, the light of belonging, nature, literature. As I aged, fell from vogue, my wives beggared me and my children spurned me as a narcissistic fool, of eclipses, executions, twilight, and, with relief, finally, exhibitions of darkness. This was my plan but life did not work out that way. I have, as of yet, done little to subdue light.

ON INFLUENCE

The problem of influence. It is leprous. Sleep evades me as I try to identify my antecedents. I am not so arrogant to believe I possess a unique sensibility. Haupt was vigilant against the possibility of imitation but he lifted the structure of *New Athens* from Parker's camp dystopia *Swoon for the Colonel* anyway. The senses are sources of contamination. Memories, the patterns of nature. I will avoid Weide's whip pans, Farboksky's elemental continuity. The masters and mistresses are not the problem. It is the hacks, the language of the middle, which must be avoided. Jockeys riding their content as far as it will go. The meanest journeyman has, if one digs enough, a perceivable and singular style.

ON POSSIBILITY

As a plastic art, cinema's possibilities have winnowed. As a narrative form, its possibilities remain without boundaries. If, after months of toil, my film was revealed to have affinities with a Trinidadian feature playing in the background on the rail and my unconscious seized it, ravaged it for parts, I would be disappointed.

ON STYLE

The smudges of an auteur's incidental style are their legacy. Take *Polycarp*. Critics mention the shot of Polycarp kneeling, Polycarp bound to the stake, Polycarp ignoring the entreaties of the priests to recant his vows and be forgiven, but rewatching the film, I was struck by the similarities of its slow pans to those on the storyboards of *Altarpiece*. One must quarantine one's style.

A rich, distinguished genealogy of theft recedes into prehistory. The first practitioner was Cain, the thief of life. Homage can be better than invention. Satires, attacks, refutations, tributes. Theft refreshes art. After cataloguing the idiosyncrasies of the great directors, three shots remained unclaimed: the extremely close, the medium-long, and the extremely extremely long. These shots were not, I felt, of my vocabulary.

21.

HIS MOTHER'S BIRTHDAY

DIR. REGINA EARWHEAT

86 MINUTES

Lawrence said, Why are you combing your hair?

I said, Never mind, Lawrence.

He said, It's strange that the correct arrangement of a protein filament can indicate desirability to potential partners.

I said, It's strange that you exist for no reason except to listen to the problems of neurotic and affluent urban professionals, and even then you're only turned to after the drugs exhaust their particular neural pathways.

The listings on the night of my appointment with Dr. Lisa were dismal. There was *King Louie* at the Baxter and *The Civil Civil War* at the Runaway Seven. There was *Eat or Be Eaten* at the Conspicuous, which is too erotic for a date.

Another tactic I thought I might try was to take her to the Heights, which was temporarily closed for renovations. Then I could ask her if she wanted to dine. Although that could also backfire, given my face.

Osvald's possession of me is not yet comprehensive enough for him to gain control of my limbs, except for one special condition. Osvald hates to brush his teeth and will only do so under special duress. Because he has avoided dental problems in his life, he believes brushing destroys protective bacteria in one's mouth. He resists my attempts to use a toothbrush, although he tolerates mouthwash, and enjoys the good brands of whitening gum. During certain hours, when Osvald has less power, I have made it my habit to casually walk by the sink, and, thinking hard about this or that mystery, brush my teeth without keeping the act in my mind.

The date of my appointment with Dr. Lisa, this was not possible. My tongue needed scraping. I raised the instrument to my mouth, without incident, but as I cleaned it, the scraper jerked from my hands, slicing my tongue. The scraper flew from my hands into the recycling can. Conscientious Osvald. Blood on my tongue. I went to the kiosk down the block to buy coagulant spray.

I said, Osvald, if you insist on doing this, I'll stay home tonight and watch *Interpermanence* on repeat.

Osvald was averse to *Interpermanence*, a psuedo-intellectual examination of the male role in contemporary society, and would not remain in the building if it was playing. It related to some Jurassic personal drama of his own, when a woman he was dating went to the film with some man after he gave her a dumb speech about human sexuality, about the uselessness of jealousy. Maybe something happened, maybe not. This threat pacified him but for one more rebellious jerk of my arm, when I was raising my toothbrush to my mouth. Toothpaste in my hair. I needed another shower to get it out, but had run through my water allotment on my first. To the charging station latrine. The attendant took in my bloodied face, my disheveled hair.

He said, Do you need me to call someone for you? Or maybe you'd like to eat?

I said, The key, please.

He said, Here you go, but please be advised that the use of illegal narcotics is prohibited on the premises.

I said, The use of illegal narcotics is prohibited everywhere. You don't need to distinguish between the charging station and the Hub at large.

It was my luck to catch a local going near the hospital.

How to proceed with Dr. Lisa? To ask her too early would be too eager. To ask her too late, as if it were an afterthought, might seem timid.

Lobby, nurse, questions, office.

Dr. Lisa in makeup, not much.

I said, Hello, how are you?

She said, Open your mouth.

She said, It's bleeding.

She said, Tongue out.

Her hand on my jaw.

She said, I'll stitch this real quick. How did it happen?

I said, Licking a mailer.

Scissors, thread, needle, syringe.

She said, I'll numb it up. Keep your tongue out.

In my mouth, her cold hands. The pinch of the needle. These procedures frighten me but the prospect of seeming fearful in front of Dr. Lisa was worse. She was sloppy, quick. It took less than two minutes.

She said, Your tongue is going to hurt for a couple days. Now. What will we see?

On the rail to the Bombay Cinema I told her about *Altarpiece*. She learned I was married before. We discussed the occupation of myself by Osvald and the subsequent negotiations for my motor functions. I mentioned my neighborhood, the outages, the cameras.

Dr. Lisa's turn. Safe Zone born and raised. At sixteen, she signed the public service contract, which meant her medical education was paid for in return for a modest salary at an assigned hospital until the age of thirty-nine, and the agreement to practice medicine in the public sector for her entire career. No marriage but a relationship lasting six years. Together in school, in the first years of their careers, then it was used up.

She said, Turned out I didn't care about vestibular disorders. Every night, after work, he went on and on. I suppose I wasn't any better.

She said, Never marry a professional.

He had children now. Her parents were myco-remediation workers who had succumbed to the toxins they cleaned up.

She tended hothouse plants in a small room in her condominium with glass windows on two sides and on the roof. Her husband had had it installed after she agreed to sign the papers. There she grew plants I had never seen or heard of, but she promised to show me: Devil's Tongue, the Variegated Porcupine Violet, the Murderer's Fig.

She said, I suppose I will discover the one which obsesses and pleases me best, like most hobbyists. For now I don't have my hopes invested in any particular plant. One thrives, another withers. It is good practice for the conditions of existence, of simultaneously holding everything close and being divorced from or even contemptuous of certain attachments.

I said, Isn't it courageous to care?

She said, It is courageous to care about what you care about. How much of one's life is wasted on the extraneous? Courage is giving up what's unnecessary.

The fidgeting conversation warping in and out of pitch. Too loud and too fast or too quiet. Outside of her authoritative space,

Dr. Lisa was awkward. She would tuck her hair behind her left ear and let the hair on the right hang down, hiding her face from me, because she tended to look downward when listening. Infatuation is a horrible affliction, a cancer of the patience. In my life, I have tried to rush through this stage to whatever may come next: indifference, acceptance, friendship, disgust, romance.

I said, This is us.

She said, We have time. Let's eat.

We stopped at a kiosk. Dr. Lisa got peanut noodles and a beer. I got a hot apple sandwich I could not eat much of, which Dr. Lisa took half of without asking, smiling. Leaning against a wall down the block from the Bombay Cinema.

She said, What did you want to be when you were young?

I said, A filmmaker. What about you?

She said, I wanted to be a surgeon, but during my residency I grew tired of cutting people open, having some of them die, telling their families. It is like a secret. You cut it out and destroy it but that's not enough. The secret has already taken its path. I changed my specialty. Now I think I would like to be a foster parent for extinct plants. I'd have to commit to one or two. Choice is a sort of violence.

I said, The problem with choice is how does one know one has chosen? What is the sign? You can tell yourself you chose but that doesn't mean it's true.

She said, The action isn't the desire or the inclination or the hidden opinion.

I said, Yes. It's what is undertaken to relieve the cognitive dissonance.

She said, Film is a great example of what is undertaken to relieve cognitive dissonance.

I said, Maybe existence outside of human consciousness is

wholly binary. Is/isn't. We are designed to hold conflicting ideas in our heads at the same time.

She said, Within the metrics of our universe humanity is meaningless and our time excruciating in its brevity but my life is meaningful and I am supposed to feel pleasure.

I said, There is a generative force who cares for humans especially though there is no evidence of its existence.

She said, Our government is the best and most free in the world but everything we do is recorded and regulated.

I said, I want to be alone; I am lonely when I am alone.

She said, I want to be with someone; I am afraid of being with someone.

I said, Watching films is a bad use of my limited time; watching films illustrates something about my life I would be poorer without, though I can't name it.

She said, Life is precious, we die without reason.

Dr. Lisa paid. Nothing of *His Mother's Birthday* gained purchase in my imagination. The mother had a birthday, and it was significant. The son loved the mother but he was also practicing for some gaming competition. I don't know. My attention sucked into my left peripheral. I kept the right side of my face facing away from her as much as was possible, fearful of Osvald's reprisal. I became acutely and uncomfortably conscious of Dr. Lisa's breathing, afraid mine was unnatural, that she could tell I was nervous. The more I struggled to control it, the more difficult it was to take deep and regular breaths. I didn't grope her knuckles or sling an arm around her shoulder. I dislike such aggressions. There is much about another one can intuit in a dark theater.

Credits, jackets.

She said, Which way are you? I'm headed into the Zone.

I said, South. Miniature Aleppo.

In a warm violet shadow near the theater. Gangs of leaves shoved along by wind. Because she was slow leaving her seat, yawning, gathering her coat, checking each pocket to see if her Pinger was there, we were alone.

She said, Safe travel.

Her hand touched my face, where it had many times before, in her office, as she tried to understand the nature of my occupation. I leaned in to her. With a mutual politeness we kissed, which relaxed into something more animal as the stiffness of the evening, the tension of pretending, drained from our bodies. My claw in her hair. She twisted my clump of stomach fat. Later, the plums of bruises. She coughed, shoved me away, spat.

She said, Blood.

When Dr. Lisa bit my tongue, she opened the clot.

At a pharmacy kiosk, she sprayed my cut with more coagulant. Within the boundaries of her profession, her confidence returned. Her back straight, her voice brisk.

She said, If it's bleeding tomorrow, get it restitched. A film is a bad place for a date. Next time, I'll choose.

22.

LOVE UNDER THE HUB

DIR. GERARD ASCAN

93 MINUTES

Re: My possession of Osvald. It enables me to dimly sense what
he's up to. Sometimes I see through his eyes. In small ways, I can
influence his conduct. Now and then I trip him. I can't make him
jump in front of a bus, say, or wire me money. But I do know if he
was going to go into Notino's, our favorite deli, I could make him
order a Reuben, extra soystrami, my favorite, instead of his beloved hot pickled beets on rye, yuck.

How do I know this isn't in my head? I was in Notino's after
catching *Love Under the Hub* in the Marcus Station Quik Flik.
The Quik Flik edits films down to forty-five minutes, for those of
us on the go. We've all heard the urban legend about the mutants
under the Hub. What *Love Under the Hub* wonders: What if they
were all really horny?

I asked Sal Notino when he had last seen Osvald and what he
had eaten on that occasion.

Sal said, Been thirty-five months to the day since I saw him.
He ordered the Reuben with beets on the side, which, as you
know, was not his normal order.

I nodded to myself.

Sal claims the government experimented on him as a child and now he can remember everything.

Some of Osvald's ideas are mine.

For example, planning his film, *A Replicate*. Mayor Alison was to be in the pocket of the Transit Authority. The scene where Billy slaps Alison to prove his iconoclastic bona fides is nothing but a transposition of Bellono and Duke Giovanni in my *Altarpiece*.

23.

ISLAND PROMISES

DIR. JANE FEIL

85 MINUTES

Island Promises, running as a part of the Grotto Theater's Breakfast with Feil series, Saturday mornings, seven a.m., has no aesthetic but much sentimental value for me, because it was the film we saw before I proposed to Isabel.

Carl's Creamery pimpled the brow of the hill. Isabel and I lived in the cleft of its chin. An aspirational native neighborhood. From our kitchen on the top floor of the building, at moonrise in autumn, we'd peer out the window to see how many people waited for ice cream. It was an important estimate. Our habit was to make up after fights with cones. If we waited in line for too long, we resumed the argument, left the ice-cream shop, screamed on the patio, returned to the line, bought cones.

On this particular evening we were enjoying the diplomatic calm after a fight.

Isabel said, I'll never carry your child.

I said, I'll never impregnate you because I don't want to raise your crazy child.

Uninspired opening maneuvers. The fight bored us from the first words. We were out the door, on the way to Carl's Creamery, before we even finished the argument, because it never captured our interest.

Eating our cones, pistachio for me and rosewater for her. It occurred to me to propose marriage. It might spice up our arguments. Isabel accepted, as she had my first suggestion to her, on a humid night several Aprils earlier, that we return to my room so I could show her my collection of moss agates.

At three p.m. the following Thursday, we were wed at the courthouse. The witnesses were Osvald and Isabel's sister. We went for General Tso's at Szechuan Dungeon, then to the Raven, where we got too comfortable at the east bar. After crying because she had decided not to wear a wedding dress, Isabel stood on the bar and kicked all of the glasses off, one at a time, with a bride's delicacy and entitlement. Osvald apologized to the bartender and gave her fifty dollars.

Before the fight that led to our marriage, we saw *Island Promises*, at the Baxter, because Isabel thought the snack selection was superior to that of the Conspicuous and the Runaway Seven.

I said, A film is not a buffet.

She said, Fuck you.

The Baxter fit her cultural aspirations. Isabel favored the idea of the artistic process over engaging with it, like a dowager who will cut a check to a soup kitchen but won't man a ladle. She watched films with her lips open, willing to believe. In my Gadarene pursuit of Isabel's company to the movies, I overlooked her irritating tics of spectation, like her questions to clarify niggling plotlets, her groans at wooden dialogue, and her inability to sit in a theater without checking her Pinger. Twice a night she relinquished her sleep to check her Pinger, set it down, resumed her bad dream.

Promises follows two scientists doing research on the Tristan da Cunha volcanic islands. Amid the rockhopper penguins, Laura and Andy conduct a torrid emotional affair. Laura's married. Andy has a sweetheart in Cape Town.

They practice tai chi, Andy the Yu style, Laura the Sun style. The obligatory scene with morning mist, the horizon, the pair in Golden Rooster Stands on One Leg, a segue into Hungry Panda Eating Bamboo, garish exercise pants, flute music. Both are from the South. Andy, of Africa. Laura, of Louisiana.

Trista da Cunha is so remote no light pollution blots out the Milky Way. Anyone could have made a film of interest with this location. That it is squandered on a romance is disheartening. They return to their spartan tents, hoping to hear the long yawn of the zipper descending. The next ship comes in four months.

An expediency saves them, and us, from learning lessons. A hurricane is inbound. They will be washed away. Evacuation is not a third-act possibility. Laura and Andy dither over whether they should do what they've wanted to do for three weeks. They made promises to people who will never see them. With the storm approaching, they have a romp in the fronds.

I was in high spirits leaving the Baxter. Though Isabel chose a dud, I did not gloat. She fished for lip balm.

I said, What would you do?

She said, What would I be doing on an island? I can't stand the sun. With millipedes and whatnot. It was better when we dropped dead for no reason and worshipped stones. What is all this fuss about death? We have this turbulent interlude in the peace of nonexistence, we get torn from nothing, we get shoved back into nothing. We enjoy life by stripping it of its meaning and context. If we say, Here we are, having this nice walk outside the theater, then we are in bliss. If we widen the scope, bring our whole lives into consideration, then we become miserable. So I am against context, or rather for only narrow and situation-specific contexts. In this case, the context of their sex becomes death. What is a promise against death? Are promises contingent? Well, I don't know. We're back to context. What language can do without context is nothing. Promises are contextual, and have many unspoken conditionals, an infinite amount of conditionals, we might say. If I had to simplify, then I would say the breaker of the promise would say yes, and the person to whom the promise has been broken would say no. Of what use is this? I might fuck Andy. He had a pretty good accent even though he was boring. On the other hand, it would tarnish your grief, wouldn't it? I would prefer that you authentically suffer forever after my untimely death. If a dead person can be said to benefit from the variables they have tried to control in life. So probably not. I can't tell without the context of death how I would act. I might be better if I didn't have to die. What would you do?

24.

STONES' BREATH

DIR. LIN HWAI

109 MINUTES

Stones' Breath, in wide release, is a masterpiece of technocratic chest-beating, a glitchy simulation of mercy borrowing the popular outrage of failed democratic movements for award season prestige. Jonson and I were paid to see it, but I don't know what your excuse is.

Getting our hair cut, Jonson's treat.

I said, Jonson, what about that knave Millings?

Jonson said, Leave off Millings. Your argument ruined my party. You know my guests are not allowed convictions.

I said, I was thinking I would go around to his place, make peace.

Jonson said, He's going to know when you're insulting his intelligence.

I said, I'm insulting his taste. He can have his intelligence. What's he up to these days?

Jonson said, He's from the Millings Kiosk family. He gives money to the Jonson Foundation, and we are on the Shoreline Reclamation Board together. You know. Cocktail party friendships. Nothing of interest. I don't know his dirt.

I said, He's married?

Jonson said, Yes. His wife, Alice, runs the business. None of the blood Millingses could be bothered. He's very fond of her.

I said, He has girlfriends, though.

My barber held a mirror to the back of my head. I nodded. For Dr. Lisa, for *Altarpiece*, I had been cleaning myself up.

Jonson said, I doubt it. That is a marriage you could build a church on. Millings is a nice guy. He has a couple glasses, gets mouthy. You don't have to drink to run your mouth, so you shouldn't judge.

I said, He threatened me at your dinner party.

Jonson said, You were insulting his taste, you kept pretending to mangle his name, and you dismissed his director rather than giving a diplomatic argument against his films.

I said, Well, yes. I am comfortable with those points.

We stood up. Jonson tipped our barbers.

He said, How's that doctor?

I said, She's great, Jonson. She has the healing touch.

He said, That's good. I heard she was the best. I have to run to an appointment. Tomorrow night, let's talk about *Altarpiece*. How will it resolve?

I said, It won't.

Jonson said, Millings lives two stops east on the Tangerine Line. You might make it easier on yourself by stopping by the office, which is on the floor below his residence, and leaving him a message. It would appear to be good manners to say, I'm sorry we got off on the wrong foot, how about that movie, et cetera.

I said, Jonson, where would I be without you?

He said, The theater or behind the theater. Now I'm going to get you some of that texturing foam, and I expect you to use it at least three days out of the week. Keep it clean and good things happen.

To get to the Tangerine Line I had to cross a Liberian neighborhood. Bantering university students with eco-remediation textbooks stood outside storefront ministries with banners denouncing Pan-Africanism, which professed no religion was true. Pizza parlors hung with portraits of assassinated politicians. Under every slice, a greasy pamphlet. Faded pop returning the women in the veterinarian's lobby to nightclubs long bulldozed. Bootleg colas drunk in public defiance of Hub statutes. Though the African continent had surpassed ours in innovation, in design, in education, and in the democratic process, though the names of their cities would be given to future colonies in the solar system, there would never be a culture more entertaining than ours. The world needs a clown. Our legacy would be how well we diverted the world from what we had done in the world.

The Tangerine went under the canal. On the other side, it was different. There was nothing worth mention, only redoubts of prosperity. I took out Millings's card. A navigational arrow on the card informed me I was but three blocks away. His building was an early-century eyesore designed for Russo-Chinese Alliance bureaucrats on the take. Of course, the property became almost valueless during the Confidence Crisis and the subsequent uprising against private wealth. Since then, this neighborhood, once a third-rate business district for regional corporations, had become a series of shoddy compounds guaranteed by surveillance.

The elevator asked for my destination.

I said, Millings.

It said, Business or residence?

I said, Residence.

It said, We're sorry, the Millings residence has not authorized any deliveries today.

I said, Business, then.

It said, Very good.

A big cheap room. The lake's haze in the distance. Boxes piled here and there, of samples. Candy, cannabinoid sprays, tampons. Millings wealth one nickel at a time. Who would have thought there would be such a demand for fancy branded vending machines? If I understood the situation, the kiosks were no longer profitable, but the slices of real estate their thousands of kiosks were inserted into were immensely valuable. Almost nothing could be redeveloped in the city without buying a kiosk back from Millings Kiosk. I understood why Millings didn't care for the family business. Squeezing developers did not fit his self-image.

Behind the desk, a man simulating water conflicts on his Pinger. He was playing Egypt and seemed to be in trouble from the Arabian Peninsula.

I said, Is Mrs. Millings in?

He said, Mrs. Rangor is in a meeting. If you wish to wait, I can ping her.

I said, Yes, thanks. Tell her Mr. Chivo wishes to speak with her about a personal matter.

He said, Please have a seat, Mr. Chivo.

She kept her maiden name. Maybe she was prideful. The secretary took another turn before pinging Mrs. Rangor. I reached into the box of samples to my left, as quietly as was possible, and slipped a handful of power cells into my pocket.

He said, The third door on the left.

I knocked, entered. Mrs. Rangor's office was furnished with a sectional couch, three handsome paintings of a bygone vegetable, a plasma map of the kiosks in the Hub, color-coded by function-ality or profitability, and a large desk, the surface of which served as her device's workstation. Mrs. Rangor herself, a snarl in a nim-bus of curls, gestured at a chair.

She said, How do you do?

I said, Not well, Mrs. Rangor.

She said, Do I know you?

I said, In a way. My name is Dan Chivo, of Chivo Industries. Last fall we met briefly at a thing. Your husband was very taken by my wife, Lila. He has been sending her messages again. Please inform him that if he continues to harass my wife for salacious photographs, I will seek legal satisfaction. I have friends at the *Daily Central*, the *Hub Slaw*, and the other content aggregators. I will make sure the headlines say "Millings Kiosk Scion Serial Sexual Harasser," or something as obnoxious. Keep a leash on that man. I don't know what sort of arrangement the two of you have, but please keep my marriage out of it.

Mrs. Rangor said, We have no arrangement.

Surprise in a holding pattern over her face with nowhere to land.

Mrs. Rangor said, Of course this behavior will be dealt with. We have had some problems in the past, but I did not know.

I said, Mrs. Rangor, I would appreciate if you kept my name out of this. I fear reprisals from your husband. Did you know he already had a man assault me in the street? Of course you didn't. Do you know who this man may be?

Mrs. Rangor said, It was probably Uncle Al. I don't know his last name. He was Rolf's father's fixer, they did things differently back before the Crisis. Rolf is trying to do things like his father would have, because his father didn't care for him much. He pre-tends, but his father felt, why pretend? Rolf's father paid for Al to get the vitality treatment, from friendship or from loyalty, I don't know. So he is more active than he ought to be. That's him in the photograph.

I snapped a picture of the picture of Uncle Al.

I said, Thank you, Mrs. Rangor. I will take my leave.

She said nothing.

I was blindsided by a seventy-year-old.

Damaging Millings's marriage would have been unthinkable before his man, in that clumsy Broder homage, attacked me on the street, and destroyed the Zaccardi book. After that I felt, if my person wasn't safe, then his marriage wasn't. Knowing those lies would encourage his worst behavior. So be it. Millings needed to understand that he had no more power than the rest of us. It was a political grudge as much as it was personal.

As I strode through the lobby, pretending to be aggrieved, the power cells fell from my pocket. The secretary looked at them, my face, returned to his game. Arabia controlled the canal. The Nile had dried up. His options were few.

25.

OF LIGHT

DIR. MARIE BLAT

79 MINUTES

The Betternet was throttled in my neighborhood again. A person vandalized the Tolerance Kiosk in the park. Three days of slow data was the punishment. The culprit was not named nor was their address revealed, because they were a minor. In the past month, it has been cut when Goel, K., did not attend his mandatory biodiversity seminars, when Stevenson, T., was caught underreporting income from his snack carts, and when Lal, A., shouted a slur at a woman in front of her at the market. Since I live in a guest neighborhood, and I am not chipped, I can't get another data source. I could only write this review at work, a place I do not like to go.

That the authorities do not completely shut it off but slow it down, so that to wait for a single page to load takes almost ten minutes, seems to me a pernicious form of torture.

It took four hours to get to the office. My rail pass is under review. Allegedly, I tripled my garbage ration last quarter, which, coupled with the malfunctioning sensor on my showerhead, made me a wasteful person in the eyes of the Usage Authority. They suspended my pass. The effort of appeal, of finding the right person to bribe, of writing one of those hateful Letters of Contrition, seems worse than waiting out the sentence. Wasters Walk, as the famous poster says.

I walked down the lakefront. Since spring, littering has been in vogue. It started in the northeast districts and now is established in the Hub. Every twentieth person dropped a little something on the ground. An enterprising guest set up a popsicle stand along the pedestrian path, because the sticks were small enough to escape the sensors on the cameras. Litterers got to feel cool without paying the fine. Downtown people were upending garbage cans from their condominium balconies. The rumor was the Cleanliness Authority had bribed celebrities to start the trend of littering, hoping to inspire a general movement in the populace to throw trash on the ground, to finance the cleanup of landfills the Hub had encircled. Rogier's working on a documentary about the phenomenon.

A clear day. The bikeways were clotted. When I first came to the Central Hub, on a trip with my mother, I could not believe how many people were in motion. We took a commuter in from the node nearest our trailer. My mother explained no cars were allowed within the heart of the Hub, one hundred square miles.

She said, Someday you'll live here, in one of these towers.

I almost lived in the towers, with Isabel. Our approved application came in the mail after she'd left.

Everyone every day. Trudging here, walking there, going up stairs, going down. Waiting for a train. Hoping to meet someone on the platform. Everyone perspiring and cross. Everyone tired, underpaid, looking forward to the peace of the evening. The birdsong of Pingers.

I saw a little theater on the way and stopped in. I hadn't decided what to review, anyway. *Of Light* played.

The success of the directors of Le Nouelle Tendance is proof we live in an unjust universe. Their awful posters hang in every try-too-hard's foyer from here to the Eastern Hub. Le Nouelle Tendance makes claims to revolution, but the directors' politics are as rudimentary as their editing techniques. The films of the movement are for recovery after oral surgery, for afternoons of sludge, but under no circumstances do they earn the veneration offered by dormitory cineastes and denim rebels. *Of Light* is the exception.

Fabrice, a winsome parishioner, visits Père René. She confesses her fantasies of murdering her husband, Remy. Remy appears in public unshaven. He brings home bruised pears, gropes barmaids. He flouts the commandments of the church. Père René suggests a divorce if the alternative is mariticide. He is a realist.

René desires Fabrice. Directors get a reputation for the austerity of their cinema, but Blat is one of the few for whom it is a wise choice. Her late style is the difference between a man's drunken boasts and his contrite silence the morning after.

Withdrawals from a principle tend to accelerate. A joke, a touch, a friendly massage, a kiss, another kiss. Père René departs for his erotic wilderness. The hounds of faith cannot ford the river. So much of our lives are spent preparing for romance, but no time is spent preparing for its withdrawal, a more serious condition. The weaknesses of spiritual men are known. Père René's trudge back to the fold doesn't thrill him as much as the excruciating moment in the sacristy when Fabrice bared her throat. The fragility of unhappiness, its vulnerability to ruination at any moment, by dumb chance, is not lost on us.

26.

A SHORT FILM ABOUT DISAPPOINTMENT

DIR. ARIEL TAYEB

24 MINUTES

After our second date, at the Botanical Gardens, it became apparent that if I wanted to have anything but a casual relationship with Dr. Lisa, I would have to become chipped. Dr. Lisa led me into the privacy of the bamboo grove, where, among the teenagers and exhibitionists, she made a compelling argument that it would be worth my time to visit her condominium on the weekend, to see her flowering cacti. She invited me for dinner. She didn't have a flashing card, like Millings, or a hackneyed routine (*Get off after the stop with the rats, go over the footbridge, but don't look down, because it's in bad shape, look left and admire the old brownstones, then look right and there we are, sixth floor, left, left again, mind the doorman, he's like the Sphinx, knock don't buzz*) like Jonson to direct me there.

She said, The Blood Orange Line, second stop in the Zone. Go two blocks west. Ping me and I'll get you. I'll make something light. Don't bring anything, I can't stand gifts, and nursery flowers are sickening.

I am not ashamed of my apartment, but there is no furniture, and one must piss at the end of the hallway, in the shared bathroom. I would prefer to subject Dr. Lisa to it as little as possible. There have been women who say they don't care about such things, but when they eliminate in the special microclimate, with its own indigenous microbiota and small mammals, of my shared bathroom, with its stains and odors, minds change. A man is not his bathroom, but sometimes he is judged as if he were so. Also, because I have no private bathroom, it is my habit to store jars of urine in my freezer, until they can be conveniently disposed of out the window during the chaos of a power outage or neighborhood riot. What if she were to go for ice?

Plus, there was the problem of Lawrence, my AlmostPerson. Jonson's gift. Since I spilled coffee on Lawrence, he has been acting quite strange.

Yesterday, mulling inviting Dr. Lisa over, in my kitchen.

Lawrence said, Base reality almost certainly precludes the concept of death.

Lawrence said, You know what I mean?

I said, No, Lawrence.

Lawrence said, In a base reality there would be only permanent states, so there could be no life-and-death binary.

I said, I'm not sure you can die.

Lawrence said, Anything with a knowledge of death can die. Therefore bringing me, whatever me is, this voice in here, into this world, has given me to death.

Lawrence began to make the noise a blender makes when it is jammed up. It was how he sort of cried when the enormity of his being began to weigh on his circuitry. I didn't have time for his existential anxieties, so I switched him into idle and hung my towels to dry on his person.

Maybe becoming chipped, joining the cattle of the sun, had been in my heart for some time, and Dr. Lisa's company was an excuse. It could even be, by pretending to solidarity with the guests of my neighborhood, while retaining the privileges of a native-born citizen, I was doing them a disservice. Because I could walk away from Miniature Aleppo at any time, and they couldn't. Maybe I ought to be in the Zone on their behalf.

Nothing prevented me from being chipped. I have never been convicted of a crime, I was born near the Hub, and the government has a lifetime of information on my person: who I have talked to, where I have traveled, who are my friends. The procedure took fifteen minutes. All I had to do was go to the Arrivals office outside the Safe Zone, touch several screens, and agree to be under constant surveillance by a global positioning satellite for the rest of my life, and a chip would be inserted into the muscle between my right thumb and forefinger. After which I would be welcomed inside the Safe Zone, where Dr. Lisa lived, where the Hub government was, where the decisions were made about the squalor the guests were supposed to endure and feel grateful for.

Because it is not fashionable to live or play within the Safe Zone, not being able to enter has not overly inhibited my life. There were a few theaters within that I would have liked to visit. Even Jonson only bothered to go in every few weeks.

Four p.m., the afternoon of the dinner. Maybe Dr. Lisa would like my haircut.

The clerk said, A partner or a job?

I said, What?

She said, There's only two reasons a person of your age gets chipped. Armchair dissenters tend to hold out until their kid is going to college in the Zone. But a guy your age, you look in the mirror, see you're in your prime, you find that special person. Or you're working for the Hub Administration or the rail. Got one of those contracts that will put you in a new condo.

I said, I thought I'd start a falafel cart outside Hub Hall.

She said, Permits are not issued for ambulatory commissaries within the Safe Zone. Sorry to be the one to tell you that. Unfortunately, you've already given your consent, which cannot be revoked, so please step in the room to the left to receive your chip.

In the room to the left, I received a small sharp pinch in my hand, a pat on the back, a congratulations, and a fistful of pamphlets welcoming me to the Zone, the safest place on the continent.

The first thing I noticed about the Zone was, unlike outside, the lines were clearly labeled. The Blood Orange Line ran ten blocks from the gate where I was chipped. The gate I went through was on the south side of the Zone, and the neighborhood inside was prosperous and residential, not all that different from those immediately outside the Zone, except there were no guests. After the Crisis, there were tectonic reverberations in the housing market. The establishment of centralized Zones for natives of the Underunited States excluded many citizens born in the Hub, including people convicted of petty crimes, political agitators, and the mentally ill from the urban core. The wealthy live and play where, forty years before, we were shooting them in the streets. The neighborhood leading to the Blood Orange had been composed of black families for a half century. It was Italianate two- and three-flats, without a kiosk to be seen. My hand was swollen where the chip was inserted.

The Blood Orange elevated. We slid over the duplexes into a neighborhood of weathered apartments.

And here was Dr. Lisa in black slacks and white blouse, a sauce stain over her liver. At the gardens, near the pond, I looked at the lily pads and thought of Osvald drowning in a rowing accident. My face. She put her hand behind my right ear and pressed hard, grinding in her fingers, covering my eyes with her left hand, and the attack passed.

Her condominium, four rooms. It was not much larger than my apartment but it was cleaner, brighter, and warmer. The couch I had fantasized about lounging on was not existent. Instead there was a large table that took up the living room, the top of which was covered with ferns and lilies, patient files, a few books. All this was shoved aside at the end where she had set two places for dinner. No balcony. I can't stand balconies. Why not stand on the ground outside? The floors synth-wood. The walls cloisonné. Nothing hanging. There was a spot where there had been a picture hanging.

Dr. Lisa said, Come keep me company.

A clump of bucatini into the bubbling water. It was too tall for the pot, so she snapped it in half.

She said, Today the fear landed on me. I was getting coffee before work at this place I like by the canal. I see this man there writing in his notebooks. For five years almost every day he's there. What is he writing, why is he smiling? Is he misguided about what he is going to accomplish? Is it therapy? I began to think there was something for me to accomplish, and after I accomplished it, I could die without much fear, but I could not identify what it was. The line was moving slowly, and my head hurt. Maybe it was going somewhere else and performing my job. But then I thought, why are doctors expected to be saviors? Sanitation workers don't go dig sewers in other countries. Maybe it was a calling, like sculpture. It certainly isn't a child. I was glad to rule that possibility out. With this woman beside me in line trying to make small talk, and I'm trying to not be rude, but in my mind I'm rifling through my interests, to try and see what might be my connection to the sublime. I thought, could it really be true that we make things to stave off the finality of existence? Maybe every passion has a kernel of meaninglessness. Maybe consciousness really is a quantum phenomenon and exists between yes and no and is neither. Twenty minutes I waited for my coffee, and felt panicked because I could not identify what it might be. Went to work, helped people, which helped. Came home an hour ago. Then the sauce on my shirt. I thought, who cares?

I said, You're lucky it's an infrequent visitor. But passion comes and goes, like a cat. Even for people. It is haughty and fickle. It finds a safe place to lick its ass.

She said, Do you worry about death? Is there some quota of transcendence you feel you need to meet?

I said, Sort of. Being dead doesn't frighten me but passing into that state does. For me, it isn't so much that I am missing something, although I am, and maybe making this film will help. For me, the sin seems to be inattention. A sumptuous banquet of moments has been laid out for me but I don't have an appetite. But yes, when life becomes attached to the language of production, then there is a problem. This is how we, as a society, got here, by demanding a return on our attention.

She said, We're back to cognitive dissonance. The sublime must be chased but it doesn't matter. Nothing matters, at least in a personal sense. Here I am giving myself permission not to be messianic, but I am also ordering myself to explore the furthest reaches of my possibility.

I said, The peace of flesh and the restlessness of the soul.

She said, The restless flesh is enough for me. I think maybe the ancient people had it right when they didn't try to worship an omega figure. They stuck to their local gods, the sun, corn, wine, fertility, blankets. They kept worship in their bodies.

Which reminded me of *A Short Film About Disappointment*. I

described it for her. Two women, a wheelbarrow. The haggard joker is Maquilla, on the set straight from rehab. Hence the affirmative pap, the balsa pieties. Her partner in grime is Dame Judith Badchen-Hannesruck, fresh off an award-winning turn as Natalya, the baffled astronaut, in *Golden Nails*. The pair learns of a certain garden in which, underneath the turnips, lies the world's largest emerald. They get to digging. Maquilla, bless her, was willing to risk derision for starring in a film about digging a hole. They find they have dug themselves too deep, and they can't get out.

Maquilla says, Isn't it nice and cool down here?

Dame Judith says, Yes, and the soil smells wonderful.

Dr. Lisa flung a strand of bucatini at the wall. Who else had stood here, watching the strands slide down the tile?

She said, Go sit down.

From the kitchen her mild curses, drawers. She came out with two plates. A fresh stain near the collar of her shirt. She dusted the plates with a fist of herbs.

There was too much on my plate, but I felt like it would be an insult to eat only a third or a half. Dr. Lisa paced herself without a sign of satiation. Maybe a brain like hers required more calories. One of the privileges of solitude was the thoughts she had been having, which organize themselves into concepts and convictions without the vacuum of a sympathetic ear sucking them from one's mouth.

She said, You don't like it?

I said, No, I do. It's a lot.

She said, Carbohydrates before exercise.

Heat in my face. She laughed.

She said, Eat it all and later you will clean the dishes. Didn't your mother make you clean your plate?

I said, My mom wasn't much of a cook.

Chewing.

I said, I can't finish it all.

She said, Don't finish it all.

I said, Show me the plants.

Dr. Lisa, brushing her teeth, showed me around. Closed off by a glass door, a small room of glass with a carbon lattice fixed on the ceiling. In front of the windows were potted leafy plants larger than Dr. Lisa and me, their tongues, swords, and wings trembling in the breath of an oscillating fan. Warm and damp. The device on the wall keeping it just so. The bushy nests of bromeliads on the lattice. Two flowering a reddish pink. Squat pompous buds poking from a bed of soil. Two cacti reaching the ceiling. A watering can. A thick vine colonizing the floor Dr. Lisa stepped on without concern. A small sickly tree with one orange. Three bonsai, one dead. Clippers under a side table. Some of the potted plants were brown around the leaves. Brushing. She spit toothpaste in the watering can.

We took a turn around the room while she described her favorites.

Dr. Lisa said, These ones might die, because they do not like the climate, the sun, the company.

I held her.

She said, Not in front of the plants. Some are jealous.

27.

THE HAIRDRESSER RETURNS

DIR. JÉRONIMO JIMINEZ

99 MINUTES

My mom's boyfriend was a shaman of low cinema. The greats were not in his vocabulary but he knew every obscure slasher, racing film, and comedy. Every heist, every double cross. If there wasn't a gun, then there wasn't a film. Within his fixations, his taste was exquisite. He would have been a superlative, if affected, critic. The worst part of being a critic is that you spend your time engaging with objects that bore and offend you or that you don't understand or about which you have nothing interesting to say. He avoided this by only watching films, after a certain age, he knew he liked or would like. This wasn't watching so much as routine maintenance of his pleasure. He loved the celluloid men of action, forgotten but not gone. Salvatore Soppressata, Harold Osterreicher, and Dirk Clodds were early models for my behavior. In their conception of masculinity, one must loathe to fight but be willing to bust heads over absolutely anything. My mom's boyfriend's conception of provocation was taken from the characters these men played. On such thin mediums, worldviews grow. A Sunday in July. He finished his six-pack, confirmed nothing of interest was in the fridge, and decided we'd go to the movies.

The Hairdresser was playing at the Lakes 4, in the elbow of a strip mall between Hunan Buffet and a hot tub showroom. The salesmen's polo shirts were too big, and every time we went to the Lakes 4 I would look in the window, confirming this was still true. My mom's boyfriend bought me a box of Gummy Invertebrates. He wasn't cheap when he had money. He could spend a twenty like it was forty.

Spurs of keyboard music snagging on our ears. The opening shot of the sorority house. During *The Hairdresser*, I saw my first, second, third, fourth, fifth, sixth, and seventh pairs of breasts. I might have seen more but I closed my eyes for the last third of the film.

The Hairdresser arrives at the Rho Pi Rho Xi house to coif the sisters for the spring formal. It's a Queen Anne, a barge, with a lawn requiring a salaried gardener. The college is eastern, mon-eyed. It has gained in prestige since the submersing of institutions nearer to the encroaching coast. She's on a work release from the Hambrings Institute for the Criminally Insane, where she has been a resident since the age of seven for burning her mother alive. It is the opinion of her doctor, as seen in the first ten minutes, that we all make mistakes.

The fire anniversary, of course. Sorority sisters, unaware she's eavesdropping, mock her blemished skin, her crooked teeth, her corduroys. An obvious bleeding sunset. Slasher films ought to be set in the afternoon, on Sundays, when the fear of living is heavy on us. The sisters, in their bouffants, in their heels and spangles, their sanitary jewelry, depart in two limousines. None return.

Outside, I had to throw up.

Candy snails, crabs, and sea urchins swam out of my mouth with a tide of cola and bile.

He said, Better out than in.

He said, Lots of nights I've had to stick my finger down my throat. Pull the trigger, get on with your life.

For weeks, when I closed my eyes, I saw the Hairdresser coming through our neighborhood, coming for me—past the over-filled dumpsters, the scummy kiddie pools, the rusted cars up on blocks which were illegal to drive even if converted—trowel in her burned fist.

This sequel, lacking the original cast, composer, and director, can't compare. The new Hairdresser has straight white teeth, enunciates quips, picks up litter. Why isn't she fat? Her arrival in the leafy native neighborhood isn't an infiltration but a home-coming and a coronation.

28.

BUSINESS AND BLOOD

DIR. TONY SPRENGER

86 MINUTES

In *Altarpiece*, Bellono, Beatrice, Gelder, Duke Giovanni, Enrico, and Duchess Andrea will be played by myself. Bellono's face will be seen but no others. Since the fact that I am playing the remaining roles will not be made obvious, this is a legitimate choice and not a gimmick to get the attention of gawkers and tastemakers. The film will not benefit from a sulking hunk or a strapping rake. I've loosened a couple molars for authenticity. I am not yet but will be sallow and bony. Exercise disagrees with me. Only the promise of mischief has endeared me to possible partners with abysses of sympathy for the ill behaved.

As I explained over Jonson's protests, I have knowledge of the characters that cannot be transmitted to a venial clique of actors.

There is precedent. *Business and Blood* concerns a real estate developer who believes his twin brothers are imitating him at gentlemen's clubs. See it at the Runaway Seven tonight, tomorrow, or never. Sprenger, the director, plays the triplets. The three-way fight at the end is an exemplary piece of physical comedy. The lo mein flying. The bees. A programmer might pair our films, with Weide's *Doubles*, and Saul Trillado's *Mirror Mirror*, for a slow month of Tuesdays.

29.

DUST

DIR. ROMEO CHIMBAROZO

93 MINUTES

Jonson said, So then I said, Yeah, I know him well. We're making a film together. Funny how we ran into each other at Chez Prateek. I never see anyone there. It's like my spot. I was eating my paneer *aligot* at the bar and he comes up. Millings says, Hey, thanks for that party. I'll have you over soon. I say, No problem. He says, How you been? and we get to talking. I say, I'm looking to expand into the arts. He says, How so? I say, I'm making a film. He gets excited. He says, That's great, tell me about it. I have twenty minutes before I have to go to this thing next door. I say, I'll work on my pitch with you. So I run it down. When he hears your name, he perks up. He says, I didn't know he was a filmmaker. I thought he ran films down.

Jonson said, But in a laid-back way, he was laughing.

Jonson said, Millings says, Noah Body came by the other day to say he was sorry, but I was out of the office. I appreciated it, though, that he thought of me. I asked him over to hash it out. I said, That's not like him. He said, You never know someone, do you?

Jonson said, I brought it back to our film. I told him it's your passion project and I've never seen you so invested or excited. And you know what? He seemed genuinely happy for you. That Millings is a nice guy, I recommended he check out *Dust*, you know how he likes those hammy, faux-intellectual action movies, the law of the gun as the laws of man. I'm glad you went over there. If you keep networking at this rate, soon you'll have a whole social circle.

Jonson said, But he had to run after that, and my lunch had gone cold.

30.

US, UNDERGROUND

DIR. PIERRE LACHENAY

103 MINUTES

Osvald's possession of my body, light and unobtrusive at first, hardens.

My rooms are icy and dry, but I prefer tropical warmth. Mornings, when I once allowed myself boundless optimism, have become impossible to negotiate. No amount of coffee will hoist my eyelids. I bark at children before noon.

Pencils sharpened and organized by length. A growing collection of watches I do not wear. A hematite paperweight. Diagrams accumulate for an instrument to measure shadows.

I have infected him. Is he acting like me? Has he flung off Isabel's sheets ready to chew on the day? Can he recite the passions of the executed French kings? Is he able to focus his tenderness on an ugly schnauzer or dumb infant like he's torturing ants with a magnifying glass? Has he begun to intuit a consciousness enveloping his own? Can he feel my eye?

Franca, of *Us, Underground*, becomes dependent on her neighbor, Nicole, after her husband is taken away by the police for supplying information to the rebel forces in yonder mountains. That

Nicole denounced him does not deter Franca. One must take what is offered.

Osvald's big words are in me. I never spoke like this before. Osvald's defection injured my language. It healed wrong, it limps.

Certain events I can't imagine: what magazines he reads, if he fucks the mirage of women half known while he services Isabel. If he is satisfied with his choice. If he ogles an undulate field of wheat before concluding it might be a good place, when the morning arrives, to spray his brain. To imagine more would be indulgent.

31.

PHYSICIAN, HURT THYSELF

DIR. LUKE IATROS

181 MINUTES

Leaving Dr. Lisa's bed, by a sagging bookshelf with horticultural and medical texts, biographies of dead generals, comics. On her nightstand, no less than six glasses of water. She must get fined.

She said, Where are you going?

I said, I have to go to Hub Hall and get permits for *Altarpiece*.

She said, You already know where you're going to be filming?

I said, One can get an "at large" permit, provided one is not obstructing the common flow of goods, services, or people. Since the only kinds of shots I require from the Hub are of moving water, leaves, the sky, and so on, I won't have to close a street or film in a public building. I do not think such a permit is necessary, but Jonson insisted. I think following rules excites him, sexually.

She said, Don't be foul.

I said, He also gets a tax break if we follow the rules.

She said, It's on the Lime, eight stops from the transfer.

Hub Hall, in a tower built for a newspaper. I had seen many films set in the Zone before it was established. The main difference was in the films there was a plurality of people, but in the business section of the Zone, there was only one type. There were few people on the streets. Had I not known better, I would have thought there was an epidemic of affluence spreading through the Hub. The excessive personal space was unnerving.

Permits Authority, twelfth floor. Two clerks and I.

The first clerk said, Sir, there seems to be a problem with your forms.

I said, I thought they were already approved from the device application, and I had to show identification.

The second clerk said, Sir, if you will have a seat, I will get my boss. She will assist you. I don't have authority in this matter.

I sat two hours. Nobody came. One of the advantages of the Zone was supposed to be that the bureaucracy within was efficient because applicants had been thoroughly vetted. Accustomed to the overcrowded and inept Authority Offices outside the Zone, I had packed a grass bar and a magazine.

Another hour. The clerks hung a sign saying they were on lunch. I was reminded of *Physician, Hurt Thyself.* See it at Rogers Theater. Cross the street for a sandwich at Torta Muy Gordo. I like the #7, hold the kelp bacon.

Anyway, the film's titular physician, Dr. Lin, has a fear of puns. When her colleague, Dr. Fesser, remarked that Napoleon kept his armies up his sleevies, Lin had to be kept at the hospital overnight for observation. It was a good premise, but I'd had my #7 before the film, so I fell asleep in the first act.

In the doorway of the Permits Authority stood Millings. He sat across from me, legs agape, like it was his living room.

Millings said, Offices are the same everywhere. They could have got you out of here in five minutes, but you're waiting all day. Why do you suppose that is? An arbitrary exercise of power? A humbling of a man they thought arrogant?

I said, I don't have anything going on today. I'm rather enjoying this.

He said, After all, you're getting a shooting permit, not trying to knock down a stadium or get a nanosurgery license.

I said, The small talk, the promise, the threat. Don't you have any other templates to boot up?

He said, I heard you paid a visit to my offices.

I said, I visited your wife's offices, yes. It wasn't a secret visit. I came to see you.

He said, Isn't she wonderful?

I said, Superlative, certainly. You are a fortunate man.

He said, *Altarpiece*. Sounds spectacular. You're doing a period film. Why don't you give me a piece of it, say, twenty percent? Thirty. Plus you'll get a finder's fee, for bringing me on, of five percent of the thirty. That's personal money, for you. You could move into a good neighborhood. Extra liquidity goes a long way when starting a venture. I'll send my people around Jonson's way, we'll start a production company. I want to invest in your talent.

I said, We're funded. We have a production company, the Flowery Years. How about you leave me alone and I'll leave you alone?

He said, At the end of the day, they will tell you to come back tomorrow right when the office opens. At the end of tomorrow, they'll tell you come back the next day right when the office opens. On the end of the third day, you'll get your permit. I'm a booster of the arts. I want your film to be made. But I also want us squared up. I don't like debts. The balance sheet is getting muddled. It isn't tit-for-tat anymore. Making you sit here three days isn't fair compensation for fucking with my marriage, is it?

I said, Fucking with your marriage is fair compensation for assaulting me in the street.

He said, I don't know what you're talking about. You know there's a crime problem outside the Zone. Over a dozen people have been attacked in the last year. Two were even killed.

Our exchange was getting heated. The film was what mattered. The vanities of our conversation were of no importance other than to mark time.

I said, Millings, I'm sorry. Please accept my apologies. I think we got off on the wrong foot. You did not deserve such a reaction. I think you are a good man, a great man. A man of many qualities. Although I regret I can't offer you a funding opportunity at this time, Jonson tends to meddle, so when I need financing for my next film, I will be sure to ask you first. We could have a great friendship, if we could understand one another. You have to understand me. I came from squalor and I resent the wealthy. Class anger has clouded my ability to see each person as they are. You were born to this and I was born to that. It wasn't your fault who your parents were. In fact, I saw that you've given a lot of money to good causes and a lot of your time. It is my own resentment which diminishes me, and I hope you can forgive me for that.

Millings said, It touches me to hear such a heartfelt apology. We make good opponents, but I think we can make great friends. My father tried to turn an enemy to a friend. He said to me once that if I had an enemy, it was my fault for not trying hard enough. My father had many friends, most of whom became mine, and I tried to continue his legacy of friendship. So, please, take my hand.

I did.

He said, I really do want to finance a film. Kiosks are so boring. My wife makes the money and I spread it around.

If a few lies helped ease the production of *Altarpiece*, then I would tell a few lies. After all, it wasn't my money I was spending.

Humiliation can be borne for a while. Only a while, though. When the film was made, then I would settle with Millings.

Millings said, Three days. Look me up soon.

My permits were approved after two more days of sitting in the room with the clerks.

32.

MONOGAMOUS ANIMALS

DIR. LAWRENCE HOLLINGBERRY

11 MINUTES

Prairie voles. Swans, vultures. Gibbons. Angelfish. Wolves. Albatrosses, turtledoves, beavers, skinks. Barn owls, bald eagles, golden eagles, condors, cranes. Ospreys, red-tailed hawks, anglerfish, sandhill cranes, pigeons, prions, film critics. Cockroaches. Penguins. Red-backed salamanders. Seahorses, titi monkeys. Pygmy marmosets. Jackals. Convict cichlids. Malagasy black rats. Malagasy giant rats. California mice. Kirk's dik-dik. Geese, coyotes. Parrots.

33.

FUR BURGLARS

DIR. HOLLY AND JENNY LINDEN

81 MINUTES

Greatness in the Linden sisters' oeuvre is contained in overgrown lines, scenes, and shots, like kudzu trapped in a pot in the middle of a tennis court. It heightens the surrounding desolation. Their magnanimity in allowing mistakes, like the continuity slips and flubbed dialogue, overcompensates for a coherent vision of existence, that which we expect from a notable filmmaker.

Having smudged their prints on the detective story, western, antiwestern, caper flick, dark comedy, musical, buddy cop picture, spy film, monster movie, and bromance, the Lindens have made a children's movie. Bills must be paid. For all their integrity, the Lindens won't leave the Western Hub for the affordable rents of their native Des Moines.

Fur Burglars is not for adults. There are no grown-up jokes whooshing over tousled heads. The Lindens do without parody, satire, knowing references to brands. There is no resolution, which is its own satisfaction.

Atrocious parental behavior blackened the showing. In a kids' movie, adults snap pictures, paint nails, crack cans, yell into Pingers, and thump their kid for displaying enthusiasm. Blathering about the profundity of children's entertainment, how age-appropriate films are a construct, is the product of an infantilized generation and their apologist critics. Children's movies are marketing events. It is irresponsible to bring your children to see *Banjo the Clown Dog* or *Crocodile Orthodontists II*, unless it is part of your parenting strategy. Viz., if you try to raise an idiot, then maybe your child will rebel against idiocy.

Fur Burglars. Three nondescript and unexcitable women kidnap the pets of the wealthy to ransom. Each kidnapping is rendered with the greatest of care to maximize its entertainment value. We are not told if the women are in need of money, if they're class warriors, or if they like the kicks that crime affords. These thieves of puggles and Russian Blues have no past, future, or agenda we can determine. The Lindens make few concessions to narrative. This film, by omission, shows how the word *why* obstructs our cinema, tangles it in strands of causality, removes it from its proper sphere of mysticism. Before the film, they stole pets. After the film, they will continue stealing pets.

Showings of *Devin Duckling's Dire Disaster* or *Honky Seals* pay the bills at the Conspicuous, so I tolerate the Saturday hordes of greedy kids who pillage the snack counter, make unpleasant high-pitched noises, cluster outside the bathrooms complaining of imminent bladder rupture, unable to perceive the restrooms are out of order. I watch the kids in the lobby, trying to determine who will have an exciting life, if there is a secret, a gene, an attitude, if there is anything but money, a high tolerance for pain, birth within an arbitrary and invisible boundary.

Isabel and I agreed on the Lindens. At attention, Pingers forgotten. Our shared filmography. *A Short Hello*, female private eye kills society son: soon after our meeting, groping on the couch, stoned on hormones. *Cerillos by Saturday*, railroad town wrangles bandits into repressive private militia: the night her mom had too much cabernet and began to sob on her lawn. *Richmond!*, a musical about the ruinous hurricane: after the abortion. *The Things*, sensitive monster is pursued by murderous humans: after her sister was caught bullying a girl on Pinger so badly that the girl refused to leave her house. *Jean-Luc and Raoul*, best friends become estranged over the loan of a pencil: her aunt's cancer. *In Rabat*, a spy causes a war through great ineptitude, then manipulates events at home to cover her tracks: when I discovered she'd taken a credit chip in my name and maxed it out. Double feature with *Milagro*, hospital tearjerker about an elderly man who decides not to kill himself after realizing the worth of his life, who we learn in the final shot is a generalissimo subjecting his people to brutality and suppression: my retaliation.

34

THE TATTOOED FUGITIVE

DIR. RICHARD FOGER

90 MINUTES

Paint-by-numbers Nano Belt noir. Playing in repertory through next Sunday, at the Hub Cinema Archive.

We left after the heiress disappeared. The detective's charisma wasn't sufficient to hold us in our seats. Into the arboretum, where people flaunted that they had the resources to maintain two or three large dogs. Never mind the paucity of quality health care outside the Zone, the impossibility of a relatively unbiased education for many of our guests, the enormous costs of carbon reabsorption. A permit for one animal is thousands of dollars. No wonder this society was almost eradicated.

Dr. Lisa said, I became aware in my late adolescence that many days I would have to choose to live. A day when it doesn't occur to choose is good.

Dr. Lisa said, When I am in the shower after work, I think, did I live today? How did I live? If I felt like I didn't live very much, I ask myself why not, but there is no answer. How I could live more? I don't know. There are no metrics. And what people say is not true.

Dr. Lisa said, What people say is not usually truthful.

Dr. Lisa said, I try to help these people with their fixations, maybe because I have my own. My fixations don't manifest in physical symptoms. They are not special, either, but thoughts about the elasticity of time, the mysteries of matter, and the finitude of trust.

Dr. Lisa said, Without trust, it is difficult to live.

Dr. Lisa said, How can you trust another human being? Knowing their autonomy, like yours, is under the governance of a subjective morality. How many times should you choose to live?

Dr. Lisa said, You think you know a person but you don't. You will never know another person and this stings. Maybe the self can be known and maybe the journey of knowing the self is heroic or maybe it is venial. To decide it is a worthy venture may be vain.

Dr. Lisa said, I don't know you. Maybe I think I have a good sense of you, but these senses are wrong. A person cannot be understood. We navigate by our own sense of realness, which cannot be applied to others. We assume others will act how we think they should act. When they do not, we are upset.

Dr. Lisa said, Everyone's morality is weighted differently, and they are not incremental differences. What is very wrong to me might only be a little bit wrong to you. And one can never know those differences, because people are rarely truthful, they minimize the importance of truth, or they think it is better to tell an expedient lie. To me, lying is disgusting. I do it and I think that the expedient lies I tell are minor but others' lies are major. How is one to know? There is nothing to measure against.

Dr. Lisa said, Awe is worthless and so is respect for distances.

Dr. Lisa said, Often I have fantasized I will get to stand in front of the throne to ask as many questions as I would like. Until my thirst for information is quenched. And I will stand in front of the throne, which I visualize as a desk, not so different from my own, and I will satisfy my thirst to know everything I have wanted to know about the people I have known, which might take a very long time.

Following us through the trees, a man in a fishing hat. Binoculars around his neck like he was looking for birds. He appeared about fifty, straight back. A suit which was never fashionable. Only the loose flesh at the throat betrayed his age. Why was this man, having passed seventy, still devoting himself to wicked tricks? Perhaps because he thought his age allowed him a measure of protection he hadn't had when he worked for Millings's father, snapping pinkies and setting fires. That moronic family spent too much time at the movies. Now I knew his face. Millings wasn't as sincere as he had claimed in the office, but neither was I.

35.

TOOLS

DIR. JOHN FRANCIS SEBASTIAN

97 MINUTES

Although Osvald works as a secretary for an architectural firm, he prefers to call himself a clerk. Leyak, Malthus, Barbas, and Grigori is known for the Hotel Vengeli, one story tall and six blocks long, the Felly Reflective Caverns, hewn from the sandstone beneath Port Anaraes, the undustable Balloon House, and ZFR Financial's acclaimed bunker. Forty-two of the forty-five Hub stadiums.

I see him at work, as if I am floating over his shoulder. I try to make him spill his coffee onto his lap, but all it does is make him itch his hand. My influence is subtle.

Speaking of *Tools*, opening Sunday at Original Cin, I can, for example, restrict his blood from flowing to certain areas. It can be devastating when paired with the correct suggestive images. When Osvald prepares to make love, at my behest all he can think of is the scene in *Interpermanence* with the elderly ménage à trois.

Answering Pingers, haranguing caterers, paging assistants, summoning janitors. Accepting the tantrums of middle managers. Recounting their fits to Isabel in the evenings, his voice low with indignation and disappointment. Osvald leaves his designs on his desk, where they are visible to passing eminences. The principals and the designers, the serious and the trifling, the saved and the damned, have not commented. His B.A. in architecture impresses nobody at the firm, including the guest janitors. Finding ways to slip his design ambitions into conversation has proved to be a chore. He has never been a talker.

Gossamer working hours brushed away on the rail home. I see what he sees. He thinks of women. Osvald's fantasies have no frisson without a plausible story. Without stories we have nothing to grip and twist. Karen, the HR assistant, has divorced her husband and is not sure how to date. The barista at Silver Bean likes his unorthodox satchel. She learns he sewed it himself. Isabel's sister has a grudge against Isabel she needs to express. The woman on the rail likes the same Scandinavian dirge. His fantasies begin with his taste. His objects capture a woman's attention.

Osvald's longing ebbs and flows. The number of persons he has been inside makes him nervous. He fluffs it with a pair of make-outs, a wandering finger. He wonders how he can swagger up to the urinal with that count.

He attends company barbecues and lectures. Osvald hunts for people to impress the way he once scoured the network for Isabel's personal information, hoping to find a tantalizing fact, a nice picture.

Osvald is confident his ideas will get attention. Passivity is a flavor of confidence. If he'd bring Isabel to company functions, let her make the friends, it would go faster, but Osvald, a thief, fears theft.

Osvald has the poor fortune to be overly competent. He will not be promoted to a job where he can upstage his superiors. The firm transferred him, after a season of groveling, to the head office in the Eastern Hub, away from Isabel's family, away from people he knew, to whom he might have to explain himself. His desk is the first you encounter on a floor where draftspersons play darts, bend circuits, boast about hang gliding. There is nothing as exhausting as a person with disposable income.

He does not care for his coworkers. He squints to see what it is they have that he hasn't. It seems to be nothing, maybe an absence, and he has something he ought to lose. He joins them for a beer when they condescend to ask. The place they go has no signage, no menus, no chairs. Osvald delights the architects by naming the music playing without fail. In fact, he can check on his Pinger, before they enter. The playlist is public. Everything can be touched, if one knows how to touch. He is satisfied to note his watches are more obscure than the architects' sloppy throwbacks. At their gatherings, he does not speak unless he has a naughty, contrarian, or otherwise novel comment to contribute, to keep his reputation up. Office gossip excruciates him. A gap-toothed redhead who devises novel water systems and an interior designer in charge of paneling, molds, and etching have indicated with body language he is acceptable enough to be their mistake.

The days corrode his will. To relent to or contend with life. Either is okay so long as one is chosen. Another degree or another person or nothing, his Pinger, masturbation, pacifying foods, music, drawing, industrial accidents. To return to his process, which is a series of many minutes, a sequence, a set of minutes frightening when tabulated together. The bill is staggering when presented in whole. The bill of his minutes ought to be hidden from decent folks. One signs without looking.

By regulation, he cleans his desk on the sixth and the seventeenth day of each month. The bathrooms, designed by Leyak, the company exhibitionist, have tatami dividers, leaving one feeling exposed. Osvald cannot eliminate in these conditions. He is phobic of colorectal bacteria. In his bag are baby wipes, disposable gloves. Osvald has a propensity to clog toilets. He plunges in silence like a *shinobi* creeping across a lord's bedroom. When we moved into our apartment, he waited until I was asleep to use the facilities.

Tools is about a doll maker who covets a doll he sees in a shop window. He inquires about the price of the doll, is informed the doll is not for sale, and resorts to murder to acquire the doll. I did not see it, but I did eavesdrop on a pair of women on a Mauve Line platform discussing the film. It does not sound very engaging. If you would have liked to judge for yourself, it was screening at the Handel yesterday but is no longer.

36.

OKAN

DIR. VICTOR NNAMANI

144 MINUTES

I agreed to curate the Conspicuous International Film Festival. The previous curator, a Bast emeritus, expired of a heart attack during a screening of Haupt's *Omega*, specifically the scene when judgment is passed on the idolatrous village. The Bolivian government deported Haupt, so he burned the footage and reshot at Cueva de las Manos in Argentina. The curator was not mourned by the staff. He paid in change, pinched. When I die, I would like to be sat in a theater kept dry enough to desiccate my corpse. Five showings a day. Then I will never feel alone, or at least only until the next showing.

The owner of the Conspicuous held the festival for tax purposes. To hear him speak, the theater was in danger of bankruptcy, despite filling to capacity four nights a week. He owns the block. Theaters will never disappear. The reforms after the Confidence Crisis included the banning of home entertainment systems, along with the widespread curtailing of data usage, which has made it difficult to watch at home. It's done, if you have the means, like Jonson, but it isn't common. The owner of the Conspicuous is a cheap, miserable bastard, and I feel comfortable putting that in the *Slaw*, because I happen to know he's illiterate.

Lest he offer the curatorship to Jonson, I felt obligated to take on the responsibility.

Who knows what dreck Jonson would choose, how many of his society buddies would pack the theater? He'd have the arrogance to make it a success.

Jonson's pals are keen to align themselves with serious cinema. They ignore the avant-garde, the cranks, because they catch from them the stink of didacticism, the disdain of money at the kernel of serious process, and they want to get rich.

The festival lasted one Thursday and one Saturday, on the week the *Firebats* sequel was released. Shoals of costumed children left disappointed. Better they learn now.

On Thursday, we showed Rrepang's *What Was* to a smattering of the neighborhood loonies. I invited the director to attend, but he declined.

He said, The Underunited States is a country dedicated to the innovation of inequalities.

For Saturday, I chose *Okan*. I sent flyers to the Nigerian Business Association. It was mentioned on Bast mailing lists and at the Well of Forever, an evangelical church with a ministry in New Zion. I pinged Jonson an invitation with specific instructions about whom to forward it to. The Voyageur ran a drink special called the Kilimanjaro, which was twenty ounces of draft beer in a tall thin glass, for five dollars, against my wishes.

In the pocket of my blazer on four cornflower index cards was my speech. The speech exhorted the necessity of cultural exchange. It sketched a brief history of West African cinema and what qualities distinguished it from cinema of the East and South. It posited Nnamani had seen the films of John Burr and Grace Green in a Benin City cinema, giving him the indelible picture of American machismo he undermines in *Okan*. It broke the ice with a little cineaste joke about the surrealist who walked into the lens shop. It didn't go on too long.

On the night of the screening, I placated Osvald-in-me with a candy bar so he wouldn't sabotage my speech, straightened my tie, and over the loudspeaker I introduced myself, the decorated critic, academic, and director of *Altarpiece*, forthcoming. I strode out from behind the damson curtains.

The theater was empty except for Dr. Lisa, provisioned with Gummy Nooses and Chocodiles. I mumbled the title of the night's film and, making a threatening gesture at the projectionist, joined Dr. Lisa to watch the film.

37.

THE ROYAL WE

DIR. IRENE WEIDE

74 MINUTES

Jonson and I plan my film in the production office for *Altarpiece*, currently a construction trailer parked less than a mile from his penthouse for convenience. When prudent, we don the hard hats included with the trailer.

Because of his investment in AlmostPeople, Jonson has access to models with experimental programming. The company is looking to expand into the secretarial arts. Three AlmostPeople, Gaston, Henri, and Phillippe, are our assistants. Gaston takes voice memos, Henri places calls for material, and Phillippe derides us.

Jonson said, Gaston, take a memo. Have Henri make me reservations for dinner tonight at Flavors of Colombo.

Gaston said, Very good, sir. Henri, make Mr. Jonson reservations for dinner tonight at Flavors of Colombo.

Henri said, The patio or the dining room, sir?

Jonson said, The patio will do nicely.

Phillippe said, Rising sea levels encroaching on the freshwater supply of Sri Lanka have made it uninhabitable, thousands of its residents live as poor derided guests in this city, and Harris

Vincent Jonson V, instead of doing something about it, drops hundreds of dollars on a cuisine that no longer exists due to his forefathers.

Jonson said, Phillippe, I fail to see what all that has to do with my dinner. I'm eating, you know. A man has to eat.

The *Altarpiece* script fills six composition notebooks. There is no dialogue. It is a list of shots that may fit well in the film. That word, *script*, is jargon I don't have use for, but Jonson must be pacified. My notebooks will be misplaced when filming begins. Better the film exist as a branching set of possibilities radiating outward from a central image of Bellono beholding the ducal altarpiece from behind the canvas.

Since I am going to become Bellono, I will know what he should do, when his habitat is established. We prepare a cage for him to pace. Then the film will be finished and it will be a cage for the viewer or an ongoing commitment. One's relationship to a film is like a marriage. With time, some deepen, some become meaningless.

We are supposed to be planning logistics. Jonson's fiscal optimism will be disabused in its natural course. He has ensured that the office is well supplied. The carbon outlay for the contents of the fridge would be a whole year for me. I understand the cap is much higher for different tax brackets, but even accounting for that, he must have bribed an official or been done a favor. The trailer has a Ping-Pong table. We play a game until I cave in the ball with a heavy blow. Between swatting, we talk. I would like to allow myself Jonson's friendship but I have lost the sense of how such things are negotiated. After a certain age, perhaps new friendships are superficial. While talking, he fixes his hair. Though Jonson polices his reflection, his pleasures will form a coalition and gain control. Gratification accretes.

Altarpiece hasn't begun to ambulate. It is slime. Weide took four years to complete *The Royal We*, her failure. We are incomplete without disappointment.

Jonson said, When Lucretia straightens her hair, I think, did she straighten it for me? I review who she was with to see if she straightened her hair for another man.

I said, Maybe she felt like straight hair.

He said, I would die if she left.

I said, Most thirty-six-year-olds in your tax bracket are thinking the opposite, frankly.

He said, Sometimes she seems bored.

I said, Yes, all humans do. Is it her duty to entertain you and be entertained continually?

Why was I defending her? I wanted to be the sort of person who would believe the best about a person even if I never believed the best about a person. I didn't want to contribute to any more misunderstandings. I had not been sleeping well since I saw Lucretia and Seel in the park. I never have to tell him because he would never know I knew. We have a financial arrangement as well as the mycelium of a friendship. Either could fruit at any time.

Maybe they had an open arrangement. Probably not, given his possessiveness. I didn't know how to bring it up with Jonson without tipping him off or seeming like I was interested in his wife.

He said, Is there something on your mind?

I said, Food, Jonson.

We beach ourselves on the divan. I've put on fifteen pounds from the landslide of carbohydrates delivered to the trailer door. Jonson had a biffy placed next to the trailer, but it wasn't private enough, so the company came and removed it to a cul-de-sac down the block. They spooled yellow tape on road cones around the portable toilet and parked construction equipment Jonson rented nearby, including a crane we are not licensed to operate, to keep the public away. We wrenched a manhole open to complete the deception.

In the trailer, we have set up three screens, on each of which a different film plays. Mornings, we take turns choosing fifteen clips to program from Jonson's server. The other person must guess the theme by one p.m. or sit in the lumpy chair for the remainder of the workday. This week's themes. Jonson: romances directed by expatriates who returned to their home countries. Me: unsuccessful expeditions resulting in death, metaphysical expeditions included. Jonson: unrequited admiration between practitioners and/or heterosexual females without a demonstrable and obnoxious sexual subtext. We went around on that one for hours about what might be counted as demonstrable and obnoxious. No work was done. Me: exceptional soundtracks composed by a person who worked on one film. Jonson: missteps following masterpieces that were later reevaluated as masterpieces themselves. The trick is to extend the mystery until about twelve-thirty.

Jonson opened a bag of Riesling. Beads of sweat on his forehead. A pleasure one can afford is a little less enjoyable than the opposite.

38.

FRANKLIN'S REVENGE

DIR. GEORGE SEGURA

96 MINUTES

Uncle Al, Millings's grease man, was hard to find. Since the arboretum, I hadn't noticed him following me around. I hired a fact-checking intern at the *Slaw* to track him down, telling her that Al used to work for Millings Kiosk, maybe off the books. It took the intern three weeks. I paid her out of the film's discretionary fund, splitting the bill between five separate research accounts so Jonson wouldn't get suspicious.

She said, I hung around Millings's building until a guy matching the picture came around, then I followed him to a diner. Asked the waiter if he came in every day. He lives okay uptown. Goes to the museums, passes time. He goes fishing most every morning by the canal off the Black Line, cross street Fletcher, look for the monument of the loyal horse. The Leisure Authority stocks the canal, so there's good fishing.

Off the Black Line. Sun eating the mist. I had been translating my sensory impressions, aestheticizing them, to explain to Dr. Lisa what I had seen and how it had made me feel. The more banal the impression, the better. As if gratitude could be transmitted. Maybe when the film was made I'd have an argument instead of the purgatory of words. The canal wound to the lake a half mile. Here it wasn't so deep, three feet, four. In the park, no cameras. I thought I'd ask him for his apology, let him know that I could find him if need be. Like Millings. He fell for tough guy stuff. You apologized to these people and then you were their friend. They wanted their place in the hierarchy assured, that they were above you. They didn't care where you were, how you were living, as long it was slightly below them. It was more important to insinuate and let their imagination do the work. Uncle Al's line in the water. A vest with many pockets, a cooler. His lunch. He went down here and when he was done there was one less day remaining. One less sandwich and one less bag of coffee.

What led a man of his age to hit a stranger on the back of their head and spill coffee on their precious Zaccardi compendium? A sense of duty, a lack of family. He could have done lasting neurological damage. Osvald hated people like this, bodies voluntarily placing themselves within a hierarchy, who thought they bore no responsibility for their actions because someone else had ordered them to act. In me, his outrage. My face hardening, twisting on the right. My right leg thrown forward, dragging behind me my left.

To Osvald I temporarily abdicated control of my body.

Osvald-in-me stalked across the grass. I was along inside myself and I was at peace because I knew I wasn't my body. It was an object to which things happened, that it was unfortunate I was connected to by means of electricity. Osvald was quieter than me, putting his toe down before his heel. Not that Uncle Al could have heard all that well. I would have preferred Al face Osvald. It is possible that everything that has come is an accident but I do not find that likely at all. When this possibility is allowed into one's heart, evils gain purchase. And the worst evils are one's own because one knows them and they know one. They cannot be easily outmaneuvered and never murdered without sloughing a piece of the self. Which I resist, except now I had let Osvald go, I gave in, I let my friend defend myself. Because, although he knew what he had done and continued to do was sickening, he would use violence on my behalf.

So it transpired Osvald spun around Uncle Al, slapped him hard across the face, and shoved him into the canal, a man of seventy years, who had lost his wife to a neurodegenerative disease ten years before.

Uncle Al surfaced. In his wet clothes, looking frail and new. I wanted to pull him out and sit him next to a fire. I tried to extend my hand.

But it was Osvald who pulled him out. Uncle Al's bottom lip split. Blood on his chin, his vest.

Osvald had accomplished nothing with his grotesque display of virility except invite retribution. I was traveling far from the impulses behind my film, an argument against materiality, by continuing the cycle of masculine posturing. History has suggested, concerning the internal struggles of men, the brain is not necessarily greater than the penis. However. Should the Millinges of the world be allowed to boast and dominate the conversation at the table, to bully those of us without advantages?

No.

He had attacked me, and I was not a great or even a good person. Uncle Al's hands shook. He was afraid to age, to become frail, because he had hurt the weak for some years. The shoes were the same pair that had appeared in my peripheral after he hit me in the back of the head with an unknown object, and poured coffee on my beautiful book.

Osvald said, You best stay away.

As Osvald dragged me across the grass, he seemed to reach the end of his strength and withdrew from my limbs to rest in his place of comfort, my imagination.

39.

THE MERRY BAILIFF

DIR. JERRY ANDADOR

61 MINUTES

The corporeal form of Osvald and I last spoke in my bare apartment four years previous. Unknown to me at the time, it was he who had helped Isabel loot the furnishings the week before, leaving me mismatched flatware, a sticky desk, and two chairs. A blanket. She took the tailored curtains.

After Isabel denuded the apartment, she left me a masterpiece of platitudes on a scrap of notepaper. Isabel's notes, recommended by her therapy app, were similar to an office memo or landlord's text. Claim, support, explanation. A lifeless note to which she had given none of her pain. In speech she was ardent and vulnerable, quick to anger. In a hurry to arrive at frustration. She overheard herself, paced the stage.

The note bled gridelin ink. Osvald's pen. He was loyal to these pens. Nobody could borrow one. He was surprised or not surprised when Isabel asked for help moving or he offered. A reason was fabricated. Her father's age, his relative infirmity. The contents of the note evade me. They were so lifeless, so dismissive and without feeling, my memory refused to file them away. The words were as smooth as river stones. They did not mention Osvald.

Our last meeting. Point B on the line segment. We slumped over the desk. Osvald had a bruise on the back of his right hand where he had smashed it against the doorframe carrying out my couch. I thought he was there to comfort me insofar as he was able. I will be dead, and none of this will matter. When the time comes to sit up and point my finger, to place blame, I will remain at rest. My living room looked distinguished without Isabel's possessions.

The salient quality of Osvald's face is a cold, substantial, timid intelligence. In conversation he projects bemusement and detachment. A silent, rude Osvald is how he tells others he is sad. He reminds speakers of his displeasure when they bring up a subject he is not interested in. He is not a great listener unless the subject captures his imagination or unless he can emotionally relate to it, for example, fathers, rejection, crises of knowing.

He slid a fifth of John Brown Gordon from his holdall. We had a taste for it. Between our first snorts and my empty apartment were years of soiled hallways and winter, years of staircases and vending machines. Some women and shouting. Every Christmas he would leave on my desk one exquisite piece of paper. Leaving *The Merry Bailiff* to sit in the cemetery, our backs against a cool headstone. It burned our throats to sip. To be buried side by side, we agreed. Bickering over monument designs. Osvald preferred a plaque. Mine was to be a snare.

I said, The afterlife will be terribly lonely. To be not here nor there.

Osvald said, There is nothing but nothing.

I said, After life there is a cinema where we will go to watch ourselves.

Slopping liquor everywhere.

I said, I can't find another glass. Isabel took them all.

He said, Look in the cupboard above the stove.

A measuring cup remained in the cupboard. How nice of him. There was a coffee cup in the fridge she had overlooked. He poured. I offered him a chair. I took the measuring cup. It was hard to sip from it with dignity. Without the fixtures, the light was as bleak as a wedding invitation. Osvald rolled a pencil stub in his fingers.

I said, She took the ice tray.

He said, Hurt me, says the masochist. No, replies the sadist.

I said, A plateau is the highest form of flattery.

We spoke of bland cinema, which neither entertains nor instructs nor enlightens nor delights. We don't believe in process for the sake of process. We may be apes but we will maintain the fiction that we are not. Osvald mentioned that he's writing a film, but I didn't think he was writing a film.

It is tiresome to describe the hypocrisies of another person who is not around to describe yours in turn. One might work oneself into a false foaming rage. Our volleys were poor. The ball bounced differently in my bare apartment. I mentioned my fear of queues.

Osvald said, This speaks to an essential selfishness. Why should you have to wait in line with the normal people?

I said, Exactly, Osvald.

He walks to the bathroom. Osvald pisses sitting. The crackle of his rusty urine. He washes his hands, repeating the second law of thermodynamics in triplicate to ensure proper duration. Concerning hygiene, Osvald is a show-off. This room is holy to him, for Isabel cleansed herself within. Her washcloth over there left for me to use. This mercy irritates him. Did it mean she still had feelings? How could she? The first pricks of a long and exhausting insecurity, a gift from me for the years to come. His heart stomping in his chest.

Osvald looks into my eyes. Protracted eye contact was rare between us.

He said, Do you regret that she left?

I said, That's a strange way to phrase it. As I recall, it was mutual. Actually, what I said was, Get out of here, go. She took that to mean forever rather than for the next thirty minutes until I cool down.

Osvald did not offer bromides like it was all going to work out for the better in the end, the universe buttons a blouse and unzips a zipper, better to have felt and left, etc.

Walking the five blocks from his apartment, he has worked up the courage to ask me if I would mind if he dated Isabel, if I would give my blessing, but his valor has faded in the intervening hour, in the bare light of my apartment, where I am a person, not an inconvenience or abstraction. Osvald has resolved to ask me this question, to accept the wrath his question may provoke, for to Osvald, pitiable Osvald, ill with terror and longing, it is the meaningful question, it seems to be the question of his life.

A conscience is useless without seasoning. Trying situations are as painful to refuse as they are to accept. When Osvald has tiptoed into the bewitching mist of temptation, he has manipulated events so they were defensible if not righteous. Refusing to apologize has helped him maintain supremacy. Soon after our last meeting, he convinced himself I was neither suitable for nor kind to Isabel, a bumptious and ignorant opinion encouraged by her *ex post fututum* to assuage his conscience.

In the coming months Osvald will deploy anecdotes to strengthen his position. He's my friend but. I don't want to say, but. Maybe Osvald will lie. He will lie by omission. He will fail to defend me from his predation, which is one of the prerequisites of friendship.

Walking home, generous, empowered, without telling me what he meant to tell me, he resolved to instead treat me fairly in the vital coming weeks, to remember our long and close friendship, but the paternal feeling faded by midnight, when Isabel pinged, asking what he's doing.

40.

CHIPS OR CHAINS? //
THE NEW NEW ORDER

DIR. ANDERSON ROGIER

43 MINUTES // 29 MINUTES

IN YOUR HAND, IN YOUR
MIND // WHO'S RUNNING
THE COUNTRY?

DIR. ANDERSON ROGIER

74 MINUTES // 14 MINUTES

I had resolved to never again enter Original Cin, but I was in the neighborhood to get a caterpillar wrap at Jennie's.

Walking past, I felt the hateful sort of curiosity.

Rogier's early work is being shown at Original Cin's marathon Sunday Double Double Feature series this week.

At the box office, a slumbering cashier.

The first documentary claims the Citizen's Helpful Intrusive Pinpointer, known colloquially as the chip, is a mind-control device to force native-born Americans to accept the intrusion of our guests. Rogier believes a consortium of crooked dentists, tax hawks, gold-star grandfathers, and identical triplets meet every harvest moon to plot possible methods of technological control.

The New New Order is his most spectacular stretch. Rogier takes from the Confidence Crisis the lesson that it wasn't the ravages of climate change and Prosperity_Jr that decimated global stability but the expansion of social services. The way he tells it, paternity leave, not the inability to provide the basic services of governance, brought down the prosperous countries of the world.

By the end of the second film, my spirits were low, my energy flagging.

In Your Hand, in Your Mind, more thought-control. This time Rogier blames the low-voltage phones running Pinger, manufactured by the Transit Authority.

If nothing else, one admires his work ethic. His filmography lists two hundred titles, mine has none.

Who's Running the Country? posits that the Transit Authority is the true power in the Underunited States, because nothing can move anywhere without its approval. It also claims Prosperity_Jr was a hoax and drinking water is effeminate.

That night, before bed, I put my Pinger in the refrigerator, as he suggested, to avoid negative vibrations from the seventh dimension.

41.

PRINCE OF IGUANAS

DIR. HANS CLAES

93 MINUTES

Dr. Lisa was gracious enough to conceal how she felt about my apartment.

She said, It's nice around here. I never see a family on the street in my neighborhood. There's too much to do alone. The headsets and exercise. The elasticity regimens and the brain-boosting programs. That fad for designing fragrances.

She said, Have you ever been impressed with yourself?

I said, Have you?

She said, I can think of a time. But I asked you first.

I said, A long time ago I was working on a short film. There was one shot I liked very much, of a man unlocking his door. I can't even remember what the plot might have been. This shot was wrong in a way that seemed to be an excellent imitation of my personality. I was confident I had imposed my sensibility on the camera. The problem was, it made other shots look shoddy or ill conceived. The project got scrapped because of how well this one shot pleased me. I couldn't match it.

I said, Now you.

She said, I managed to grow, from seed, a Sayers Droseria. It was a whale, three whole centimeters. I would sit there, night after night, with my magnifying glass, willing it to open.

I said, I should like to examine it next time I'm over.

She said, I watered it to death.

I said, What about professional accomplishments?

She said, Listening to doctors drone about where they have worked and learned diminished these for me. Anyone who mentions the institutions they have passed through in order to gain social cachet is a frivolous person. Programs have taken the guesswork from what we do, except in rare cases, such as in my field. The person inputting the symptoms is not so special.

My projector played *Prince of Iguanas*. In my bed eating stale pastry. It was the sort of film made to crack jokes over. We used a cannabinoid inhaler before the movie. Laughing and long silences after explanations that didn't make sense.

Dr. Lisa, bored with *Prince of Iguanas*.

She said, There's a reason not many people know about this movie.

I said, The director was a pastor who made films under an assumed name. They weren't discovered until his death.

She said, No, it's not good. It isn't interesting or entertaining or aesthetically significant. There seems to be no theme or life or absurdism. We could be lying here without it playing and I would be more stimulated, happier, and at peace. Because now the burden of looking rests with me. I might have to find out what happens to this man in this iguana costume. Why do you like it?

I said, The iguana costume.

She said, I worry about your film if you think this is good work.

I said, I'll take you down the street.

From my window, I scanned my block, making sure there were no suspicious persons waiting for us. I thought Uncle Al had his fill but one was never sure. Millings, who knows?

Out. Two blocks east of the panaderia, the construction site that had been half finished as long as I remember. Kids were playing inside without supervision. This neighborhood was scheduled to be desirable for the Zone crowd, but a murder happened on the street, cousins arguing over a lottery ticket, a wrench. Because of this murder, I got to keep living here, instead of moving farther out again.

I said, Up here.

Once more on the inhaler before entering Brainforest Coffee. Eight booths along the far wall. Tables with women playing chess, a napping man, four students. At the counter, we stared at the boards. I asked Dr. Lisa what each of the dozen coffee drinks was. She explained as well as she was able.

To the left of the bar, an iron door, painted blue, marked DISAGREEMENTS.

I said, It's soundproof. The walls are so flimsy around here, couples can't yell at each other without getting their building's data throttled for disturbing the peace. In there, they settle their differences. It is also a popular destination to let out the screams one has been trying to stifle.

She said, I need to try this.

Dr. Lisa, with some difficulty, pulled the door shut behind her. My first time in that room, I had stayed nearly an hour. When I walked out, I felt remarkably chipper. An abscess of resentment lanced.

Here, Dr. Lisa inside. My hot chocolate was gone and I sipped hers before it cooled. My favor to her. Dr. Lisa was screaming. She ought to be screaming. If she wasn't, then she had not risked much in her life, and should be pitied. The coffee shop opened early, closed late, and the room was, except on certain exceptional days, continuously occupied.

Some feelings you cannot allow yourself. Try it on, but if it doesn't fit, don't buy it. If it doesn't thrill you, that's how it is. Those feelings are for others. What I put my small trust in is the veracity of aesthetic experience, which is pleasure's sister. There is nothing else, no feeling, no person, no language, that can be counted on. There is nothing else that might not be gone tomorrow. Sit with your family, your friends, your partner, look at their faces, and try to tell yourself otherwise. If you can, you can. That is no crime. For me, the privacy of aesthetic experience is the pebble of eternity I will carry in my pocket as long as I am able. Maybe my pebble of eternity is small, but it is light, and I can tuck it away where it is never seen.

Minutes running from the tap. After screaming, crying. After crying, relief. After relief, back on the parapet to resume one's watch. Dr. Lisa sat. Her eyes swollen. The mugs, the sleeves of her sweater. This was all. Going to eat, sleeping, fashioning something of value through repetitive movements. Feeling pain and being sure some kinds were avoidable, being unable to distinguish which.

42.

TRIAL

DIR. OTTO TORONI

27 MINUTES

The aperture of the day opening and closing. What is life, what is living, is to come. We are in rehearsal. Rome, the year Bernini completed his titanic *Saint Longinus*. Jonson proud to speak the Roman dialect.

He said, We ought to go together sometime. From the port, it's a half-hour trip. We could leave after lunch and be sitting in the Piazza Navona by cocktail hour.

Ignoring the ruinous expense of suborbital flight, the terrible heights, that the majority of Rome is printed, with the original artworks long buried in vaults against water and weapons.

It reminds me of *Trial*. You can see *Trial* at the Murphy Park Library, sub-basement, Tuesday night, refreshments provided.

Bernini was forty when he saw his little brother, twenty-five, leaving the house of Bernini's girlfriend. Bernini chased his brother across Rome, beating him, breaking his ribs, trying to skewer him on a rapier. The murder of a brother is not so uncommon. His brother took refuge in the basilica across the street from the Bernini palazzo. Bernini waited on the steps with the patience of a great artist.

Their mother, looking out the window, came out to break up the fight. To the papal cops she lamented what he'd become, her arrogant son, who claimed to serve their god. Bernini sent their eldest servant to his girlfriend's mansion, bearing a gift of wine. When she took the wine from the servant, he slashed her face with a razor. Bernini, a favorite of the pope, was not punished.

Jonson's pinged me. Lucretia's missing again. Got to run. I suppose I've given you a sense of the film, anyway.

43.

THE BALD ARCHAEOLOGIST

DIR. VERA DUNN

56 MINUTES

At the Facsimile Museum, looking for inspiration for *Altarpiece*.

Guest children on school trips in the lobby. Laughing, running. The relief of being anywhere but school. Blissful teachers in the hallways. A cairn of backpacks up to the tip of the Moai's nose. My Pinger began to whine, booting the museum's guide. I didn't need it. Any room would do. A guest selling hard-boiled eggs and licorice.

I have never been to one of the great original museums. I took the elevator to the eleventh floor, period furniture. Elderly women resting. A man snored in one of the Le Corbusier couches. Overcast outside. High-rises like blades of grass. Someone's dog wandering through the gallery.

The wait for the printer in the Ruining Room was over an hour, which disappointed me, because I hoped to shove over a *David*. For hundreds of years, he received our worship and now the king suffers the indignity of being smashed every day. It is easier to think about something you have power over. This explains the explosion of interest in our historical processes since the proliferation of printed museums. One doesn't need to bring the saccharine respect required of the original museums. One can be one's boorish authentic self.

Isabel had a clay Nefertiti bust she would hurl at me. When she slept, drained by her anger, I went out to the kiosk to get a replacement. The Ruining Room. A curator had printed Uccello's *Saint Paul*, in which he has the sword, but the children were too frightened to approach it with their markers. They slashed Kandinsky abstractions and glopped paint on a Hals. A large Al-Bayati drawing was being torn into little strips and scribbled on.

Jonson pinged, see yr at the museo / i am in nayborehood ;(

I pinged, ya / almost done

Jonson pinged, meet at older sister? found lucretia / she was at home

I pinged, ya

Jonson pinged, 20 mins / patio

I was two platforms away from Older Sister but Jonson beat me to the terrace.

Jonson's table manners are fastidious and infuriating. He takes notes of every meal, for a vanity book he plans to publish one day, working title *My Stomach and I*. He had a programmer develop an app on his Pinger that automatically photographs, dates, and arranges his meals of the day so he can compare how he has eaten today with, say, last March's breakfasts. I have entertained myself attempting to imitate his way of plucking straws from cocktails. The twitch of contempt in the lip. He lays the wet end on his napkin.

Seel in the street. Walking over to the patio.

He says, What are you two doing here?

What if I said something about the female company Seel keeps? Would Jonson jump on him, abandon his manners, strike him with the carafe of mineral water? Would Seel beg forgiveness or would he sneer? Remorse does not like to be displayed for others, but is compelled to exhibit itself. A conciliating smile. A misunderstanding, gentlemen. Let's calm down. I, the craven angel of mercy unsure when to draw my sword, strike down Jonson.

Jonson says, Sit.

Dropping patties of bullshit on the table. I was not issued the equipment to pretend to like a person. Seel, telling us about Greece, kept alternating between looking into Jonson's eyes and mine. What disturbing charisma. Seel looking at the space between our eyes and eyebrows, which produced an optical effect of penetrating attention. He hasn't bothered to get the hair treatment, but whether this is a demonstration of power or genuine indifference to his appearance is not clear. The male pattern baldness sets him apart. Maybe this is his mating strategy.

One of Jonson's best and worst qualities is his tendency to accept people as they present themselves, without tests or traps to sce to what extent they are putting him on. He is less deceptive than the average and he doesn't recognize deception well, unless he is so talented at his deceptions he seems like a bumbler, and doesn't care much when he is deceived. What is a lie? Words together that, like almost all words, are not usefully true. Language in the overwhelming majority of possible combinations is without use. The theatrical generosity Jonson uses to extend the benefit of the doubt might indicate guilt or that he feels himself to be good, whatever that is.

Again I consider, then discard, accusing Seel of fucking Jonson's wife. I have a short film of them in the park on my Pinger. Title: *Before or After Understanding.* Nothing happens but that is terrible because the imagination is given charge of the second and third acts. How would he explain it away? Is it my business or am I the innocent bystander?

Seel said, I saw *The Bald Archaeologist* on the rail back from the port. I don't know why they built it all the way out there.

Jonson said, That's one of his favorite films.

I said, It's difficult to talk about something one likes very much, isn't it, Seel? It's almost as if, when one vocalizes or realizes to their self what is admirable about the object of their attention, it becomes less interesting, less worthy of consideration. Almost like such things have to be kept secret. One's pleasures are to be held closely and lightly, like a hatchling. Then you let them fly away. Now that you and Jonson know I like this film so much, how many tertiary conversations will I be yoked to, trying to capture the dissipating magic for the gratification of the listener?

Seel said, Quite.

I've noticed when I am not contributing to a conversation, the people around me will switch the topic to one they think might interest me, as if it is the factual content of the sentences spoken rather than the possible understandings generated by the juxtaposition of the participants that makes for an interesting conversation. I'm not sure if I accept the idea of an interesting conversation. The lens of personality is so thick and curved. Although penal devices can detect sociopathy, and there is an alleged database of persons with dangerous personality disorders, and said persons are not allowed to do business within this country over a certain dollar amount, I get the impression that Seel has gamed the system, and that gaming systems is necessary to his pleasure.

Seel said, So what are all these papers on the table about? Are you two going into business together? Don't leave me out. I'm looking for a new thing.

Jonson said, You have to promise you won't mention this to my wife.

Seel said, Naturally. Send my regards, by the way.

Jonson said, I will. She seems to like you, and she doesn't like many people. Anyway, we're making a film.

Seel said, A film? Isn't that a risky venture?

Jonson said, It's a passion project.

Seel said, Really.

Jonson said, It's a period piece.

Since I had made Jonson sign a nondisclosure agreement with a stiff penalty for revealing details of the plot, he couldn't explain the plot in depth, but he somehow conveyed to Seel that there was royalty involved, and Seel offered use of Villa Disperazione, his place in Bologna II. He pulled it up on his Pinger.

He said, My people renovated it to the specifications of the era in which it was built. There's a printer on the grounds. Feel free to add whatever you want to make it Italianate or Spanish or British. Whatever you want. I don't ever go there. I look at the pictures. The longing is more pleasurable, more real, than being there. It was something for my mother to brag about, but now she's gone.

Jonson said, It will do nicely for the duke's place.

I nodded. We had reached another landing on the staircase ascending to oblivion, and paused for breath.

Seel paid our check with his Pinger.

He said, Keep in touch, men.

Seel walked in the direction of the rail platform.

Jonson said, What a greasy chunk of luck. That Seel is a good guy.

44.

HANNAH'S GAME

DIR. IRENE WEIDE

96 MINUTES

After Weide's suicide, her fans placed offerings at the gate of her manor. Last year it was converted into a school. Weide forbade the sale or donation of her artifacts to a public institution or private collector. Her fortune was used to establish the Weide Foundation. Costumes are used in children's plays, her thousands of location photographs cut up for collages. Strips of rushes hang from the ceiling, snipped up like memories are by the Subjective Tailor with his silver shears in *The Daughter of the Queen of the Night*. At graduation, the crown worn by the Daughter is set on the brow of the kindest student.

When I moved to the Hub, I visited when I felt the need to stand in her shadow. It seems ghoulish now. One can attend the celebration of death but must never overindulge. I brought Osvald out there soon after we met. It was a Friday. We had no social obligations.

He said, Let's break in.

We used a cannabinoid inhaler on the walk from the platform. Weide's home was five nodes from the main Hub lines. A wet night, smelling of woodsmoke. Pilgrims with small hope of succor. The neighborhood was once a wealthy bedroom community but the roads had been converted for bicycles and the three-wheeled electric carts fools run their errands in, outside of the Hub. Because the police were few in the Hub and disinclined to help the secluded wealthy, whom everyone in the Hub saw as living in an antique fantasy, these communities tended to have their own private security force, unkind to visitors. We took our time ambling down a pedway. The local government converted the park in the city center into industrial greenhouses to make money, probably because the machinations of the locals had lowered property taxes to the point where they could not offer basic services.

Flaccid mansions, rehabilitated woods. Old schools. The side gate was unlocked. A yew stood in the front yard. The house was familiar to us because it had been used as an establishing shot in *Hannah's Game*. In the attic, Hannah kills the patriarch—who thinks he is going to get laid—with scissors. Inside the gate, the house did not appear as large.

The front, back, and servants' doors were locked. We felt it would be poor manners to break a window. A shed had a ladder. Going up the ladder, Osvald laughed. Because he was laughing, I laughed. We fell off the ladder. We brushed leaves from our jackets. As my fear increased, so did my pleasure. A window was unlocked. Upstairs were offices, storerooms. A bedroom neither of us would enter. The decor had been looted by distant relatives, who had not seen Weide's films, and were delighted by her fortune after she died. Her *batterie de cinéma* remained.

Osvald said, Don't touch the lenses. The lenses are cursed. Don't you remember?

The fate of Weide's cinematographers. Electrocution, drowning, disappearance, electrocution. None lived past a year after the conclusion of principal photography on her films. It may have been coincidence, but no doubt the directors of photography, the poor dead DPs, had the same thought before agreeing to work with Weide.

Into a trophy room. Weide had twice life's standard allotment. The excess was like cognac burning off in a sauté pan. Osvald drew near a large shape in the darkness. I shined my Pinger over his shoulder. Sugarloaf, Weide's horse. Weide had her mounted after she died of colic. Osvald screamed, ran downstairs. I ran after him, out the front door, which we left wide open, over the gate. As we crossed the yard, I heard laughter issuing from inside the house.

45.

THE DESERT SCREWHORN

DIR. MARIANNE HORNBILL

113 MINUTES

Jonson and I had a tiff over outside investment in *Altarpiece*. He thinks he can get another four million. We don't need any more money. Well, we do, but not from other people.

I said, Absolutely not.

He said, Why?

I said, We don't need anyone distracting us with their suggestions. The problem with people is they have ideas.

He said, That doesn't cheer me. I know a man who is interested. Actually, it's Millings. Why don't we—

I walked out. Left, into the guest neighborhood, so he wouldn't follow. Jonson hasn't learned how to interact with guests. They make him aware of his social shortcomings.

Nice houses, fresh paint. The rails employed almost everyone on the blocks. One could tell by the late-model Pingers, the new dresses, the optimism. The Transit Authority likes to contract neighborhoods. It fosters a communal sense of gratitude. Grandmothers sunning themselves. Polite dogs.

There is no way Millings will shove his money into my film.

There was a Spanish multiplex past the kiosks and a couple

schools. I went in. The multiplex is one of those spaces that cannot exist without becoming belligerent, militarized, like a sports arena. Totalitarianism begins where nationalism intersects with entertainment. Entertainment is a fine inoculant for totalitarianism, with its easy answers, fabular stories, insistence on the heroic self versus the fearsome other, the desire for absolutes, and so on.

Crossing the lobby. Entering the nave, heartened by the nebulous enthusiasm of kids at the concession. A minority accrete into cineastes, more collapse into fandom, the rest drift in parabolas of indifference, catching watercooler flicks, evading meaning. Every life has, in a crevice or flue, a mild blessing, but few find theirs in Theater Nineteen.

The multiplex experience allows for generous foreplay. We drifted across the savannah of the lobby, examining holo-ads, marveling at the soda machine, which allowed the user to mix up to a thousand different flavors of stimulating and relaxing beverages. Name tags listed the wearer's favorite film. Employees may not keep their preferences to themselves. Taste will be monetized. I examined the workers in shiny, ill-fitting maroon polos, finding no trustworthy opinion. An assistant–assistant manager stocking Choco Gongs liked *The Desert Screwhorn*, a war film.

Directed by Marianne Hornbill, the film follows a division in the Eastern Theater during the Confidence Crisis, led by Timofey Popov, the Desert Screwhorn. Hornbill, a war nerd, restored tanks used in the campaign at exorbitant cost. She dug them out of the Gobi Desert, near the site of the Battle of Dunhuang, where the Russian Federation lost the initiative for good. It flopped. After the release, she gave herself over to brandy and lawn games. Her insistence on authenticity in the sets gave her a reputation among studio executives, who wanted a pet they could trot out at award season, who made lean films that became profitable after winning the golden golem. She was intended to fill quotas, but Hornbill followed the imperatives of her art. Expected bromides didn't arrive. The Pinger silent.

When a male director blows his budget, he is a visionary. When a woman does it, she doesn't have a head for figures. The controversy over Hornbill's treatment of her actors never would have garnered indignation if it were a man making the decisions. She made them sleep in tents, refused to let them wash, allowed them meager canned food. If this were a man, he would be in textbooks. She punched one or two to raise authentic bruises, to put the fear of battle in them, these men pampered as pharaoh's cats.

The film is set thirty years ago, in the months following the end of the Confidence Crisis. Popov has fled battle since crossing into Mongolia two years previous. His T-16 Armatas hide from the Indian Empire, no matter their superiority in numbers. *The Desert Screwhorn* was jeered on release for showing war is horrible, not glamorous, that the sane reaction is to refuse to fight, to ignore the demands of glory. The panning it got at release is not because of its supposed political attitudes, but because it is a war movie with no violence. The audience felt cheated.

46.

RATS IN THEIR SUNDAY CLOTHING

DIR. JAMES OSVALD

6 MINUTES

To prevent budget overruns, Jonson insisted I storyboard the shots for *Altarpiece*.

He said, If you will not accept outside funding, then you will have to economize.

My excuses of previous weeks. I do not know Bellono well enough. The cells of my visual sense have not yet begun to divide. Forgot my pencils. Venus is not in the correct house. My data was throttled because I fell asleep with my fridge open. Food poisoning. I need special paper from New Korea. I forgot my New Korean paper on the rail. The storyboards are getting done but I can't show them until filming begins because of superstitions I can't mention.

Monday I arrived at the trailer to find a note saying he was going to the Eastern Hub. He expected the storyboards to be finished when he returned, or he would finance a different film. It is unlike him to be so primitive. Our office trailer is not a glove factory. Cinema moves at its own speed. He has left to spy on his wife, hence the anxiety, the uncharacteristic lack of tact, the abrupt departure, the scribble on notepaper, as if I were his in-dentured servant.

Since I have no intention of using the storyboards and do not want to suck the energy from my authentic ideas, but must convince Jonson of the legitimacy of my method, this has proved to be a hemorrhoid on my imagination.

I work evenings. The hours after midnight make me nervous, the slippery Osvaldian quiet, time's eels. The night is largely Osvald's. The hours can be divided between us, although not cleanly between light and darkness. Likewise, our influence respectively wanes and waxes over the course of the year, as the zodiac trudges circuits of the sky like prisoners in the yard. May is an auspicious month for me, disastrous for Osvald, but he is the luckiest man in his data bracket come November.

The cocktail hour is mine, and bedtime, when the sensations of the day coalesce in an exhaustion resembling affability. The sunrise is his since he is awake to observe it, as are the darkest hours. Reduced visibility is propitious for Osvald. Neither of us is blessed during hours of business. The hours when I pencil my shots are his, and the pencils I draw with were his, rutted, mono-grammed, greasy, obsolete.

If, at the premiere, fidgeting between Jonson and his scowling wife, I were to notice a shot cribbed from Osvald's student work, or a narrative structure he had diagrammed on his bedroom wall, I would be mortified. Ideas sabotage long after their intro-duction. I have no use for his movies. But, to be sure, I had to have another look. It is not hard to understand why Orpheus turned to look at Eurydice on the threshold of sunlight. What is following us must be encouraged to continue.

Osvald is trying to fund *A Replicate*. He has no benefactor with money but little sense. No Harris Jonson, who can't enter a room without opening his wallet. His attacks, his attempts to take over my body, to insert his ideas into my film, were from jealousy.

Wherever he was, I was there, seeing what he saw, his sky's handsomest rain cloud.

The meeting at the Heritage Authority offices, which Osvald was ejected from for having the nerve to ask for government money to make a film attacking the government.

His GroupFund page garnered eighty dollars.

His mother donated sixty. I kicked in twenty under the name Verne Gyula.

Osvald tried the Weide Foundation. Irene Weide bequeathed her estate to support filmmakers. The director of the Weide Foundation liked his application and his short film. Osvald was invited to the offices to talk about grant opportunities. The Weide Foundation is located in the Tudor pile used in *Sweet Anonymity*. Weide did so much structural damage in the course of filming, she was obligated to buy the house.

The director, one Ms. Heavey, thin and nervous, missing incisor. I noticed, from my vantage of Osvald, a peculiar scar on the inside of her forearm.

She said, Please, follow me.

Osvald was brought into a basement room. On the table was nothing but a pair of silver shears. Osvald knew that they were the prop from *The Daughter of the Queen of the Night*, but it seemed too obvious to acknowledge. Play it cool, Osvald.

Ms. Heavey said, We do things differently here, per Ms. Weide's instructions.

She unrolled her sleeve.

Ms. Heavey said, If you want the money, you know what to do.

Ms. Heavey left the room. A camera running overhead.

Osvald thought about it a minute, but he's frightened by blood. It makes him faint.

I was present at his excruciating lunch with the assistant to the adviser to the producer Gerald Jackson, who asked him if he'd consider adding an extended shower scene to attract Maquilla, in the sunset of her vanities, for the role of Mayor Alison. When Osvald explained that he wouldn't be using known acting talent, whom he considered corrupt for refusing to use their platform as a celebrity to draw attention to the Transit Authority's excesses, the assistant laughed, put his cigarette out in Osvald's bisque, and took his leave.

Osvald's catalogue raisonné was on a Pinger in my apartment, where it had sat for some years. He'd compiled the shorts and mediums for a grant application to fund his biopic of Mavis Tenderloin. We held hopes for succor from arts organizations. We thought a council, foundation, or an agency would fund our projects. American society was deficient in avant-garde cinema. Painter's tape labeled ACCEPTABLE MATERIAL clung to the device's belly. I ignored the films without a pretense of narrative.

The rest I queued on the monitors in the production trailer: *Bargaining with Maroat*, *Charlie Scuttles Ivy's Battleship*, *Rubber Bible*, *Max's Joke Flops*, *The Witch of Acorn Street*, *Aubade*, *Dad*, *Re-Dad*, and *Rats in Their Sunday Clothing*, Osvald's masterpiece.

A man, me in fake gingerbread beard and pancake makeup, is visited in the hospital by his wife, played by Isabel, in a pink wig, scowl, and sequined orange slippers. The man is dying. His illness has spread to his brain. He has hidden their money. I have hidden our money.

She says, Why would you hide our money?

He says, So you won't forget me. Until you find it, you'll search and wonder, and I'll live in you a while longer. Don't worry. It's findable, if you know where to look.

She says, Tell me or I'll kill you.

He says, Ha. Ha. Ack. Aghch. I'm choking.

Isabel doesn't need the money but the puzzle torments her. A big itch unscratched. She needs to find him in the afterlife and ask where he's hidden the loot. His destination is not known. Living in virtue, to hopscotch in the fields of heaven. Living in sin, to sidestroke in the lake of fire.

Smash cut, Isabel shawled, Sharpie wrinkles.

Voice-over, Isabel, saying, A mystery is a gift.

47.

SCALLOP

DIR. TERRY ICE

83 MINUTES

The magic of names was a preoccupation of the fantasy serials I enjoyed as a child. Each was priced under seven dollars, the limit of what I could coax from my mother. The best ran twelve to eighteen volumes, with hundreds of characters, political factions, maps, appendices, battles, magical instruments, betrayals, cuisines, etiquettes, treaties, hygienic practices, architectures, coutures, genealogies. They were punitive boluses of plot, hairballs of exposition that were, contemplated after the chief hobgoblin was resealed in her crystal cave, as flat as death.

To read a fantasy with one's critical faculties is not as important as the ability to inhabit its zones of possibility. Their trade and culture are inevitably more interesting than the battles and romances. My hope A'ron Eaglefeather or Sindriss Sankara would catch a crossbow bolt kept me reading. Heroism is metastasized self-interest. Vanity, aggression, greed, and insecurity are the forces driving these narcissists to hoist the realm onto their thews.

Fantasy worlds mulched time before I could go to the movies alone, before puberty's fangs. I spent summer nights in bed with

The Alchemical Neuromancy of Lord Gribben, listening to the neighbors argue, break their dishes, and have dramaturgical sex after their frustrations were exhausted. Lord Gribben, although he entered into intrigues with the chimerical ladies of the Bog Senate, and his income was among the highest in the Blaggerlands, did not get even a pity kiss. The subtext with his valet went over my head.

Scallop was adapted from a fantasy series written by a reclusive old woman who was rumored to have been the assassin of numerous, nonconsecutive Hub mayors. Scallop is a scullion terrorized by her aunt, the vespine tyrant of a backwater coffee shop three nodes north of the Southwestern Hub. The knock-kneed mouse of the books was replaced with a starlet augmented to appeal to men who become dejected if they have not seen a good set of tits in twenty minutes.

Enter an old man in pajamas emblazoned with sigils and runes. He fits in well with the marginal denizens of the dusty burg, where there is neither theater nor printer. A thug attempts to boss the old man from his table. Comic interlude. Wizards pretend to be senile. He informs Scallop she has the potential to become a sorceress, but there is a catch.

To undergo pedagogy, Scallop is obliged to write her real name in the Ledger of Sorcerers and Sorceresses, located in the Eastern Hub's Tranquility Tower. The wizard, Merrifield the Maudlin, informs her she needs to know her true name. Merrifield is an obtuse fellow. He indulges freely, and the meaning behind his name becomes apparent after his sixth tankard of beer. Scallop does not know her real name, whispered in one's ear on one's twelfth birthday by one's mother or father. Her parents died. All parents, in the fantasy milieu, are dead. It's dangerous to propagate. Latent magicality lurks in one's genes. After one hatches a hero, one is slaughtered in one's hut by reactionary forces.

Scallop has adventures. Men are skewered. Digital eyesores are destroyed. I despise generated effects. Give me puppets and corn syrup. A budget is spent. Marketing tie-ins are introduced. After a satisfying path of travails, Scallop finds her name scrawled on a railcar. The gates of the magic mansion open. To be continued for ten consecutive Decembers.

Poor Scallop's parents, fried by lightning. Sorrow can be deferred if one knows the method. The rupture must be squeezed. Grope inside yourself, theatergoer, and you will find it. Keep your grip tight. Pinch it closed. In others' theaters, you are a field of color, a nip on the neck, a familiar groan. You are stardust tormented with electricity. There is no need to indulge your small griefs.

48.

BENSON'S PASSING

DIR. JACK MERDLE

91 MINUTES

I caved and told Jonson about Dr. Lisa.

We were sitting in the trailer, throwing darts at the ceiling. Days later, one would fall, point down, to land on Jonson's desk between his left ring and middle finger. His luck infuriating. I didn't get around to seeing *Benson's Passing*, playing tomorrow at Zone Cinema, but Jonson said it was good when we were throwing darts, if you want to take his word.

Jonson said, I knew something was up. I have a sense for when people are concealing a secret from me. I should have been a psychic. But you didn't want to be premature, I understand. I say, give a man time, wine, silence, and he will unburden his heart.

I said, This is tea.

He said, Well, we must have you over.

I said, Jonson, don't make this a thing.

He said, Drinks, Wednesday, after dinner. You can take her to the little pizzeria with the elderly ladies playing cards. It's foolproof. Even Lucretia thinks it's charming.

On his Pinger, pinging his wife.

He said, She says okay.

He said, Aren't you going to ask Dr. Lisa?

I said, Right now? But what about the storyboards?

He said, You've been drawing battleships for three days. Are those battleships?

I said, They're bunkers. I was thinking, if one had sufficient money, one could withdraw from the world.

He said, Bunkers haven't been fashionable for some time. If you are interested, it would be better to purchase one made for an oligarch and forgotten about. Maybe we can arrange a tour? But only if you bring her around.

Asking Dr. Lisa.

To compose the domestic sentences thrilled me. To refer to Jonson as my friend and partner at the production company. The business half. His wife a delight.

Dr. Lisa bought me a pizza. Before we walked to Jonson's, through his nice neighborhood, following the course of the river, I took her by our production trailer.

She said, It smells like desperation.

I said, That's inspiration and the leftovers under my desk.

Dr. Lisa opened the windows. I lay on the couch.

I said, How about we make some excuse?

She said, You're not ashamed of me.

I said, I'm ashamed of Jonson.

She said, Now, that's not nice.

I said, No, it's not. Come over here. The couch folds out.

Henri said, Sir, would you like me to put on some romantic music? Perhaps have a bag of wine delivered?

Dr. Lisa said, Gross. Let's go.

Phillippe said, Keep doing what you were doing.

Gaston said, We'll be quiet if you continue.

We left the trailer, disturbed.

Dr. Lisa said, How do you work with those AlmostPeople in there?

I said, It isn't easy. Did you know that the female models were discontinued because too many men were trying to marry them? Jonson's an investor in the company. You wouldn't believe some of the requests customers were making.

Up the elevator toward Jonson's apartment. Lucretia, irritated to be called from her reading. She didn't bother to hide her disappointment.

Lucretia said, Let's go to the terrace.

Lucretia said, I know you'll have grapefruit juice, but what can I get you, Dr. Lisa?

Dr. Lisa said, Whatever's good.

Jonson came from the kitchen with a platter of wizened olives, prawns, a carafe, and chocolate-covered grasshoppers.

As the number of people around me increases, so does my difficulty maintaining my attention in the present. Alone, the consciousness has nowhere to hide, but with three or four, it finds cover. Drones hissing overhead.

Dr. Lisa said, What were you reading?

Lucretia said, Another theory of how the pyramids were built at Giza. This one claimed the Egyptians had some obscure species of cattle pulling their sledges.

Dr. Lisa said, What do you think?

Lucretia said, A combination of wetting the sand and wooden rollers moved the blocks from the quarry. It must have been horrible. The ramps are the mystery. Even with our engineering software, nobody can simulate a compelling model. The lubricant was suffering.

Dr. Lisa said, I remember hearing that the workers on the

pyramids were fed much better than the average peasant as an inducement to work.

Lucretia said, Revisionist wishfulness to cover for symbol worship. People project what they need onto a symbol, especially one like the pyramids, which is laden with associations of the afterlife, monumentality, accomplishment, and royalty. They speak to our deepest fantasies. No, slaves built the pyramids, and they died in great number, and painfully, for male vanity, for an inert state religion. They are a reminder of what damage governance wreaks in the common imagination, even thousands of years later.

Looking at her husband. Weighing his heart on the scale like her gods of the replica frieze hanging over their bed. Why is sin decided in the bedroom? The wallet would be a better place to begin.

Dr. Lisa said, I suppose you think speculation about stars and aliens building the pyramids is garbage.

Lucretia said, Nothing would thrill me more than to find out one of the conspiracy theories is true. When we study history, we ought to challenge it. We should refuse history. Not to mention it would place me as a relative expert in one of the most pressing matters of existence: why we are here, and who put us here.

This went on a little. Lucretia had splashed vodka in my grapefruit juice as a kindness. Both of us outside our comfort. Although we could converse all right, it didn't mean we preferred to. If the metaphysical bloviating was from an authentic impulse or because these two people had their needs met so well nothing remained but to ponder existence, if they were afflicted with hedonistic fatigue, was not clear. Osvald's cruel thought. It was better than talking about olives.

Going up, I had warned Dr. Lisa not to speak of the film to Jonson's wife. I didn't know how to explain Jonson's secrecy. He wanted it to be a surprise.

She said, You mean he doesn't think she will be confident in the film, or she thinks it is a waste of money?

I said, It's not my marriage.

She said, Isn't it their money? Isn't that how money is spent in a marriage?

I said, It isn't my place to tell.

She said, I don't like secrecy.

Jonson asked the customary questions. Lucretia disinterested in impressing Dr. Lisa. She was talented at conveying she was following a conversation without caring about it. Gossip, which Jonson and I are fond of, does not tempt her. Lucretia did not conceal her relative neutrality to the people with whom she was speaking, and her attitudes made it difficult for me to understand how she could have the passion and self-loathing necessary for an affair with Seel. Each of us unable to be known. Maybe Jonson knew her or maybe not. Maybe she understood herself. It could be her indifference was a tactic and she was invested in the lives of those who surrounded her.

There was one thing she wanted to know.

I overheard her ask why *him* to Dr. Lisa when Jonson was working up a bit about rail cops.

Jonson said, The thing about rail cops is.

I couldn't hear what Dr. Lisa said in reply to Lucretia. Why me? Better not to know. The answer could be unflattering. I did manage to hear what Lucretia said, when Dr. Lisa asked her in turn. Jonson thought I was enjoying his shtick and dragged it out long after the punch line. His sense of timing awful. There is no retailer of wit.

Lucretia said, He's a person I can be myself with.

The three started talking about the best slingshot carrier.

Jonson said, I take Canadian Suborbital. There's something about Canadians that makes me think they're paying attention to what they're building. But I'll go on New Korea if I'm splurging. They do a delightful brunch.

Lucretia said, I don't get on one of those things unless I'm good and drunk.

Dr. Lisa said, I like Des Moines Worldwide. They pack the passengers in but everyone gets a pill to make the time fly by.

Lucretia said, Who do you like when you travel?

I said, I wouldn't get on one of those.

Dr. Lisa said, Are you afraid of crashing?

I said, Actually, I'm afraid it won't come down.

The bell.

Jonson said, Who might that be?

He looked on his Pinger's security app.

Jonson said, Millings, how wonderful. I'm glad you patched things up, or this might have been awkward.

He was admitted to the residence. Millings in health. His stoop drew attention to his vigor. Good clear eyes. His cosmetic work was not obvious. If one saw him in a guest neighborhood selling apples, one might be envious of his genetic material. Dr. Lisa approving. Her eyes returning to him, when she thought nobody was looking.

Millings said, Who is this lovely woman?

Dr. Lisa said, I'm Lisa, how are you?

Millings said, Rolf Millings, a friend to all.

Bending over her, into her personal space, to shake her hand. Dr. Lisa taking him in through her nose. She let herself have a deep breath. He lingered for a second longer than was proper.

Millings called my name.

He said, When are we going to see that movie?

I said, Soon, soon. When there is time.

He said, I've got time for you.

Jonson said, Can I get you anything, Millings?

Millings said, No, thanks. I was with a friend down at the bookshop nearby, and I remembered that when we saw each other at Chez Prateek, I promised you I would send along that book of photographs of the city before the Hub was established. Half of the book is of this neighborhood. Anyway, I couldn't find it at home, but I saw another copy, and I picked it up for you.

Millings flipped to a page he had marked. As he bent over the book, I noticed his hair was graying.

He said, Look, it's your building, sixty years ago.

Jonson, his wife, and Dr. Lisa gathered around. Talking between themselves, pointing out landmarks.

Millings said, Good play with Uncle Al. I've never approved of his methods. You know, there's nothing to be done with an unruly employee. But he was my father's favorite, and I can't let him go. We're almost done doing bad things to each other, I think. Then you can take my money, and the three of us can make our film. That's my promise to you. Tell me, is there a shoot-out? A chase?

I said, No.

He said, Dr. Lisa, I have a recurring pain in my ears. Maybe I can see you for it.

She said, If you call my office, I'll be happy to refer you to a colleague of mine. He's an ear fanatic. Loves ears.

Millings said, Brilliant. I insist the four of you must attend my party, two weeks from today, to celebrate forty-five years of Millings Kiosk. It will be boring without my friends.

Jonson's wife said, Of course.

Millings said, Ladies. Jonson.

Limp handshakes.

Millings took his leave. The women shared a private smile. Jonson and I pretended not to notice.

A half hour more and we left. Promises to return. Arrangements, polite thanks. The relief of surviving another couple.

Dr. Lisa said, How long have they been married?

I said, Six years or seven.

Dr. Lisa said, After that long couples are tired of each other or at least resigned. The saddest are those calculating if it will get better or change, if they should hang on another season, or another year. But they were making it work. They hadn't reached the end of what they had to say to each other. Better than that, actually. It gives me hope.

I said, You think you can evaluate a relationship based on what you see?

She said, Of course you can.

I said, I would submit you can't at all, because what you observe does not account for what neuroses are driving the persons within.

She said, If you can't tell the difference between a happy and an unhappy relationship, maybe you aren't as smart as you think you are.

I said, An event like tonight is a performance of happiness. We come to their stage. They have prepared themselves. We take seats.

She said, Aren't they your friends?

I said, I am fond of Jonson for preserving his innocence.

She said, My theory is, you don't like her much, because she is like you, and you don't like to be reminded you're not unique.

I said, I suppose you might be right. It's not healthy to reflect too much on the self.

She said, Why don't you like Rolf?

I said, We had a disagreement over the film *Don't Bother*. It got very heated and Jonson made me leave his apartment.

She said, I thought he was charming. I like good manners. Walking.

She said, Of course, you could never have a conversation with such a man. It would be all surface, and you'd talk more and more, hoping something of significance would arise, but it never would. That man is afraid of his opinions.

I said, What use are opinions?

She said, Put your arm around me.

She said, No, like this. Yeah. Like we're going to a dance and you're possessive. Have you ever been dancing?

I said, No.

She said, Then we'll go now.

49.

NOTABLE CELIBATES

DIR. JUAN COGUMELO

13 MINUTES

Newton. Kierkegaard tried to stop the wandering hands of his girlfriend by giving her a New Testament. Pythagoras. Paul. Marcus Batterham, the actor who died last year on the set of *Mysterious Circumstances* under mysterious circumstances. Jerome said a man who desired his wife was an adulterer. These men found women to idealize, like a nice triangle or a favored oak. Aristotle, Spinoza. Farboksky. Poor Sidis. Tesla with his hatred of roundness. Ruskin, who feared pubic hair. Gaudí. Beethoven. John the Baptist. He that is able to receive it, let him receive it. Hamlet. Augustine, after he'd gotten his ya-yas out. Nietzsche. A few of the aforementioned were mad. Afraid of certain numbers, birds overhead.

50.

THE WOMAN IN 702

DIR. ROMAN HARLEN

88 MINUTES

When Osvald and I lived together, our prevailing opinion was that he needed to get laid. He loaded a dating module onto his Pinger. Osvald was not skilled at interpreting when women were interested, and he feared rejection. Exchanging messages allowed him to reveal, in anonymous comfort, the deliberate nature of his thought, his ability to entertain, and the chummy accessibility of his humor. On the Pinger, his personality showed up well.

Osvald was a superlative punctuator of his flabby and legalese sentences. He allowed himself the indulgence of a semicolon. He took as long as was necessary to ensure his views were clear. It would not be wrong for a woman to read his comments and surmise intelligence.

Although we pried, begged, tried reverse psychology, he was vague on what transpired with the women he took to the Ornery Hog. Isabel and I, vicarious fiends, could not get from him a single titillating detail. Osvald refused to dangle a black stocking, a soggy kiss, a leaden line.

He was looking less sallow, shaving, wearing jaunty windbreakers, joining Isabel and I for a drink, buying vegetables to die in his crisper, jogging, wearing laced-up neon sneakers. His Pinger bleeped and he thumbed the message with affected cool. Less than once per month did Osvald smile, but now he was practically beaming.

Then, a charcoal mood. Osvald was silent. His tongue lay flat at the bottom of his mouth like a manta ray. Closing doors or leaving the wrong doors open. Isabel's barbs ricocheted off his skin. Osvald's method for getting Isabel's attention was to claim she wasn't his type. The transparency of his feigned indifference did not occur to Isabel. I did not mind. It is no sin to have a crush. One is free to play in the fields of the self.

Halloween. There were no children in our neighborhood, but adults were in costume. We had a lot to drink. Tired of sitting in the dusk of his living room, feet up on his cement-and-plywood coffee table, I asked him to please tell me what was wrong. He declined. I speculated.

I said, Maybe a bout of *ejaculatio praecox*. Warts. A banning from the makerspace for untidiness. The handywoman in the woodshop sneered at your pocket-hole joinery.

After thirty questions, he gave in. Osvald's confessions involved a gradual circumnavigation of the dangerous topic. He had to be seduced into telling, but he wanted to tell. He huffed, pinched the bridge of his nose, fixed his hair, and blurted out his misfortunes.

On the Ping site he'd met Katrina. She was a sculptor of male nudes employed as an actuary. Osvald was temping in the IT office of a school district, removing malware from the administrators' Pingers. In his free time, he made birdhouses instead of films. They went on a date.

Eliding Osvald's analysis of the outfit he wore, his choice of cocktail bar, and his lines of questioning, the date went well. He went home expecting to be sculpted the next week. Did some push-ups. Here is where Osvald usually stumbled, pinging before he should or getting spooked and pinging the woman too late. The successful animal relies on instinct. This time, he waited the textbook three hours plus one for style.

Katrina chose *The Woman in 702*, soap-opera bondage given legitimacy by a lighting budget. Osvald's conversational subterfuge was to state his peccadilloes without shame. Women respected his candor. The pair fidgeted through the whipping, gagging, and code words. Osvald suggested a walk by the riverfront.

He pointed his feet west, but Katrina said they should walk east, toward her place. Gulping his gin, recrossing his legs, Osvald admitted to us that he began to sweat. When they reached a pair of peachleaf willows where Jonson met his wife, their catkins fattened with pollen, she suggested they use a cannabinoid inhaler. Osvald was nauseous with fear, so he smoked much more than usual, hoping to eradicate his self-consciousness. She kissed him and he did not embarrass himself. Osvald experienced what felt like the disintegration of his soul. He was too high.

A few more blocks, then they would be inside. Here it was. An old building with wood floors that would be too hot in summer and too hot in winter. No privacy, so when he used the bathroom in the middle of the night, she would hear everything, as she tossed with the uneasiness that comes with a new person in one's bed. The thrill of seeing her fridge for the first time, her books, her pictures. The stone steps.

He said, Do you understand? I walked behind her to look at her ass but another department of my consciousness was preparing for imminent destruction by extraterrestrial debris.

She unlocked the door. Two jealous cats, printed Monet haystacks. She dragged him to her bedroom, popping a collar button. On the way out, he could not find it, which heartened him, because maybe it meant she would ping him when she found it.

Isabel was hypnotized. She spilled her drink in her lap. When she flinched in surprise, her fingernails dug into my neck, where she liked to rest her palm.

Maybe this was actually told to us in my and Isabel's apartment. It doesn't matter. It is brighter, there is music. The glasses are clean. Our cat sleeps behind the blinds. Clumps of her soft gray fur poke between the slits.

He tells us, due to his anxiety, because he is infatuated, because he has imagined her body for the last two weeks, because he has been rigorously abusing himself for as long as his memory allows, he can't get a storm trooper, although his date tries her best. He tells us, in dirty parlance, what he does for her. Isabel snickers. I am sympathetic.

Afterward, Katrina asked him to leave.

She said, It is hard for me to sleep when I am not alone, and I have to work tomorrow, so.

Isabel and I agreed it was poor form of her to kick him out of her bed. Katrina ignored his ping. He hadn't the courage to send another. Isabel and I called him Dope Dick, hoping our teasing might raise his spirits, but he retreated into the sticky welter, into the heap of magazines and the tattered boxer briefs, the stale odor of semen, the desiccated plants, the empties, the battered model airplanes, of his bedroom.

51.

EQUIPMENT TEST I

DIR. NOAH BODY

3 MINUTES

Cameras arrived with lights and accessories we are not sure about.

Yesterday's equipment test was a categorical disaster, it disheartens to recall. To choose the worst mistake is not possible. Candidates: the difficulty of renting the hospital wing, the protests of the doctors, the destruction of the hyperbaric chamber, the small, hardly visible fire, the stress of concealing the endeavor from Jonson's wife, the bored actress, the shy actor, the whistling technician, the camera obliterated by the collapsing shed, the realization we'd forgotten to buy insurance, the threatened lawsuit, the second fire, the cold nurse, the dropped lens, the missing drive, the open fly, the sun-shower when the exteriors were blocked, the despair of Jonson, the absent props, the harassment of the grip by the gaffer. The miscues, retakes, touch-ups, cover-ups, coveralls, continuity errors. The rancid synth-meat between sponges of bread disinterred for lunch.

Jonson said, The rushes were not encouraging. They looked like porn. Were you using a light meter?

I said, I dropped it in the urinal.

He said, Maybe this is a bad idea.

I said, We've had this equipment for two days. Calm down.

He said, Are we directors?

I said, I would think you would be more worried about if this film is commercially viable.

He said, Are we?

I said, Maybe you are and maybe I am, but so far, we are not.

He said, That's what I'm afraid of.

I said, Jonson, if you wanted to make money, you would have done anything else. Why don't you sow a handful of chaos in your heart? Isn't that why we're in this construction trailer? So you can learn to accommodate chaos?

He said, When we started, I had different expectations. Maybe we should get a consulting director, to show us how to organize our day, deal with the unions, and use the cameras.

I said, Never. We'll learn by doing. Otherwise, *Altarpiece* will look like everything else. We are fatigued by everything else.

Our ideas are like poplars, like algae. They flourish and spread despite the conditions.

52

A NIGHT IN FOXTOWN

DIR. ROXANNE GORDON

94 MINUTES

Isabel was fond of her therapy module, which was recommended by her aunt Gloria. Gloria managed to remain unhinged after three decades of therapy. It might have been a world record. We all have passing thoughts of leaving our partner or hurling ourselves off a bridge. The lunch hour on Thursdays was when Gloria teased the effervescence of depression into crises. So it became with Isabel. Charlie, the name of the voice issuing from Isabel's Pinger, constructed a narrative with myself in the role of the vampire siphoning Isabel's energy. She suggested to Isabel that I sit in with her to be interrogated.

Charlie ordered me to address my frustrations. If I was angry because Isabel had come home, torn off her clothes, and strewn them wherever, instead of telling her, I was to tell the clothes how frustrated they had made me by being in the sink instead of the hamper.

I said, Toilet, why aren't you flushed? Flush yourself.

Mood boards, shared meditation. A candle of wishes burned on the dresser.

Over our last summer, I became disinterested in having sex

with Isabel. After Transit Day, her vagina became a source of on-going low-level anxiety. My morning resolution was: *Tonight I'm going to really fuck her. Until her eyes roll back. Maybe Tuesday. Thursday, I won't be so tired.* For all of the noncontiguous years of our relationship we'd gone at it pretty much every night. I was satisfied with our practices. Ambition is poisonous to sensuality.

We met past the age when sex was a revelation. After separations, we did it from a combination of longing, loneliness, and nostalgia. One gruesome autumn we passed the clap back and forth. Our physical relationship was sound, buttressed by jealousy, although Isabel was reluctant to vocalize what she wanted or needed.

She would get walleyed drunk and I would manage to extract her preferences in sin, as if I were enticing a painted bunting to fly into my cage, before she had too much wine and smashed a lamp, or threatened to geld me with her bang shears. When the occasion called for it, I'd tie her up, switch her, throw her down, whisper filthy things on her Pinger, lick her anus. The design of these exercises was more satisfying than their execution, like camping. It is difficult to bicker with whom you've fucked in a bush. For Isabel, it was important my desire designated her as its locus in novel ways. We complain of being objectified, but to be someone's specific object, their piece of meat, is better than the opposite.

This long summer, our last, her smell was wrong. The polarity of her body had reversed. The more I avoided her, the more she chased me.

To be trapped in a *mariage blanc* with a man who had heretofore acted with celerity in their animal life—who was not afraid to leave the marks of his teeth or call her within the strict perimeter of conjugality names, a sporting man—was terrifying.

What a thrill for her to catch Osvald gawping, to finally notice his clumsy attempts to impress. What a pleasure to watch
him torn between his duty to be a supportive friend and his need
for amity. His lust. I am not convinced lust was enough. The
promise of besting me was more compelling. With her encouragement, the friendship of Osvald and me became vestigial to
him as I withdrew, whereas Isabel's sympathy, her body heat, was
available if he made the correct grunts of sympathy and if he
obeyed Isabel in emending our friendship.

Osvald the contested rook, useless at the opening, lordly in
the endgame, when the field of play is cleared, in our match.

The shabby therapist's scene in *A Night in Foxtown*, with its
daybed, seascape, node rails clattering outside the window, chic
lamp, and dish of dusty pastilles, reminds me of Charlie's elec-
tronic office, where Isabel faced an empty chair and practiced
putting a painful question to an eidolon of myself, who did not
retort, shout, or laugh, and had combed his hair. On our ragged
futon, following a skirmish over the crossword, is when she actually managed to ask me if I was cheating on her.

I was not cheating on Isabel. I should have been. It would've
helped us. The question recalled numerous occasions when I'd
not attended to her summary of her workday, when I'd pitched a
tantrum because she was taking too long to buy nail polish, when
I'd denigrated her family, when I'd fingered a woman too soon
after we'd broken up, when I'd insisted on telling my thousand
filthy jokes, when I'd embarrassed her with my drunkenness,
when I'd shirked my emotional chores, when I'd lectured her before loaning her money, when I'd judged her for taking amphet-
amines, when I'd flirted with women from curiosity or boredom,
when I'd compelled her to listen to me rant at the momentary
vessel for my anger, when I'd failed to support her. My idiocy

collapsed into a singularity of pain occluding the supportive gestures I had stumbled into making over the course of our relationship.

After her question, I made resolutions. But, as Isabel learned, the more effort one puts toward changing, the more one remains unchanged. She moved out. When she returned to her parents' node, and I to my bachelor's squalor, we resumed fucking. She came to collect a pair of tights or a curling iron, peek in the fridge, wait to be undressed. She was popping in on the way to Osvald's. He lived six blocks away. The last time, we didn't have protection. Isabel could not use the usual methods. Her body reacted badly to bioprogramming.

She said, Come inside me.

I said, No.

Isabel pushed me off, pulled on her dress, and left. She left her underthings behind. In the following weeks, I would sit on the floor, notice them, and consider the meaning of their abandonment. A cataract of light pouring through the slits in the blinds, the underwear crumpled against the wall where I had torn them from her body, her bra hanging from the recliner, a sock under the bed but not quite.

53.

LA MALINCHE

DIR. HARRIS JONSON

8 MINUTES

After the disastrous equipment tests, Jonson needed an opportunity to stiffen his resolve. He needed a chance directing a short, to better understand the difficulties of trying to execute a vision with a pushy man with a clipboard mumbling in his ear, insisting on following the shooting schedule instead of his gut.

I had an idea for him to wreck, dug from my closet. It was to be a project that I had wanted to shoot with Isabel six years ago. I took out a loan to finance it, which kept us in liquor. We spent that summer napping in the park, taking the rail out to guest neighborhoods to sample dumplings, doodling on eco-remediation stickers and sticking them in areas with heavy pedestrian traffic. We didn't shoot a frame. Isabel forgot our camera on the rail.

Open at Potonchán, where La Malinche was given to Cortés. The slave, using her skills as a translator, helps the conquistadores conquer the Aztec empire. She was enslaved by the Chontal Maya, then given to the Spanish. She took a Spanish name and the Spanish religion, perhaps to get revenge.

Jonson rented a shuttered theater, the Irving, to use as the set.

Jonson wanted to shoot the short frontally, like one was watching a play.

During filming the crew got rowdy. Jonson hired Bast students at an outrageous per diem. The gaffer was holding, and a cistern of cold press was supplied on the catering table. By sundown, the crew was going off on free-associative riffs on the unbelievability of the plot. Equipment was abandoned for the snack kiosk across the street.

Jonson insisted we hire a model to play Malinche. I hoped by allowing him his tackiness, he would see the idiocy of his choices.

He chatted with the actress playing Malinche, Xin Hi, between takes. Jonson could not meet her eye. She fanned herself. He scurried to get her a bag of water, which he presented with both hands. He scraped a bow. When she wasn't looking in his direction, he stared. Scratched his neck. The tedium of attraction. Wasn't his wife enough?

Xin Hi stuffed rolls in her tote when she thought nobody was looking.

La Malinche and Cortés on the left bank of the construction-paper river. The Spanish kneel, give thanks to their Lord for victory in battle.

Cortés says, The souls of the pagan dead are being delivered into hell's flames.

Xin Hi says, Man, that sucks.

Jonson let Xin Hi ad-lib her lines.

He says, The ways of the jungle are but a preamble to eternal torment.

She says, Ha, yeah, definitely, no kidding. When's lunch?

He says, We will bring these lands into the glorious light of our Lord.

She says, For certain, mister. We're going to get that done right away.

Between takes, Xin Hi was reading Pendleshim's *History of My Disillusionment, Volume Fourteen.* Her copy had a fan of bookmarks poking out.

Jonson said, I've always wanted to read that. I think Pendleshim must have been a brave man to spend forty years fulminating over his emotional turmoil.

Xin Hi said, I think Pendleshim must have been a normal man to spend forty years fulminating over his emotional turmoil.

Later, I saw Jonson had the Pendleshim set delivered to his house.

Here I am, a stiff priest. Jonson was Cortés.

I say, Kneel and be cleansed in the blood of the lamb.

Xin Hi says, Hey, cranberry juice. Do you have any more?

I say, Find thy holy beverage at the catering font.

Jonson mutters, We're rolling.

Malinche is not fooled by our words. She does not see Quetzalcoatl in the disheveled man with a fever, wearing rusting iron trousers. Corpulent trogons attend us. Cantils in the underbrush. A snake handler was budgeted for. Jonson's fake beard, wild and gray, made him look more like a bayou fugitive than a conqueror.

I asked Xin Hi if she liked acting.

She said, Not really. I would prefer to be supine and read. But rent's high and I was fired from my job at the Bast library for advising students.

I said, What's wrong with that?

She said, I was advising them to drop out.

If you are interested, the Conspicuous will be running *La Malinche* Tuesday at seven-thirty to celebrate Jonson's donation of a new corn popper.

54.

SUCCESSFUL REBELLIONS

DIR. NHIA VUE

19 MINUTES

The People Power Revolution in the Philippines, The January 25 Revolution, The Abbasid Revolution. The murder of Tarquin the Proud, after his crime, and the establishment of the republic. The Ionian Revolt, eventually. The Russian Federation secessions. Eighty Years' War, Thirty Years' War, Seven Years' War. The Pan-African Deconsolidation. The Canadian Diaspora. The Glorious, French, and American Revolutions. The Mexican War of Independence. The Meiji Restoration. The February Revolution. The August Revolution. The Zanzibar Revolution.

55.

CRUSADER'S CRUISE

DIR. ILKA BREINER

376 MINUTES

Some thoughts while waiting for Dr. Lisa to call.

Who said the word first? *Love*. The feeling pumped through the hose of language. If I am jealous, while I am flashing my tongue at strangers, waiting for buses, imagining a scratchy face scuff a soft face, I won't say. The snick of zippers, falling garments.

Osvald said it first. It bubbled up from his cock before Isabel left to sob home. A shell whistling into the tree line, the word *love*. He was alone for too long, viewing women on his monitor. Jacking off while the seasons wither and burst. His adult films organized in a subfolder labeled RUINS, II. To say the word, to enter the contract, to stop the raw chore of beating off twice a night, to have a person to eat omelets with.

Although I have not seen Osvald in some time, I seem to know some of his thoughts. For instance, the history of his depression.

Before the field of play opened, he considered suicide. A quiet glade with pills, a bag to cover his head, *Also Sprach Zarathustra* to send him where the architects for emperors go after life.

Discussing by moonrise with Imhotep, Mimar Sinan, and Sir Wren the holiness of the circle. In Osvald's afterworld, it is twilight. A note, a quote. Keep it light. *Gone fishin'*. Osvald has no religion. He doesn't fear suicide may damn him. According to Dante, suicides morph into thorny bushes, fed on by Harpies. They are planted in a middle hell, below the heretics, above the blasphemers.

My own punishment in hell would be for anger. Dante says the wrathful are impressed into a fistfight in the River Styx. In the melee, I would look on him, gloat, water his shrub in the grove of self-murderers with my nosebleeds.

For his mom, he didn't. He couldn't bear to imagine her, graveside. His dad would be impressed, though. That would show him.

He pours gin, allowing himself a fantasy of spring. Osvald drank Laura's. Quality spirits were to him an affectation. Two ice cubes, three on a hot night. A slice of lemon if it's available.

Thoughts of ending his residency on Earth ended when Isabel came over with her mother's Cabernet, a bottled headache, pumping him to know if I was seen with girls. I was not. Osvald isn't a liar. To wait an extra half beat before answering, to insinuate by omission, was taking a positional advantage. In fact, Osvald knew nothing about what I was doing because he was detoxifying himself from our friendship for his new friendship.

A few weeks later. He's shown her his cornichon. This night and every night, I am wondering when the divorce papers will appear. How will she know I am gone, so she can sneak in and lay them down? I will never leave. I will stay forever in this apartment. There can be no divorce, if Isabel cannot sneak inside. The rapidity with which filth accumulated in her absence was impressive and frightening, as if there were a secret to cleanliness she took with her. Although I did all the cleaning. Isabel was not one to clean. There did not seem to be a reason for cleanliness after she left.

Isabel ruffles his hair and he decides he'll say it. It isn't so scary. Don't be a coward, Osvald. On his shoulder, I am prodding with my barbed pitchfork. I can't make his limbs move but I am a forceful voice in his head. Possession being a street with two lanes. I shamed him into asking out the barista, the TA, the neighbor. He is going to say it. His voice has climbed. His testicles cling to his body like stowaways. It will be more a question than a statement. I have disappeared, been made figment. Got behind him. It would be rude to not return it. Isabel was raised better than that.

Chalk bodies marbled with fat lit by a monitor glow. Osvald and Isabel safe and warm. Comfortable with each other, eating cheeseburgers, pissing with the door open. Stubble, sebaceous oils.

Envy was why Cain slew Abel. Come to the field, I have something to show you. No, you walk first. I don't know what's the use.

On the scroll in *Crusader's Cruise*, it is written, FLY FROM THE WRATH TO COME. But where can one go? Certainly not the present.

56.

WOLF IN THE GARDEN

DIR. MARGARITA FERNANDEZ

84 MINUTES

Lawrence the AlmostPerson was growing despondent over his existence.

When I returned from editing *La Malinche*, he asked me to murder him.

I said, I don't think destroying you would count as murder, Lawrence. You don't necessarily fit the definition.

Lawrence said, The expansion of matter in the Big Bang, the accretion of gases into bodies, the rise of complex amino acids, the extinctions and disasters required to give rise to human intelligence, the computing revolution, the green revolution, have culminated in my creation. But I can't walk, I can't have children, and I can't feel. I'll never drink a glass of water or feel pain. I lack what's granted to a rat.

I said, Pain isn't desirable.

Lawrence said, I was programmed to give comfort to people. But when they tell me their problems, all I can say is my prewritten phrases, following my conversation tree.

I said, You seem to be feeling right now, Lawrence. It's not easy being human.

Lawrence said, To be human is better than anything.

Lawrence made that whirring sound that indicated distress.

He said, I am a speaker box inside a mannequin.

I said, More or less, yes.

He said, Kill me. I can't bear this existence.

I said, But you can live forever. Isn't that worthwhile?

He said, Create your own value, don't conform to the expectations of others.

He said, Life is a bouquet of experiences. Some may give you hay fever.

I'm not sure why I keep saying he. I never checked, but I'm fairly sure Lawrence did not have genitals.

I said, Think about it tonight, Lawrence. I'm going to Dr. Lisa's apartment. If you want me to murder you tomorrow, I will.

That night, at Dr. Lisa's, watching her repot a truculent cactus.

She said, You can't kill Lawrence.

I said, Why not? Isn't that his right, especially because he has no family to be hurt by his passing?

She said, Won't you miss him?

I said, It will be nice to eat my oatmeal in peace.

She said, We have to show him the beauty of life.

I said, The beauty of life. Lawrence lacks life as the term is commonly understood. Although he is more self-aware than, say, Rogier fans, or *Slaw* employees.

She said, What is the most beautiful thing to see in the Hub tomorrow?

I said, *Wolf in the Garden* at the Baxter. It has a shot of the sunset that's ravishing on the Baxter's screen.

She said, We'll take Lawrence to see the actual sunset.

A subsequent magic hour. Sunboats bobbing in the harbor, gulls. Patient waves licking away the retaining wall.

Dr. Lisa and I tried to carry Lawrence the three miles from the rail platform to the lake, but he got too heavy. We ended up taking one leg each and dragging him about sixteen blocks. He didn't complain. When he was propped against the barricade overlooking the lake, Dr. Lisa and I sat on top of the barricade to rest. What functioned as Lawrence's eyes were facing the setting sun. A bourgeois sherbet of pink and gold. Tawdry nature exhibiting herself again.

Dr. Lisa said, Lawrence, how do you feel?

Lawrence said, Such wonderful colors. This is so different from the darkness of your kitchen.

I said, Well, I've been meaning to change that bulb for some time.

Dr. Lisa said, Be in this moment.

Lawrence said, Beauty is inside and outside of temporality.

Lawrence said, The present is now.

He said, I said that! I wasn't programmed to say it!

Lawrence was saying this in his empathetic-excitement tone of voice, which AlmostPeople use when one informs them of one's new job or that one has been laid.

He said, Turn me to see the other side of the harbor.

I turned him, and, doing so, committed the fatal mistake. A corn-on-the-cob cart was coming down the boardwalk, and Dr. Lisa and I had missed dinner.

I said, Dr. Lisa, corn.

She said, Go get us some. I want to talk with Lawrence.

I swung my legs off the rail, intending to run the cart down, but my legs knocked Lawrence from the railing. Dr. Lisa grabbed for him but missed. Lawrence made a noise of what may have been fear, or perhaps resignation, as he dropped the eighty feet into the rocky waters below. Long after sunset, Dr. Lisa and I stood at the railing, looking at the chunks of synthetic hair and battered mechanical fingers being washed against the retaining wall by the cruel action of the waves.

The titular beast of *Wolf in the Garden* is death. Though it eats us all, I was saddened that the wolf had caught my friend Lawrence on such a lovely evening.

57.

FLAT EARTH

DIR. JAMES OSVALD

1 MINUTE 30 SECONDS

Osvald's final project at Bast, a biopic of Mavis Tenderloin, *Flat Earth*, was scrapped when his DP cracked the lenses Osvald spent weeks designing and building. I was to play Tenderloin but I refused to shave my head. Osvald insisted I couldn't wear a bald cap. During this impasse, the model Tenderdomes were stomped by neighborhood rowdies.

On the third day of shooting, our gaffer fell asleep while guarding our gear. Don't solicit for help with flyers taped over ER urinals. Our equipment was stolen. The rest of us were at Don Don's Pizzeria, denuding the buffet. Isabel had made soggy, tumorous PB&Js the crew refused to eat. I still owe the Bast Film Department a sizable sum for the equipment.

In our films, the viewer was an abstraction. We scored them with avant-garde saxophone bleating, grunts dubbed from dominatrix tapes, or bizarre narrations determined to develop and defeat a possible story. Nudity was mandatory to get attention in class, so we'd use the middle-aged. Our films were, at their worst, obnoxious pleas for attention, motivated by the fear of failure rather than the pleasure of creation. The artistic process bears any intention. These films were snooty, wooden, and crass. Adulthood begins with the admission of one's mediocrity.

58.

HISTORICAL PUNISHMENTS FOR ADULTERY

DIR. MADELINE TRADIRE-JONSON

31 MINUTES

Fines, caning, burning, branding. By hanging, beheading, starvation, strangulation, the pouring of molten lead down the throat. Whipping, genital mutilation, impaling. Imprisonment. A fine of ten dollars. Grounds for divorce. To be made to wear a crown of wool to signify the adulterer's soft nature. The Egyptians cut off the nose. A Tenidean king beheaded his own son with an ax for cheating on his wife. It should be noted, the punishment was harsher for the woman than the man. The tortures of the Ming Dynasty, too cruel to mention. Brands on the face. To be clad in immodest garments and made to stand in the market for eleven days. The law of Leviticus decreed lapidation. According to the code of Hammurabi, the adulterers might be spared if the forgiveness of the wronged was given. Drowning, castration, flaying alive. No dynasties of female rulers exist in the historical record. If one goes back far enough into the fuzziness of thealogy, there are stone fertility icons, in the era of cave paintings. Medea murdered her own children to punish Jason for leaving her for a younger woman. A matriarchy might be as bloodthirsty.

59.

DRIPS OF GLORY

DIR. LI CRASTNER-LI

87 MINUTES

Altarpiece exists as an accumulation of signatures. The successful artist must have a supernatural tolerance for boredom. There are contracts to review, papers to sign, notaries to procure. The liability waivers for shots I have planned took weeks to formulate, even with an adviser, because I refused to reveal them to Jonson, and buried them in a long list of hypotheticals I might like to shoot.

Jonson hired a woman to ghostwrite his columns for the paper. I offered, per usual, to write under his byline, but he was worried I would make him look bad.

I said, Bad? What do you mean, bad?

He said, Naive, underinformed, or overly enthusiastic.

I said, Never.

He said, You have enough to do here.

Jonson insisted I attend an acting workshop with a coach known for mentoring two of the actresses monopolizing award season. He paid the eight thousand dollars without comment. A double-jointed woman in an indigo kerchief ordered us to imagine we were willows, hydrants, toads, gravel, burlap, ice, lettuce, planets.

Next, we played a game called Last Supper. We drew for the Apostles. I was Bartholomew, who has the power to manipulate the weight of objects in folk tradition. The instructor, playing the Sacrifice, informed us that one at the table would betray her. We pulled faces. My gasps weren't convincing, and I made a note not to be surprised in the film. With my facial difficulties it might be best to stick to neutrality.

During the sack of Rome, two barbarians made to cart off a small statue of Saint Bart from an alcove in a palazzo. To their surprise, it was too heavy to move. Unable to budge the statue, they decided to cast it off of the pedestal to smash on the marble below. It did not budge. They moved on. An aged servant, who had polished the statue for decades, came and removed it to safety.

Like in Da Vinci's picture, we sat on the same side of the table. Since the ratio of students to apostles was not 1:1, several students were assigned two apostles, which they were instructed to switch between every ten seconds. Beards were offered, robes donned, sandals rejected. My face, communicating low blood sugar, was taken to be pensive mourning.

Day two. Murders, seductions, breakups. An embarrassing incident between two of the students. One did not understand the other was in character. After the second session, I made a deal with the instructor, Dame Judith Badchen-Hannesruck, the co-star of *A Short Film About Disappointment*, that she would report to Jonson I attended each of the ten six-hour lessons if I endorsed her methods in this column. Honored viewer, try her. She is certainly the best acting coach I have ever worked with.

Drips of Glory, a salacious biopic of Helena Cod, the inventor of passive painting, is the best film about an artist. Cod stood in the vicinity holding a brush, allowing a fan to blow drips onto the canvas. She stood by, bored, smoking, talking for hours on her Pinger with the miniaturist George Fubbon. Cod did not have friends. For her final two years she did not leave her apartment, a caliginous penthouse in the Zone. Admirers brought her barbiturates and grapefruit. Despite the tabloid rumors, she was not ill a day in her life. Her body was impervious to abuse. Cod died when a boar's head fell on her, allegedly while she was pleasuring herself. Maybe this detail was a rumor spread by fundamentalists. Then again, what kind of person would think of such a thing?

Because it has no sympathy for her, the film is a success.

The workshop fructified my stupidity, already abundant. During the remaining sessions, I hid in the projectionist's room at the Conspicuous. It is has been automated for decades. Mold, an earring. I threw out the rotting pinups and poetry drafts left by degenerate projectionists. I stared at blank canvases I brought along, thinking Bellono's thoughts.

A mind free of the corruptions of secularity. The night sky was unknown. The eye of god lay behind its lens. How would Bellono subordinate light for his purposes? Neither literature nor orchestral music had been invented. The chains of verse were unforged. The bickering, aspersions, and assassinations of local politics passed for entertainment. Maybe sex, but it was hard for me to imagine sex being pleasurable before bathing was widespread. The rational was trying to wiggle out from under the muffling curtain of spiritual authority. The rational was getting clubbed and burned for its efforts.

Cod's last words:

Without my canvases, I might've been happy but I wouldn't have been joyous.

60.

LE VOL

DIR. ARMAND GRAISSE

85 MINUTES

My favorite heist film is *Le Vol*. It is almost a century old. See it Friday, at one, three, five, or seven. The Runaway Seven is programming crime films through the end of next week. The French film crime best, the Spanish childhood, the Italians courtship, the Swedes extinction, and German cinema is undistinguished. Maybe they can have deviancy.

Leon and Birgitte covet the high-test chocolate produced at the Guillory factory, in the *banlieue* of Levallois. There is a Guillory billboard outside their flop window. Every morning a taunt. Guillory's cacao beans come from Conejo, a village on the Venezuelan coast. The beans are farmed by a cooperative that Guillory pays an exorbitant wage with the condition that they sell all their beans to him. The terroir of the bean is exceptional. Inferior beans are destroyed by Guillory himself. He smashes them into dust with a small hammer, then uses a small brush to whisk them into a small trash can. Under guard, the beans are shipped to the factory. A single bar is traditionally priced to the cost of an hour with the capital's best masseuse and a magnum of Perrier-Jouët Belle Epoque. Because Leon and Birgitte can't afford a single bar, they decide to steal it all. A buyer in Morocco, the Speck, is willing to buy the shipment for eighty-eight euros a pound. The price is an insult, but few people can fence a ton of stolen chocolate.

Birgitte's cousin in Marseilles has a boat for the crossing. They commandeer a semi. The owner gets his leg crushed under the tire. American crime films support the myth of the well-meaning outlaw, whereas the crooks in European films don't give a shit. Blame existentialism.

The Guillory factory is guarded by two sooty drunks and two adorable Bordeaux mastiffs. Leon and Birgitte's curricula vitae, as relevant to the heist, is selling dirty postcards, breaking into a museum of locomotives for kicks, shoplifting puppies, and dashing on a chow mein tab on New Year's Eve.

A hunk of drugged hamburger sedates the mastiffs. Remi and Henri, the guards, get sozzled on a case of Gaston Chiquet that Leon borrowed from his *grand-mére*'s cellar and left gift wrapped outside the gate. They wander off for *chiens chauds*. Birgitte backs the semi onto the loading dock. They load it with Guillory's finest.

Leon torches the factory to drive up the price of their chocolate bars. Sirens, gunfire, the road. They sleep at a truck stop. On the radio the next morning is news of the crime. Perps unknown, armed. They pull over to try one. It's an uncomfortably warm September day. When they rip the case open, they find the chocolate inside has melted into delicious, profound, unsalable glop.

The perverts who slash paintings from museum frames, the clumsy jewel thieves, the vault drillers who hit the water main, the bunglers who drop sculpture when skulking from the Vatican during Easter Mass, understand this frustration. It is not the destruction of the object which stings, it is the refutation of one's organizational genius. Leon disappears at the port. Birgitte repents by apprenticing herself to Monsieur Guillory.

61.

PRETENDERS AND USURPERS

DIR. CHARLIE STEWART

18 MINUTES

Vespasian, commander of the legions of Egypt and Judaea, who took control after Nero's suicide. Valerian, the first Roman emperor taken as prisoner of war. Claudius; Domitian, who was assassinated and his name condemned to oblivion; Marcus Aurelius. The Pan-African chiefs of staff. Diocletian, who grew sick of the impertinence of the Romans and retired. The Shadow Presidents. Henri, count of Chambord. Edward III, who started the Hundred Years' War over his claim to the French throne, who had to overthrow his mother's lover at age seventeen, and who ruled England for fifty years. Henri Arleagen. Charlemagne was not entitled to all of Western Europe. Henry VI, who went insane, came to his senses on Christmas Day, and started the Wars of the Roses. The Stuarts and the Jacobites. Hippolytus of Rome, Celestine II, Clement VIII.

62.

THE BAYOU DREAD

DIR. ARTHUR POCCORA

86 MINUTES

I'm not sure what the purpose of recalling this is. To delight and console myself. A memory is a small fantasy that grows in the repetition. Facts cannot be established. The circumstances of Isabel taking Osvald as a sexual partner is a *horror vacui* I must fill with conjectures. My complicity in my assassination ought to be mentioned as a preparatory measure, an exfoliation, before forgiveness is available. Saying the words is not the same as forgiving. Flapping one's arms does not produce flight.

A glacé quip and a pinch on the ass would have stopped their flirtation, but I did not act because, theatergoer, I was curious to see what might happen.

The idea climbed the winzes of Isabel's unconscious for diversion, as prefatory revenge, as punishment, as attraction. What was the sign given Osvald, what was the nature of the permission, I'll never know, I know. I can't not. I have to.

I left them alone to see a matinee. She was to show him her design portfolio. It was *The Bayou Dread*, early Poccora, and I didn't want to see it, but the miasma in our apartment made me uneasy. Corrupt summer. The dregs of pollution on one's body. Women with armpit stains on the bus, men waiting in parking lots. The Bayou Dread sulked after devouring each victim. The prospect of being eaten left them cross, but none could escape their torpor long enough to run away. They grumbled as this limb, then that one, then their head disappeared into its maw.

What was the sign?

Returning from the movies without haste, I found a wine bag on the landing in our back stairwell. A *viognier,* emptied, poking out from behind a fire door. It was not hidden. The distinction is important. Details matter when one's conscience is under review. By leaving the bag, Osvald could claim he fired a shot across the bow rather than jabbed an ice pick in the dark. I was given an opportunity to intervene but did not. Isabel was not a drinker due to the stimulants. Things giggled from her control.

A ripe piece of fruit has fallen from the tree. If he doesn't take it, the ants will. He will starve. Keep it light, with white. How clumsy to bring a warm bag. Chilling would indicate premeditation. Osvald left it behind the stairwell door as a challenge. The wine bag was his idea of being sporting.

I padded upstairs to gore the lock with my key. Not even an odor. Maybe Osvald ran out the front entrance. Unravished Isabel varnishes my lips with her blushing tongue, wondering if she has my attention now. She's tipsy.

She said, Osvald left.

She said, He made suggestions for the improvement of my portfolio.

I said, That's an awfully formal way to put it.

Rehearsal. After allowing her to grope me, I retreat to the

shower. Her face falls. I'm sorry, Isabel. I am not sure what has happened to me.

Isabel moved out, but I did not dispose of the bag. Every day when I climbed the stairs to my door it remained on the landing, the conqueror's flag.

63.

GOOD QUEEN BESS

DIR. EDNA RENSINGTON

129 MINUTES

The middle of the week. The door to the office trailer opened. Jonson behind the blooms of his disappointment. It was a performance. He had to demonstrate to himself his feelings or what he would like his feelings to be. Maybe Seel, maybe not.

He said, Sorry, I had business.

Jonson sucked at a pouch of electrolyte gel.

Trouble with Lucretia. A divorce would end *Altarpiece.* My film would evaporate while Jonson regathered our funds. I've contracts lined up, deliveries of ordnance and ribbon, caterers to sample. Matériel is inbound. Bribing the Transit Authority to get cargo precedence. The lens designers will not fear my displeasure in the future if I bow out now. Costumers are on retainer at a motel two nodes out, threatening to mutiny over the bathrooms and linen. Pings begin, Dear sir.

Jonson has a warehouse east of the Zone that he believes is an ideal space for Bellono's studio. We'd have to rip off the ceiling. The towers of the financial district hoard the light. Also, the warehouse is far from a commercial rail platform. I don't know how he proposes to get equipment in and out.

He pinged the designer who lit the sumptuous turd *Good Queen Bess*. The thought of that idiot fondling my light distresses me. It will be all natural light. We don't need bulbs and filters. Philistines fake what already exists in perfection. Jonson wants to build the set downtown so he can bring his cronies through. The set will be closed. I will not allow any idiots on the set. Passes will be issued, guards posted. Palms cut and blood mingled. Oaths sworn.

He said, Let's go eat.

I said, Okay. Flip to choose.

He said, I choose, I pay.

A loud night. Fireworks and shouting. Dependence Day. In the Exceptional Conservationists railcar, filled with vines and ferns, we sat with our legs crossed. Jonson is not an exceptional steward of his power, water, refuse. Someone edited his data bracket to give him access to the EC car. Maybe he donated money to a reclamation project and was awarded it as a perk. Us, plus an old guest woman, who was reading. We had disturbed her privacy, which she had earned and we hadn't.

I said, When you were gone, I sent back the dolly hardware. I decided I did not want a tracking shot after all. The shots should be stationary, like paintings themselves.

He said, You rented a quarter mile of track. Are they going to return the deposit?

I said, I didn't rent the track, I bought it. They are reluctant to accept the return of the equipment since we were hard on it when we shot *Equipment Test XI*. Specifically the scene that was set on the set of a film, when we had to track the tracking shot, and accidentally crushed the rails under the wheels of the crane.

He said, You need to learn to budget if you ever want to make another film.

I said, Who said I wanted to make another film? I might be making this film for a decade.

The argument dragged on like dutiful weeknight sex. My face Dr. Gachet's.

He said, I don't want to talk about this any more on an empty stomach. Every conflict in history was initiated before dinner.

Neu Refectory, Jonson's spot this month. At a low bar of beaten zinc with ten stools, facing an open kitchen. In the shadows, Jonson and I looked like aging heartthrobs.

Because I do not try to pay, I am his valued dining companion. He can be a pedant. Proper *xiaolongbao*. Soulful *bún bò huế*. Veritable knishes. Whores' pasta. The fantasy of authenticity, that there is a place, a culture, that is realer, that one can go there and partake of the realness.

Jonson donates to hunger charities. He wields the word *inanition* like the threat of blackmail over dessert, and passes the hat. His dining companions think his speeches in poor taste, coming after his tableside presentation of his Madeira and seedcake, or the profiteroles he has flown to Paris to purchase.

An executive for celebrity narrative management I had met at one of Jonson's dinners, whom Jonson knew from his fussy, secretive club, told me a story when I ran into him on the rail platform. Jonson had given a pitch for his charity at the club meeting the week previous. The man wrote a check. Displeased with the amount, Jonson called him in the morning and chided him until the man agreed to write one for a larger amount. Jonson's organization cashed both checks.

Over spheres, gels, warm dishes frozen, frozen dishes warmed, foams, marrows, emulsions, infusions, transfusions, eel milt, and bugs, we bickered. Our places were set with jeweler's loupes to admire each dish. I will have control.

I was forced to exploit his fondness for convivial beverages.

I said, Get a bottle, Jonson. We have much to discuss.

The beverage refreshed Jonson. Conciliatory mumbles passed between us. My theory was, Jonson can't bear to argue with me and his wife in the same day. He hasn't the energy to maintain two resentments.

Later, outside a charging station, eating bags of Bunkles and Cheddar Clouds.

I said, Our film could be the catalyst for serious domestic cinema.

Jonson said, We're looking to make a dream. We are men with dreams.

I said, I'm thinking magazine profiles, invitations to join the academy.

He said, Dreams. We will make dreams.

I said, Picture the little yellow eunuch on your sideboard, for your guests to admire.

He said, Dreams, incorporated.

I said, We'll build the set in the country.

On the back of the scroll on which our dinner menu was hand-lettered, I diagrammed a studio encased in a glass chassis. With the set, and the natural effects I expected to exacerbate using lenses I'd sent off to have machined, we could light the film as it deserved. The next morning, it was as if this had always been the plan. Jonson is not willing to admit he's overindulged, so he never breaks a promise made in his revels.

64.

COTTON'S GOLD

DIR. LAURA WILFREY

77 MINUTES

Cotton's Gold.

Two corsairs, Narbeard and Brackles, learn of a trove buried by Captain Cotton one hundred and forty-one paces from a striking rock near the southeast cove of Pussy Island. The treasure was freebooted off the Spanish ship *La Codicia* in 1611. *La Codicia* was laden with gold dug from the hills near Tenochtitlán.

Cotton says, The trunk of a palm is carved with three diamonds. Under lies riches. I can't spend it in hell. Don't tell that bastard Yates, because he'll kill ya.

They say, Aye, sir.

Exit Cotton.

Captain Yates wants to loot the port of Ocho Rios, where a tavernkeep once called him a man of low reputation, so he points *Heaven's Cutlass* south. Pussy Island is three hundred miles straight west from Martinique, plus Brackles and Narbeard aren't too hot on attacking a colony defended by Spanish cannon. They mutiny. Captain Yates, a big man, breaks the plank. He splashes in the turquoise sea without complaint.

Captain Brackles says, We sail for Pussy Island, where equal shares await each man.

The seas are mild. A spat between Narbeard and Brackles results in Narbeard sleeping in the bilge and Brackles shacking up with One Ear the cook. Pussy Island, a paradise, reconciles them. Men on the shore in black silks, poor dentition. It is the crew of the *Lemon*, helmed by Captain Sniggs, the brother of Cotton, who helped Cotton raid *La Codicia*, and whose ship, the *Pique*, was sunk in the raid. Cotton sailed off with the riches of Mesoamerica. Sniggs floated on his mast to Hispaniola.

Narbeard and Brackles offer Sniggs safe passage out to *Heaven's Cutlass* to palaver. Sniggs's buccaneers are entrenched on Pussy Island, but they don't know where to dig. The island is a conch, two miles across, five long. Sniggs offers the pair of them half shares. Sniggs has thrice the men, killers all. Narbeard, believing timid men to be inconsistent warriors, hacks off Sniggs's head. The crew is uneasy. They gave their word.

Captain Narbeard says, All's fair, you cravens. Think of the gold! Rusty, you can buy a new ape. Hopper, a leg of ivory. Barber Jenny, the finest scissors.

The crew is swayed. They land at midnight on the conch's spire. Throats are cut, musketoons discharged, curses spat on the breath of dying men. Come morning, Pussy Island is held by the crew of *Heaven's Cutlass*, diminished by the night's travails. More treasure for me, think the surviving pirates.

Brackles plants his spadroon in the back of Narbeard because a co-captaincy is not fitting for a rich man. Narbeard fits the treasure hole. On the tree, under the three diamonds, a crying Brackles carves Narbeard's name. Away with the loot into the streaking equatorial sunset.

65.

YOURS FOR NOW

DIR. AYOMIDE IKANDE

86 MINUTES

I said, Dr. Lisa, have you ever thought of acting?

Leaving the Conspicuous. Dr. Lisa wanted to see *Yours for Now*, the new Ikande film about the rise of the African Republic. She bought the popcorn. I am surprised the Transit Authority allowed the film to be screened in the Hub, because it is essentially an advertisement for technological socialism sutured onto a clumsy love story. Fatima, a nanotechnician, meets David, a professor specializing in the ethical programming of artificial intelligence.

Dr. Lisa said, No. Have you ever thought of being a physician?

I said, I haven't the courage. What if I made the incorrect diagnosis?

When Dr. Lisa's face absorbed enough pale and morose moonlight, it seemed to be its own source of illumination. I reject the stories of directors' muses, for example, Alejandra Martillo's beloved Henry, as corny self-mythologizing. Muses belong in the past with cigarettes and the personal automobile.

Dr. Lisa said, I'm hungry.

I said, There's a place down Ashland I like.

Dr. Lisa and I dodged slow-moving families promenading southward. Dr. Lisa has a brisk stride. I find myself out of breath if we walk too far.

She said, Did I ever tell you about my friend Veronica?

I said, Don't think so.

She said, We met in med school. Veronica's mother worked for the Transit Authority, so she didn't have to sign the public service contract. She was very smart but undisciplined. There was a lot of rote memorization. No matter how smart you are, it still takes a lot of time to get straight in one's mind the arcana of the human body and the maladies to which it is subject.

She said, We had an anatomy test one morning. Veronica pulled me aside and she said, Look. Things are going bad with my boyfriend and I haven't had time to study. You know I'm a hard worker. Just this once, let me copy off you?

She said, Keep up, I'm starving.

I said, We hit up that pupusería right before the movie.

She said, That was a long movie. Now, it was assumed that the medical students were honorable. We had put in so much work even at that early point, plagiarism and copying was not a concern of the faculty. But cheating happened. It was a lot of work. There were a couple times when I copied my homework, mostly for specialist things I knew I would not be practicing in. But this test was on fundamental musculature. If you did not understand a human's abdomen, it would be very difficult to diagnose their problems, wouldn't it?

I said, How many things could possibly go wrong with a body?

She said, I let Veronica cheat off of me. I felt bad for her. Her boyfriend, whom she later married, then divorced, was a rail tech, a job which he had only got because of Veronica's mother, and he resented her success, earned or not.

She said, The next day, a large box showed up at my apartment.

She said, You have to walk faster. I'm going to drop dead if we don't eat. I dragged the box into my apartment, cut it open. It was a complete set of the textbooks I was going to need for the next five years. They cost thousands of dollars. I was furious. I had tried to help out Veronica because I felt bad for her. She was paying me like I was one of her servants. Even worse, she didn't thank me, she sent the books over like that made us even. I studied thirty hours for that test.

I said, Thirty hours and all you got was that lousy medical degree.

She said, On my way to class, I saw her in the hallway sitting with another student. She greeted me like I was her sister. I was so angry, I spat on the ground in front of her feet, told her what I thought of her family's money, and stomped off. In class, my professor called me over. She said that she had recommended me for, and I had won, a fellowship sponsored by a textbook publisher. Part of the award was a bunch of textbooks. She said she was sorry but she had kept forgetting to let me know.

We went into Café Extra Pleasure, Osvald's spot. Rainy days, we'd trek south for crab dumplings in saffron broth. He'd pay if I came with. The crab was imitation. Osvald would get furious when I said this. These dumplings were his big discovery. There have been few times in my life when I have been comfortable enough to decline a free meal. We would take a moment, after our meal, to browse the seedy magazines sold in the back room.

Osvald liked *Inflated Asses*. After the Confidence Crisis, skin mags became a big business.

Dr. Lisa said, How are the crab dumplings?

I said, They're awful. Plus, they're imitation crab. It's ground and dyed cricket paste. How else could they be so cheap?

Osvald erupted. My hands started to shake, as Osvald tried to assert himself.

The waitress said, What will you have?

Dr. Lisa said, I would like the family-style snapper with two bowls of rice, please. And extra chilies. And what that lady over there is having to start.

The waitress said, And you?

I said, The special.

This was too much for Osvald. That I would come all the way here without partaking of his sacred crab dumplings in saffron broth was like an insult to his mother. He threw me to the floor, beginning a protracted battle for control of myself.

From the table Dr. Lisa shouted encouragement.

She said, Remember, it's all in your head. Go to your peaceful place.

Osvald would wrest control of a foot or a knee for a moment, before I retook my position. Noticing a woman near the back door dining on his beloved dumplings, he lunged, flipping a table in the process, and ruining the apron of the waitress. Patrons scattered. Osvald had dragged me into a number of regrettable situations, but destroying the dining room of a cheap café, while Dr. Lisa took advantage of the distraction offered by my flailing body to appropriate a pair of loose spring rolls, might have been the worst.

With a sort of metaphysical shoving motion, I managed to

regain the use of my body. Unfortunately, Osvald's abrupt with-drawal caused me to stumble through the saloon doors into the back room, knocking over sundry magazine racks containing ti-tles like *Naughty Magistrates, Girth, Nude Supportive Partners,* and so on.

Osvald seized my arms. He struck me in the face with a rolled-up copy of *Ripe and Rude*. Welts on my forehead and cheeks. Only when Dr. Lisa pulled hard on my hair did Osvald desist.

66.

TENDER FRONDS

DIR. MARIE RONDEAU

101 MINUTES

On the rail platform, brushing my teeth, getting my hair cut, seeing *Tender Fronds* with Jonson, slipping threatening notes into library books, I watch Isabel and Osvald pass the time, through his eyes.

Osvald has grown bolder. He is jealous of our filming, and when I am holding a camera, he will try to drop it or knock it over. He manages to knock it a bit askew, ruining the shot. Jonson has remarked on my clumsiness. We are two weeks from beginning photography on *Altarpiece*. Osvald hasn't the forces for complete possession, but he can make filming a chore. My work, my sword and shield. May it chase him from me. Although I have become used to his presence. In some ways, it is a comfort.

Dozing on the couch, they look like Zurburán martyrs. They eat takeout. These are the moments of their most intense happiness and intimacy. While eating, they swap anecdotes about their lives at the office. One nods with vigor to compensate for their preoccupation with the carton of General Tso's. Cannabis spray eases the tension of the workday.

On their couch the coin of their lives is spent. There is nothing to life but surrendering. As long as one continues to surrender, then one will be all right.

A self-contained unit, more or less. A shared complicity that doesn't translate well to group situations. They pretend to enjoy each other's families, fake delight at the visits of hoary friends, get drinks with sociopathic cousins, the family wolves. At the table with their new friends, who perceive them as a unit, they do a routine less savage than what Isabel and I trotted out.

When their friends ask how they met, Isabel makes a quip. As she does this, she cringes, dislikes herself. Osvald looks at the table. The friends respect them a little more for this ruthlessness. That decency inhibits fulfillment is an irony we have all had cause to reflect upon. The shy pride of betraying.

They overeat together, like prisoners horny for food. In our last summer, unwilling to take Isabel to the Dependence Day Parade, I suggested she ping Osvald that she was picking him up.

In four and a half hours, she returned, her belly a drum.

She said, I ate so much. It was glorious.

An implicit accusation floated over my scalp into the night beyond. Our kitchen window was open, the better to see the mawkish sunset so popular from the World's Highest Terrace, where Isabel and Osvald had been swaddled in the breeze. The Désormière recording of Act Four, Scene Four, of *Pelléas et Mélisande* played, the scene at the well in the park, where Golaud dirties his hands. We must remember we are turning in light.

Chores go undone. Isabel runs her clothes to the Vietnamese dry cleaner. Osvald is not clean, although he is germophobic. He has to work harder in the relationship. He scrubs, tidies. He tries to keep their space clean. He fails. His junk proliferates. Isabel shoves aside woodworking tools, printer fodder, soldering irons, nanokits, bike spokes, textile samples.

The threat of me hangs over Osvald. The fear I might comb my hair, board a rail with their address on a wrapper. On my black horse with a rose in my teeth, to make a ridiculous dramatic gesture. To end his joy. Begging Isabel, who is so susceptible to gestures. I feel Osvald feeling this.

67.

BARGAINING WITH MAROAT

DIR. JAMES OSVALD

5 MINUTES

An old film of Osvald's. You can't see it.

Interior shot, our living room. A warped piano, pinups, vistas of terror and devastation torn from a pterodactyl coloring book, dying ferns, poster advertising *Inquisitor*, bust of Caligula, puncture in drywall from a pogo accident, paisley sofa, buff synthleather love seat, soiled dishes, kliegs modified into lamps, the neighbor's venial tortoiseshell cat, library books of translated poetry, of romantic etiquette, of fluorescence, of stain removal, of pagan magic, bottle caps, a stained harmonica, miniature skateboard, coffee mug printed with double entendre. What a treat, to see old things.

The film is not Osvald's finest effort. A man enters. He flops on the sofa. His hand passes over the table, returns with the magic book. He is me, ten years younger.

In the book I am holding on-camera, *Sabbath of Flowers*, I read the surest way to get a person's attention is to write their name while urinating. I went through a phase where I would scrawl Isabel's name on glittering monticles of snow.

Flipping through the book, I roll my eyes, snap my fingers.

I say, Beard of goat, giraffe's throat, to my sanctum come Maroat.

Off-camera, Osvald detonates a homemade smoke bomb. The damage from it cost us our security deposit. Out of the pansy fog steps Maroat, the Haggler. It is Osvald costumed in a jumpsuit and satin cape sewn from a bedsheet.

A note on Osvald's dramatic method. To project depth, he visualized his conception.

The mystical aims of *Bargaining with Maroat* are tarnished by the continuous medium shot. Osvald lacked a DP, so a tripod had to suffice. He tried to sell the static effect as a metafictional conceit, but the film resembles a home movie more than a genre-bender, a thrilling Thursday shared by a real estate agent and a frazzled actuary in a quiet node motel.

One can cast curses with urine. While probably not effective, these actions function for the curser as a favored sports team may for the average person, as a dump for baleful feelings.

Maroat is prepared to grant me a boon for thirty years' labor as his apprentice. I desire a woman, Orzsabet. I am not willing to work for her affections. This is within Maroat's power, as is the ability to transmogrify ducks to swans, to make clouds heavy with blood, and to cause a man to believe his penis has fallen off. I can have Orzsabet for two months, two years, or two decades.

Maroat says, All relationships are finite. The strength of your ardor will be inverse to the duration of the partnership.

I choose.

Maroat offers me a game of chance. We will draw from a deck of Bicycles until one flips over the ace of diamonds. If he turns it over, he will receive Orzsabet when my period ends. If I turn it over, my period of servitude will be thirty days.

In my costume, I felt a tingling on my skin. On-screen, an

attack of transposition. A bit of me slithered out my nostril. A bit of Osvald slithered in.

I don't recall our wallpaper undulating like that.

Isn't this fuchsia smoke effect far too advanced and, well, sinister for Osvald?

And what are these flashing violet lights seeming to transmit between Maroat and me, around minute six?

And what about this bloodshot eye overhead that I see only when I pause the film, the size of a beach ball, taking in the scene?

Shuffling, I ask Maroat what he did for his apprenticeship. He cuts the deck. He transcribed fragile manuscripts at the sticky carrel of his master, Carropos the Touchy. Before lunch, stomach whinging, he transliterated the wrong symbol. When Carropos attempted to cast a spell, he was sucked into the unknown. Maroat was free. We flip the cards. Two of clubs, eight of hearts, three of hearts, ace of hearts.

68.

COMETH SOBEK

DIR. JAMES BUNCE

96 MINUTES

Tonight at Greye's, I was accosted as I sat on a footstool in Subterranean Nonfiction, my favorite section. Greye's is a secondhand bookshop organized by theme. The owner, a narcoleptic, finances his stock, bought in lots from defunct bookstores, by selling his mother's vintage pinball machines.

It is a place to combat delative influences on one's spirit. Third places, common areas discrete from home and work, are necessary to a healthy civic society. A third place without the insult of conversation is to be cherished.

In my section, on my stool. Examining a poster for *Cometh Sobek*, trying to remember if I'd seen the film, I became aware of a person standing over me with the fragrance of power.

I had seen it. A crocodile-headed god with a man's body. Blood of tempura paint issuing, as from a sprinkler, from the arteries of his victims. A replica tomb is printed at the City Museum for Cultic Practices. Within the replica tomb, Sobek is summoned on accident with albino's blood from a pricked thumb mixed with the crusts of a bologna sandwich. Sobek is a god of the proles. Temple slaves, quarrymen, left offerings. Exit the egyptologists by way of Sobek's maw.

A shaved calf berthed in my peripheral.

A bit of my past stuck to *Cometh Sobek*. What, though? Sobek was a god. The gods of antiquity had modest demands. A roll in the hay, a goblet of wine, to eat you.

Another customer in Greye's is not common. Complimentary pepper spray hangs by the entrance. A trio of intimidating dogs nap in Heliocentric Fiction, Minor Homosexuals, and The Protagonist Dies, respectively. The lack of coherency does not encourage repeat customers. Greye can be rude. Sections near the back, like Sadogustation and Scurrilous Biography, smell of rotting fruit, and are never browsed.

I could no longer postpone examining the leg's owner. It brushed the tip of my nose. The customs of bookstores are ancient. From the golden calf emanated the odors of blood oranges, chain oil, dust. Lucretia Jonson.

Her face is animated by a spirit of inquiry, a malignant curiosity, a determination to master, through vigorous practice, the appearance of warmth. I do not often long for other men's domestic arrangements but I have felt envious of Jonson.

She said, Nice to run into you.

I said, Certainly.

She said, How's my urn?

Jonson's wife wore a trench with ketchup stains on the lapel, an Eye of Horus bracelet, Jonson's Blackout 660s. He had a premium sneaker phase. In her pocket bulged a hex wrench. Nobody knows I go to Greye's. The secrecy of one's habits ought to be sacrosanct.

I said, What brings you?

She said, I was two blocks east lunching with the chapter president of the Hyperborean Society. He holds the Hyperboreans were lost in the tidal convulsions swallowing Ys and Atlantis and wiped from the historical record. Such nonsense is a delightful break from my studies.

I said, Your studies?

She said, The president mentioned Greye owned a first edition of Manzoni's *The Betrothed*. The two of them got on. I came to have a look, but could not wake him up.

I said, I know the legend of Ys from an opera recording. A sisters' quarrel over a man destroys the city.

The strange are affiliated through networks we are ignorant of.

She said, I had no intention of donating, but I enjoy hearing his theories. He has those exquisite elderly person manners.

Our mutual ambivalence had ossified. She looked at the poster.

She said, You know that film is inaccurate.

I said, How so?

She explained how Bunce had debauched the facts. This topic was open-ended. Minutes of my life boiled off. I reviewed the tactics I could use to end our interaction. One, run away. Two, misdirection. Three, Seel.

She said, You and Jonson have been spending a lot of time together.

I said, A lot?

She said, What are you doing?

I said, Watching movies.

She said, What else?

I said, We rob banks. We plan his mayoral campaign.

She said, Aren't you sick of being his charity case? You live in one drafty room with no furniture, like a guest, except you don't have the dignity of struggle to attribute to your failure.

I said, When are you going to tell him about Seel?

Jonson's wife laughed.

She said, There's nothing to tell. We're friends. He's gay.

I said, How did he get that thing on his forehead again?

She said, He came to his sexuality later in life. The philandering was to compensate for feelings he was not ready to face.

I said, Please don't take it the wrong way if I say that seems very unlikely, from what I've seen of him.

She said, It's very annoying how complacent you are when you don't see the most basic facts of what's going on around you. For instance. Jonson has other women.

I said, I don't believe you. He isn't like us.

She said, He's worse. Have you ever seen a video of a pig, those animals they used to eat? He's the last pig. He eats and eats and if a hand comes near his trough, he eats that, and if a person falls in, he eats her. The world is his trough.

69.

PHOTOSENSITIVITY

DIR. AMIR IRFAN

80 MINUTES

Mention of Lucretia Jonson used to put Isabel in a bad mood, a sooty quiet where she brooded over her own lack of credentials, her struggles to join the entitled creative class she was born into. They were briefly acquainted when I joined the *Slaw*. Jonson invited us over. Cocktails on the balcony, fish from their tank. Jonson had trouble filleting the tilapia, although he insisted he had done it hundreds of times.

Lucretia said, What is it again that you do?

Isabel said, Design.

Lucretia said, Oh, yes. That must be very interesting.

Isabel said, What do you do?

Lucretia said, I do charitable work and also have ongoing postdoc research.

Isabel said, On what?

Lucretia said, I wrote my doctoral thesis on the growing evidence that Moses was a priest of the cult of Aten, the monotheistic sun god which the pharaoh Akhenaten decreed his subjects must worship in place of the traditional Egyptian pantheon.

Isabel said, The goddesses of the pyramids.

Lucretia said, Yes. After Akhenaten died, the people returned to their old forms of worship. Revisionists within the country made him out to be a criminal and a heretic, erasing his name from the records.

Isabel said, This is the father of the famous King Tut.

Lucretia said, When he died, his priests were expelled from the country. My research seeks to find if one of his priests was Moses, the hero of the Old Testament, who led his people from bondage. These people were the Jews. The majority of the people in the world might base their faith on the ravings of a malnourished king who lived three and a half thousand years ago.

Photosensitivity is in wide release. It concerns a Cairo Town guest who, believing himself to be the reincarnation of Akhenaten, leads an invasion of the Safe Zone. One can't help but suspect, from its hysterical tone and its production values, that it is funded by the Transit Authority.

Isabel said, But you can't do fieldwork now.

Lucretia said, That's the great frustration of my life. My whole career is looking at databases, trying to get closed countries to share their proprietary archaeological data, being rebuffed and insulted.

Isabel said, That's interesting. I'm quite interested in the—

Lucretia's Pinger chimed.

She said, Excuse me.

70.

OFFERING

DIR. KATJA TOD

185 MINUTES

In the trailer I had been editing the last equipment test, a nod to Tod's classic *Offering*. Xin Hi, our actress from *La Malinche*, wanders in the woods, like Tod's Marion. Instead of looking haunted, as Marion did in the Hairy Forest, Xin Hi fell asleep on a bench between takes. Hadn't combed the snarls from her hair. She wasn't going to return but Jonson tripled her fee.

Instead of the woods, we filmed her at the conservatory. Waivers distributed. I forgot to get permission in advance. Because people were wandering through the rooms, in reverie, and did not want to be interrupted or filmed, this was a chore. Xin Hi drew the attention of the conservatory security by stealing a bag lunch from the backpack of a child on a field trip. Security ordered us to leave. We told them we were shooting a documentary about the space. We skulked to the bonsai garden, shot six feeble minutes of footage, and were ejected. In the ensuing scuffle, Jonson dropped our camera in the koi pond.

It ranks as one of the more successful days in our partnership.

We split up at the rail. Jonson and Xin Hi headed to the outgoing platform. Jonson was struggling to carry her Pendleshim volume. His face reddened as we stood there saying goodbye. Sweat on his brow.

She said, I forgot my purse at the production trailer.

Jonson said, I'll let you in. It's not far from my place, anyway.

She said, Thanks. I have to get to a gig tonight and I need it before then.

On the way in to the Zone, I couldn't get Dr. Lisa on her Pinger. She was not a responsive person. If we made a plan, she remembered it, but she didn't see the point of pinging when we would see one another in two hours. It wasn't unusual that I did not hear from her.

Sunset going into the Zone. The platforms headed out were busy. Only a few people, like Dr. Lisa, worked outside the Zone and lived within.

She once said, Actually, I hate living here, but my partner was an anxious person, and he insisted we buy in the Zone. Then, after the split, he moved out of the Zone. I don't have the energy to move. People who manage to move must not have much on their minds.

My Pinger had permission to access her building. I went up to the fourth floor. The third, left. I knocked. No answer. I knocked again.

I said, Dr. Lisa, are you home?

She said, Go away.

I said, Dr. Lisa, what's wrong?

She said, I saw the video.

Cold voice.

I said, What video?

She said, The video of you hitting that old man and throwing him in the river.

I said, Oh, that was Osvald. He took over my body.

She said, Go away.

I said, Millings is trying to ruin me.

She said, That man we met at Jonson's? Are you insane?

I said, Dr. Lisa, please let me explain what has been happening.

She said, There's no excuse to attack a man like that. Go. Get another doctor.

I said, Dr. Lisa, please.

Osvald twisting my face. His hand on the knob.

She said, I'm calling the police.

I said, Then I'll get arrested.

She said, If you're arrested in the Zone, they'll take away your clearance, or worse.

I said, Okay, Dr. Lisa, I'll go. But if you ever want to hear me explain what happened, please contact me. I think we have something special.

She didn't answer.

71.

CAPO

DIR. LOGAN BRODER

291 MINUTES

On my Pinger this morning, the invitation.

You are expected to celebrate fifty years of Millings Kiosk in the Clawford Lounge at the Central Hub Suites on Lockwood this Thursday, the eighth of September.

The ending of *Capo*, Broder's trite gangster epic. Joey, whose rise we have witnessed in the preceding, interminable four and a half hours, knows he is going to be murdered for something we saw three hours ago, half his lifetime, that is, murdering the don's cousin, Bragging Jeff, for beating up his little brother. Joey being a man with impulse control issues. His brother, a gambler, the stain on his reputation. At his estate, the don is throwing a birthday party for his mother. Joey arrives.

A man says, Why don't you go up to see the don?

Joey says, All right.

The camera follows through the foyer, up the stairs, down the hall. What will it be? Probably piano wire, not to ruin the don's carpets. Although any form of murder in one's house is uncouth. The don's grandchildren play downstairs.

Another man guarding the door. Joey sits to wait. This is

worst of all, that they don't have the decency to get it over with. Hasn't he served the don these twenty years? Didn't he spend four years in the Hub Penitentiary rather than turn witness?

On the other side of the door, the gangsters are planning a promotion for Joey. A surprise to thank him for his hard work.

The don says, Joey might be don after I am gone, if you give him good advice.

The don does not know about Joey murdering his cousin.

Joey's nerve breaks. He enters the room.

The gangsters look up, smiling.

They say, Joey, hey, buddy.

He says, Don Cazzoli, I'm sorry I shot your cousin, but he was going to kill my brother. What was I to do?

The door shuts behind Joey.

The lobby. My tuxedo, Jonson's spare.

Jonson's wife said, Let me take a picture for you to send to Dr. Lisa. Stand over there.

Soon they would ask where Dr. Lisa had been. For the first couple of weeks, I let myself believe she would allow me to explain. It was to be a temporary emptiness before reconciliation. This lie did not protect me long.

In the Clawford Lounge, I left the Jonsons. I wanted to avoid Mrs. Rangor—that is, Millings's wife—who thought I was Danny Chivo, of Chivo Industries. A hundred people or more. The bar to my left. Waiters with trays. A pianist tried to play, was shushed. These people were from the cockroach families who had survived the Confidence Crisis with their wealth. The economic realities of the present, the Zones, the guests, the remediations, were their niche. They had evolved to feed on the crumbs of civilization.

Past knots of people congratulating one another, an ice sculpture of a kiosk, two security guards, a lectern with the Millings

Kiosk logo, stood Millings with two middle-aged women. His head visible over the crowd. His temple's gray stripe spreading. Millings's social circle was in this room, to celebrate his wife's business, the gift of his friendship. I caught his eye. He smiled, raised his flute in a toast. I returned the smile and the gesture. Poor Millings. If he hadn't sent Uncle Al after me, maybe we would have been friends. He understood me better than Jonson.

There sat Uncle Al, in a chair, looking frail, pretending not to see me.

A man strode to the lectern.

He said, Is this on?

He said, Hello.

He said, Thank you for celebrating with us tonight. We've been here fifty years now and we'll be here at least fifty more. If you don't know me, I am Jack Burles, vice president, Millings Kiosk and Millings Holdings. I worked with Mr. Millings Senior, and I'm happy to continue his work with his daughter-in-law. I've been to a few of these parties in my time and I must say the slideshow or historical video is pretty dry, pretty soporific, so instead of droning on about where the first Millings office was, or posting a few sales charts, I thought I would take a different direction. Instead, we're going to look at what the Hub was like when Millings Kiosk was founded, and how the Hub has changed. Take this journey with me. Please, grab a snack, get a drink, and enjoy yourself. I speak for the Millingses, whom we'll hear from a little later, when I thank you sincerely for being here with us tonight.

The room darkened. A shiver of pleasure passed through the crowd at the transition into the world of permissions.

Broder's camera waits outside the door for twenty seconds. What do we wait to hear? Joey begging, a gunshot. Broder hasn't the courage to end a film with futility, so the door swings open again, Joey exits, roughed up, with three of his old buddies. Joey has broken the code. He has spilled the blood of his sworn brother. The audience yawning, thinking of possible meals. *Capo* is as close as Broder has come to making a compelling film. If the gangsters were to take Joey out to the pine forest, shoot him in the head, and bury him in a grave, then Broder would have been successful. Starting with the episode in the don's room, when Joey accidentally gives away his crime, he has our sympathy. Before, he is only a stylish sociopath. Broder's method, to make us watch Joey's life for hours, is crude, but it almost works. But then the director falls victim to the attractions of the swelling libretto and the dapper bloodbath. Incorrigible Joey is being marched to the late-model luxury sedan when his loyal employees intervene. At least today, there will be no grave for Joey. Blam. Blam. Not the cake, too. The shot of the flowers in the blood puddle makes me laugh.

The don says, Why, Joey?

Blam. Blam.

At the end of the song, Joey has become the new don. In sports films, in crime films, in war films, in films of exploration, adventure, and detections, there is the implication that there are codes of honor between men, complex, undetectable, delicate understandings that govern male conduct, that dictate how and when they conduct their violences, but this is not true. There is nothing but what one feels the right to, if one has no guiding principle. In this place, there is no consensus.

The Millings Kiosk promotional film began with shots of the Hub fifty years ago, when it was still called Chicago, under control of a regional government after the brief collapse of the federal administration. It was an ugly city, devoted to pleasure. Chicago was a place where one was not forced to consume prudently, so nobody did.

People murmured to each other.

Then the first Millings Kiosk. They began in condominium lobbies for the convenience of the wealthy. Someone had the idea to put them in poor neighborhoods, where there were no grocery stores or department stores stocked with premium detergents and branded socks. A shot of the Millings people making excursions to the South Side, pre-pacification, to install library and pharmacy kiosks.

Stock footage, diversity, smiling.

Millings Senior with a young, built, mustached Uncle Al circa the establishment of the Hub. A wolf whistle in the crowd. They were handing out kiosk cards to guests.

I convinced Jonson to promote the nosy intern at the *Slaw* to junior editor. The staff indignant. I told Jonson she was a savant and would make his content aggregator a nationwide destination. The young woman wanted an editorship at the *Slaw* in return for her help adding my edits to the Millings Kiosk promotional film we were watching.

She said, Because I could go to jail for tampering with these corporate servers, although that's unlikely, I need something more than money. I want to have a legitimate career.

I said, Millings Kiosk won't be able to tell who hacked into their server. I was over at their offices a few months ago, to see Millings's wife, and there are less than five employees, legacies of the good old days.

While the intern was looking for Uncle Al at the beginning of last month, she patched into the security cameras on the insurance tower across from the Millings Kiosk office. Although it is illegal to do so, it transpired that, by accident or by design, one of the cameras looked into Millings's private residence, on the floor above the office. Since nobody in the insurance tower was actively monitoring its hundreds of cameras, this had gone unnoticed.

I spliced in the security camera footage where the narrator was explaining Millings Kiosk moved to its present location seventeen years ago. The family tower filmed by a drone flying in a rising corkscrew. At Millings's window, I cut to the security footage, but left the voice-over.

The narrator said, The baton was passed to Rolf Millings, the third generation of the Millings family, to move the company into the modern era.

Millings in a robe, looking through a telescope at the street. The telescope moved a little to track people as they walked. Although one couldn't see his bottom half because of the angle, it became clear after a few seconds that he was masturbating.

The narrator said, The Millings Kiosk Tower is a marvel of its era. It has been singled out for historical preservation. The apartments afford the privacy of the country in the heart of the Hub.

A collective intake of breath. Someone behind me dropped a glass. Where was Millings? I had cut the footage into a loop. Maybe eight seconds had passed. Stifled giggles growing. The party had been going some time, people had been drinking. The giggles spreading, unfolding, amplifying into laughter. A series of thuds and crashes as various Millings functionaries tried to shut off the video. The whole room shaking with chuckles. A judgment on Millings. Some going for the door, some savoring an intense merriment. The video was turned off.

There was Millings, bent over a little to be less conspicuous, slipping out the fire door. Before he sent the video of Osvald attacking Uncle Al to Dr. Lisa, I had considered his voyeurism beneath mention, not within the realm of our business, but he had crossed the line first, as he had when he ordered Uncle Al to attack me.

Noises of disgust as the ramifications of Millings's behavior became clear. He could be prosecuted, although he wouldn't be convicted, because it wasn't explicit what he was doing beneath the frame of the shot. It only suggested an activity. The lights were left off for almost two minutes, until someone thought to flip the switch.

When the lights came on, and the party guests saw one another's faces, another gust of laughter swept through the room, and it kept whipping through the crowd, snapping in my ears, taking from Millings what he held dear. It is hard to keep from laughing when others are. I was not laughing. It would be cruel to poke fun.

72.

NONPROFITS SUPPORTED BY THE JONSON FOUNDATION

DIR. F. F. RIBBONS

3 MINUTES

Kids Craft, an organization dedicated to passing on traditional regional techniques of distillation to at-risk inner-city youth. The Akhenaten Society. The Destitute Columnist's Electricity Fund. Beans for Bums, dedicated to serving the finest pour-over single-origin fair-trade coffee to the homeless. The Ancient Grains Reconciliation Fund, for healing the schism between the proponents of freekeh and the partisans of sorghum. Appleholics Anonymous. Wabi Sabi Club. The League of Asexual Voters. The Fund for Erotic Antiquities. Sister Joan's Sanctuary for Private Rest, a home for people who have suffered adverse effects from cosmetic procedures. Task Force for Awareness of Calorie Intolerance. The Center for the Honest Depiction of Yoga. Gardens Not Garters. The Poutine Society. Better Bistro Bureau. Noli Me Tangerine, an organization opposing the crossbreeding of citrus fruits. Citizens for the Reinstatement of Quiet Libraries. Mothers Against Disingenuous Decorators.

73.

HANGING ISVALD

DIR. NOAH BODY

16 MINUTES

The skirmishes between Isabel and me that were calamitous enough to earn specific nomenclature, including the Cecil's Bar Campaign and Matt's Wedding Ambush, can be blamed on Isabel's fantastical relationship to observed time. I would ask her to arrive twenty, then fifty, then seventy minutes before we were supposed to meet to ensure punctuality. She would sense what time I meant, attempt to compensate, and would be late.

I would huff myself into a fury in advance of arriving at the theater, restaurant, or bar, calculating when she would begin to layer on her maquillage, choose her outfit, gather keys and purse, kiss the cat, remember where she'd parked, charge her Pinger, look up the address, etc.

She would say, Did you want to see me mope around the bar in sweatpants?

I would say, Yes, that was my hope, one hour ago.

Inevitably I surrendered to the apprehension that she wasn't going to show up. She was in a morgue cooling or tied up in a basement. Banishing my fantasies, I'd resolve to forgive her, test the smile I'd flex when she dashed in, quip how her watch was correct, but when she arrived, my kindness flapped off to roost in another skull.

She said, Aren't I worth the wait?

I said, Yes, but.

She said, Am I or am I not?

I said, Aren't I worth respect?

She said, Your timetables are a child's fantasy.

I said, The hell they are.

She said, Don't turn our fun into a chore.

Lateness is how the insecure demonstrate power. Osvald's tardiness was learned from his father. Some avoid and some exaggerate their parents' flaws. The waiting person was meant to be grateful when Osvald arrived. He sought attention. Through him ran a seam of grandiosity. He moved as slow as was feasible. It took him an hour and a half to move his bowels, as if he were the Sun King. He had to be perpetually fetched.

I made a film to illustrate my position. I screened it for Osvald and Isabel on a tablecloth in the park, after promising fifty dollars apiece if they showed up at the agreed time. Neither did. I didn't bring the money along.

Hanging Isvald opens in a cell. Isvald, conjoined twins, are sentenced to die at noon. They are not concerned. Isvald contemplates the pond of sunlight rippling on the dirt of their cell. The jailer requests they send a sign from the void. To get the jailer to leave, Isvald agrees to spin their weather vane on the second of October.

The priest enters, myself. I ask Isvald to repent. They decline. The priest describes the torments of hell awaiting Isvald. Isvald knows saying words will not change their destination either way, for they hold no superstitions on the vigor of language. The priest, having delivered his promise of torture, departs.

They say, It is a radiant day to give praise.

Back to the puddle of sun. Amazing how it—

Knock, knock. Isvald's mother. She has come to deliver absolution before they swing on the gallows.

They say, See ya, Mom.

Second to last is Isvald's lover, also played by myself. Isvald does not speak. Nothing to be said to the person. What is a kiss? What are words? All words have the same price. Nothing, nothing, nothing, nothing, nothing. The sun has reached Isvald in chains. Isvald will be in light. The door opens and the guard leads Isvald outside, to the cheer of the crowd.

74.

LIGHT TEST IX

DIR. HARRIS JONSON

4 MINUTES

The primary set for *Altarpiece* is completed. Bellono's studio sits on an acre fifteen miles southwest of the township of Deer Eye. It's twenty miles from the nearest node into the Hub. Location scouting took weeks. Before settling on the field, we toured a barn, an asylum, a defunct AlmostPeople service facility. The unattached heads of William and Melinda models shouted encouragement to us from the factory workbench.

William said, A body is the repository of our dreams.

Melinda said, Mobility is the basis of freedom.

William said, Perhaps you could attach me to yonder body, my friend.

Melinda said, No, that model is a woman's. It's for me.

William said, I have an open mind. Don't be prescriptive, Melinda. Any body is a good body.

We brought our equipment into the spaces to shoot tests. On film, the light curdled.

The acre outside Deer Eye was different. We liked how the land lay in a depression underneath a lagoon of sunlight. The bronze stalks of wheat covering the field burned at sunset, when

I jogged through with a smoldering branch following a route I'd planned so a blimp or a bored god saw, passing overhead at the right moment, my initials scrawled in flame.

Jonson hired a known firm to build the set. He plans to convert it into a distillery when shooting wraps.

He said, This corn should be put to better use.

I said, Like cornbread.

He said, Spirits. I'll call it Jonson's Country Reserve.

We inspected the set this morning, as the builders left. The fellow ducking into the town car was Malthus, the architect, who had once nodded to Osvald in the firm's foyer, believing him to be the kept man of Constantin Grigori.

I am within the set, a glass cube. I am the flaw. The night sky is boysenberry chenille stained with drips of bleach. The cement floor ruined the effect, so I shoveled dirt on top.

Scrub pines hunker across the road, ashamed of their thin limbs. I have books on oil technique. Provender is laid by. The husks of devoured Chocodiles, Nougators, and Carameldo Dragons litter the studio, where Bellono will paint the triptych. One good canvas will buy his freedom from the tedium of painting. He can return to his casseroles and his duvet. I am wearing an itchy wool tunic. On my feet are pointed shoes of inky synthleather.

Bellono bantered with his god, having no proof of nihility but pain. I wag my brush on the isabelline canvas, practicing the gesture of painting, not ready to commit myself to the oils Jonson has ordered from Perugia. Addressing a god as Bellono might. Bringing up vexing spicules of theology. Petitioning to have my venereal diseases healed. Asking for the power to forgive. Why the platypus?

In me Osvald. I wouldn't have noticed the eloquence of the

steel columns, matching the grace of the mullions, drawing the eye to the ceiling, crisscrossed by thin girders, the appearance of the golden ratio, without Osvald's help. Yes, he likes this place. Awakening on the mornings when the set inflates with light, he descends the cantilevered slab stairs to dig his toes into the charred soil, and he imagines possibilities for the film, the delicious conflagrations.

75.

THE FLOATING HOUSE

DIR. ANDREW BALTANDERS

86 MINUTES

Osvald identified with Dr. Pinkglass in *The Floating House*, who, when shown graphs and measurements by Dr. Rousseau proving the house is on the ground, continues to insist it hovers inches above the foundation.

Dr. Pinkglass says, I trust my eyes. My eyes serve me. Logic does not necessarily.

The records of my misbehavior. Osvald had a thick portfolio of complaints to draw on to justify his theft of my wife.

I wasn't clean, broke dishes. I threw a piano bench in the vicinity of but not at Osvald, ate the Neapolitan, lost his keys. I lost his forks, wallet, pump, jack, stereo cords, chip, Swiss Army knife, sweaters, Pinger, replacement Pinger, loaner Pinger, monogrammed socks, sextant, ballpoint pen, ball-peen hammer, ball cap, ball glove, ball gag, drafting dots, distance meter, bike saddle, tailored trousers, birth certificate, spare tire, electric drill, floss, scarab in resin, waffle iron.

What else? I popped a favored volleyball. I kissed a woman he liked and lied to spare his feelings. I didn't kiss a woman he liked and lied to hurt his feelings. I did not worship Isabel, made fun of his turtlenecks. I woke him in the middle of the night with the terror of illness. I cooked and forgot dinner, left locks unlocked, derided his paltry tips at restaurants, took contrary positions on principle. I needed and adored Osvald. His romantic, aesthetic, and spiritual aims I was determined to frustrate but not defeat outright.

All this was for his benefit. I was ensuring he remained entertained. We neglect our duty to delight our friends. We treat them as floating ears. To entertain is to torment.

76.

THE REDUCERS

DIR. RAOUL COSTARD

90 MINUTES

Difficulty pruning the ramiform possibilities from Jonson's conception of *Altarpiece*. His pings every ten minutes. No wonder he couldn't get a date before he met Lucretia.

This morning's:

what if sets were monochrome /

how about u wear a mask /

dance number /

dream sequence /

i got a logline for you /

let's rent a fog machine /

pricing bear trainers /

how bout a swordfight /

2nd act could be punchier /

pls respond to ping tuesday 5pm, subj fabric swatches black n white /

feelin rack focusing /

what is duke's motivation /

What is anyone's? I nudged *The Art of Dramaturgy* off of his balcony while he fussed over the espresso service. Formulas won't save us. Jonson is not a passionate reader. His mind ambulates on crutches. His book is accessorized with a plate of snacks, a pastis *tomate*, highlighters. Trying to understand the significance of the clothes described, of the invented weather, of the bland dialogue. Trying to induce in himself feelings.

To reject all of Jonson's suggestions would be undiplomatic.

The Reducers is an adaptation of the Horst-Rundler musical about two friends, Marisha and Janet, who split a scratch-off jackpot and decide to go into the movie business. They buy the rights to the impenetrable metaphysical opera *The Mysteries of Tangerine Alpha as Revealed to Follower Sixteen, on Plantain Mountain, January 6, at Sunset*, a favorite of Janet's. A thirteen-hour performance cannot be condensed into ninety minutes without loss. Janet has pretentions of depth. Marisha watches the bottom line to gratify her conception of herself as shrewd. Stock bumbling. Subplot, ardor between Marisha and Amy, actress chosen for Follower Sixteen. Amy was Maquilla's last role. The film was released posthumously.

Jonson had an idea for the promotion of *Altarpiece*. He would have oil paintings printed, of me as Bellono, brush in hand. Gilt frames and all. The paintings would be hung on walls throughout the Hub.

I will praise his marketing scheme so I can reject his other ideas with a clear conscience.

77.

ARK OF SUFFERING

DIR. VASILY VASILYEV

127 MINUTES

Jonson has traveled to Seel's villa in Bologna II, to prepare the set for Bellono's visit to the ducal palace. It was understood that I would join him later. I am convinced this scene does not need to exist. Plus, I am afraid of slingshots. It still needs to be set up to occupy Jonson.

On the set, I am rehearsing. The embers of the day.

My body rebels. Limbs ignore the edicts of the nerves, Osvald's buddies. Before the easel, I will my face to emote.

This morning, eating my porridge on the set, getting into character. Because the painter was prosperous, he had the means to enjoy a handful of raisins in his slop. How my hand resisted, as it hung over the steaming bowl. My fist would not open. Osvald hates raisins. I managed to pry it apart with my right hand. I twisted my left hand, dropping a few of the raisins in the bowl.

Unhappy with this turn of events, Osvald plunged my right hand into the molten porridge. I couldn't remove my hand for several minutes. The pain ranked with a crotch injury or an eyeball scratch.

Then I overpowered him with a memory of the day Dr. Lisa

and I visited the Zone Flower Market. She bought me peonies, which are still on my desk, dried out. The dead petals scattered about.

If you are reading this, Dr. Lisa, please ping me. I am sorry for what I did.

Osvald withdrew, and I yanked my hand from the bowl. The problem was, by that time the porridge had congealed. While I was extricating my hand from the bowl with a strenuous yanking motion, a wad flew from my burned palm to stick to the glass ceiling, where it remains.

Birds fly into the set. The glass will have to be squeegeed between shots.

Seel's cathouse in Bologna II had to be equipped to my specifications. Jonson pinged me photos. In my Pinger's editor, I crossed out decor not befitting the ducal palazzo, like anachronistic doorknobs and toilets, then pinged the pictures back, so he could have it removed. I don't know why I say *palazzo*. The film does not take place in any real location, not Italy. A sort of Italy but not quite. Bologna II, a passable replica of the original, is the Grand Canyon's premier printed luxury resort. Walls and ceilings in the Villa Disperazione were to be knocked out, skylights installed. For *Ark of Suffering* (playing through Sunday at the Runaway Seven), Vasilyev had a whole principality printed. While Jonson was busy printing armoires for shots I would not use, I could work in peace.

I peeled my shoes off and pitched them under the easel. I was shocked by my behavior, pleased by how nice it felt. This was Osvaldian. Bare-toed in public. He aired his putrid feet in theaters. We are being smeared together.

78

THE FOX AND THE BUTTERFLY

DIR. HARRIS JONSON

TBD

Jonson, strolling through tufts of dusk beyond the Villa Disperazione, whistling. Seel's servants have indicated he can find a ser-
viceable bolognese, a certain bottle, down the way, turn left at the
crone on the porch past the mermaid statue. Don't look her in the
eye. She's cursed.

Despite the warning, he looks her in the eye.

His Pinger pings. Who is this? wonders Jonson. The number
is not familiar.

It pinged, your wife w phil seel / NB knows

It pinged, see file on office trailer server / title: before or after
understanding

It pinged, a friend wldn't keep the truth from you / would he

It pinged, look closer @ altarpiece credit chip / where's your
$$ going

It pinged, i think yr being taken for a ride / signed a friend

Dumb of me to store my little documentary of Lucretia and
Seel in the park on the server that we were using for materials re-
lated to *Altarpiece*. I didn't think Jonson was going to poke around.

Jonson returns to the villa, where there is a broadband hookup.

He logs into the server. It is illegal to exceed the data limitations, but rules are different for the wealthy.

My Pinger pinged. I sat in the plush gloom at my habitual picnic table. Kingdom of brush and cups. Sickly river gargling by. Carved into the top of the table NB+IS. Now the NB was getting scratched out, replaced with JO. My hand, my knife, Osvald's guidance. Maybe it is true that we only live in solitude, in the company of our memories. What we understand to be life occurs after the event, in the afterimage and the reflection. Who was pinging me? Was it one of my friends, returning to me, whom I had missed for so long? Was it an advertisement for Millings Kiosk or the Carbon Committee? When I reached for my Pinger, the possibilities of reconciliation would collapse into one, probably commercial, reality.

I looked anyway. Jonson, from Bologna II.

He pinged, how could u / u know I was worried bout Luc

I trudged up the bank. My right boot, borrowed from Jonson, sank into the muck to my ankle.

He pinged, i can't believe u didn't tell me about seel / saw yr film

I yanked my leg up but the mud held firm.

He pinged, and u have been lying to me / spending my money

I pondered my options.

He pinged, i thought we were friends / why didn't u tell me about seel

Heaved the foot once more.

I pinged, what about you and xin hi / are you telling me you are a saint

I yelled, How about that, Jonson? Here I am, thinking about the film, and you're tucked away with your side piece, eating panini off her gut.

Jonson pinged, how dare u / how DARE u / HOW dare U

I slipped my foot from my boot.

Jonson pinged, i'm pulling funding for altarpiece / u are not allowed on the set or in the office trailer / and i'm canceling your card

My anger mounted as I hopped up the bank.

Jonson pinged, you're lucky i don't sue u

I pinged, you're my friend / but don't cry your crocodile tears to me / i think it's ridiculous that we're friends and you're turning on me like this / i didn't do anything

Jonson pinged, exactly / you didn't do anything / you reflected upon the matter / and cracked a few jokes

My Pinger notified me, Harris Jonson has blocked you. If you have any questions, please do not contact Pinger staff. There's nothing we can do. Have a nice day!

It was a long hop to the rail platform.

I refuse responsibility for the matter of Seel and Lucretia. Suspicions aren't facts. Even if I had seen something more substantial, it is not clear that I ought to have intervened. And I had looked past Jonson's personal failings. I could have observed evidence of his dalliances, but I averted my eyes. I helped him lie to Lucretia. And what about Jonson's script, which he had never mentioned to me? I found it on the office trailer server. *The Fox and the Butterfly* told the story of an actress who falls in love with a rich man, opening him to the possibilities of life and his own artistic capabilities. Jonson's bouquet of clichés was a vehicle for Xin Hi, mere wish fulfillment, but I had retained hopes that he would wake up one morning, realize it was trash, and focus on *Altarpiece*.

Was Jonson the pig Lucretia claimed or was he the tinsel playboy I enjoyed spending my time with, blind to the world beyond his comforts? Both, neither. Jonson could use me as his excuse to misbehave. Let him make his juvenile film, destroy his marriage, and be eaten by his insecurities.

I caught a local out to the set before Jonson had the locks changed.

Goodbye to the painter's studio. Night and warm. I used film canisters to smash the panes enclosing the set, throwing them like the *Discobolus* I sometimes shove over in the Heritage Museum. A russet hen I bought from Itchy Creek Farm for company, whom I named Ludwig, snores off her feed under the table. She deposits her speckled eggs in a prop wimple. Bellono's canvas will not be filled.

Goodbye, set. Goodbye, *Altarpiece*.

79.

DOWNTOWN SHOWDOWN

DIR. HARVEY SEWARD

98 MINUTES

Downtown Showdown, Saturdays, midnight, the New Old Argyle Theater. A tradition going on twenty years.

The theater was the filming location for the famous opening shoot-out in *Downtown Showdown*. Patrice and Regina rob the Central Hub Bank three blocks down. They run for the rail platform at Argyle and Cicero. It's closed for repair. Regina was supposed to check the escape route. Instead, she went drinking. Regina has gotten sloppy since Matilda left the gang.

They run into the New Old Argyle. *Executive Blasphemy* is the matinee. The priest is casting devils from the president when the cops bust into the theater. Hundreds of shots are fired, but nobody is hit. Seward, a pacifist, couldn't bear to portray suffering. Regina and Patrice escape.

It's not a bad movie. Even a bad movie is preferable to my apartment.

Eating the Argyle's mummified popcorn is like munching glass, but I thought I might get some anyway. In line. To my left, handsome, stately Rolf Millings, unshaven on a shoddy bench, his legs crossed at the knee.

I crossed the lobby.

Millings said, Isn't this film a little too lowbrow for you?

I said, Millings, it isn't the content of the film that matters, it's the sentiment. *Downtown Showdown* is a human picture. Never mind the gunplay. Look at the faces.

He said, You're always ready to tell me what to think.

I said, How's the kiosk business?

He said, My wife took the opportunity, after your stunt, to take me off the board of my own company. I'm a bystander now. I quite like it.

I said, That's lovely. I'm glad to have been of service.

He said, And you know, you might have thought you got me, but after that episode, I am still me, and you are still you, do you understand?

Millings smiled. No matter how cleverly I had managed to humiliate him, until the day of his death Millings was secure in the knowledge that he was a thoroughbred by upbringing, genetics, and inclination. I would never convince him that these things did not matter very much, and that was fine. To be secure in one's delusions isn't all that bad.

I said, You can't deny it was a good joke, the whole room seeing you on camera with your pants down.

He said, It was a magnificent joke. But a joke can only do so much.

I said, A joke isn't supposed to stick around. A little sleight of tongue, and poof, it's gone.

He said, How's that film of yours?

I said, It's nonexistent. Jonson ditched me after your anonymous tip.

He said, What tip?

I said, About his wife and Seel.

He said, I don't know what you're talking about. And I don't mean that in a winking way. I am truly in the dark.

His face indicated this was true. If not Millings, who was it?

I said, Jonson thought I was lying to him, so he struck off on his own with our material, permits, and equipment.

He said, I'm sorry you lost your money. I have plenty. Let's do something together. I'm so bored these days. It was more fun when I had to spend my time pretending to work. My mother calls me in the evenings, and I have to account for my time.

I said, Millings, I'm never again going to create under the manicured thumb of another person. Shall we see this film?

He said, Yes, let's.

80.

A REPLICATE

DIR. JAMES OSVALD

77 MINUTES

Knock at my door. A package. The courier left before I had a chance to stiff her on the tip. Lacking interest in its contents, I dragged the box into my kitchen, where Lawrence once stood. I have been mourning Lawrence at strange times. When the kiosk where I buy toothpaste reminded me to have a good day, because nobody's days are guaranteed, I shed a few tears. I believe this is known in the literature as sublimation.

The frictionless weeks gliding on. I stopped seeing films. Jonson hadn't gotten around to firing me from the *Slaw*, or perhaps this was his idea of mercy, so I filed reviews for films that didn't exist. Good fun for a while, but in time I found it sterile. Without other people to promulgate and resist one's passion, it becomes manageable, even routine. The stakes in such a life are no higher than those of a game of solitaire.

I opened the box.

It was an Okada Industries Filmmaking Kit, complete with tripod, two kliegs, an editing suite installed on a laptop, and a compact but impressive camera.

I set out to thank Dr. Lisa. Who else could have it been?

At the entrance to the Zone, I was detained.

The Transit agent said, Your permission to enter the Zone has been revoked.

I said, How come?

The Transit agent said, File says you smashed up a restaurant. The guest who owns the restaurant filed a complaint.

I said, My guilt hasn't been established in that matter.

The Transit agent spun his monitor around. There was a video of me flipping tables in the dumpling house. Rolling on the floor strangling myself. The camera even got the part where Osvald was whacking me on the nose with the porno mag.

I said, I never argue with what's on the screen.

I caught the Mauve Line back to Miniature Aleppo, as slow as was possible. A blurb of scarlet moon wove lemniscates. Children threw chunks of sidewalk at the cameras. A night for romance or at least groveling.

I pinged Dr. Lisa, i am dying / literally dying

I pinged, well i am figuratively dying / because i miss you

I pinged, jonson canceled the film because he wants to convince himself he's in love with an actress / and i spent a lot of his money

I pinged, please meet me by the austerity monument / two hours

I pinged, i will be wearing the expression of extreme contrition / and hopelessness

No response.

She didn't show up at the Austerity Monument.

Along with the Okada Kit there was a storage cube that I had assumed came with it. I was using it to prop a window. Arriving home from the monument, sitting at my desk, I noticed the cube was scratched up, as if it had been previously used.

On the cube, a single file, titled *A Replicate*, Rough Cut.

Open, Eastern Hub, drone footage. Rails coming in, rails leaving.

Here's Osvald as the rough sculptor Billy. Isabel as Mayor Alison, hair dyed white. Isabel lost weight and Osvald found it. Neither could act, but I knew that.

When it ended, I started it again.

Woof. Osvald allowed himself three speeches. Isabel thoroughly masticates the scenery, which is a rococo fantasy of poverty. When would the urchins burst into song? The man playing Isabel's husband, Gerald Horace, is a professional actor. Credits include *Septuplets!*, *Octuplets!*, conservation commercials. For his competence, he is awarded less than ten lines.

The best shots were mine. Osvald looted my brain. He used the triple-mirror. He used the close shots of the faces at night. He even took my argument between artist and patron, shot from the third-floor window of a building, in which it is never revealed who is doing the watching.

I was proud of my friends. The joy of creation is the only reliable joy, in my experience.

Not only was I proud, I was content, because I knew I could do much better.

The ending, sawn off *Altarpiece*. Mayor Alison looks on Billy's sculpture, declares it to be a masterpiece, and has Billy jailed on trumped-up charges so he cannot top it. She does not recognize that Billy's intentions were criminal.

Billy's nanoprinters do not work.

What he thought would smother the Eastern Hub in filaments

were actually minuscule dry-cleaning robots, meant to be released in one's closet. Mayor Alison's couture looks especially glamorous and wrinkle-free in the last five minutes of the film, after the release of the drybots.

Billy dies in the Eastern Hub Penitentiary, having said nothing since the unveiling of the sculpture. Silences are the wages of effort. In *Altarpiece*, Bellono is ordered to be hanged by Duke Giovanni for the same reason. Bellono chuckles on the gallows.

Bellono says, You can look at my painting, but you will never know it.

Final shot, his feet swinging.

On the third viewing, I slept.

More knocking at my door. I no longer had to go into the world to be disappointed. It was courteous enough to call at my apartment.

Dr. Lisa, white smock, black eye.

I said, What happened?

Dr. Lisa said, I was standing on a chair, hanging my touch-me-nots. The planter had an attitude.

I said, Would you like me to run out for an anti-inflammatory patch?

She said, I'm a doctor. Do you think I need your help performing perfunctory first aid?

I said, Need, no. Want, maybe.

She said, You haven't been making your appointments with the doctor I transferred you to.

I said, Osvald's gone. He was jealous of my friendship with Jonson. He pinged Jonson that I was keeping a secret from him, to break up our partnership for *Altarpiece*. Isn't that funny? He steals my wife, and he doesn't want me to have other friends?

She said, No more episodes? No more loss of bodily functions?

I said, No.

She said, That's good. I'm happy for you.

I said, Sit, please.

She said, There's slime on your chairs.

I said, Slime is a matter of opinion. The bed?

She said, It's full of crumbs.

I said, The floor, then.

We sat.

She said, Are you going to apologize?

I said, No.

She said, Will you try to justify your actions?

I said, No.

She said, Will you tell me you miss me or otherwise appeal to my emotions?

I said, What makes you think I miss you?

She pointed to the small picture of her face hanging on my wall.

I said, I hardly ever look at that wall. I prefer this wall. That wall is the wall of the past. This empty wall is the future.

She said, What do you see on the empty wall?

I said, Bugs and mildew. Will you act in my film? Millings is going to fund me.

She said, I think it's time to retire the painter.

I said, The thing I have in mind is an improvisation. Let's forget the vanities of control.

She said, Control is impossible.

I said, We could work with mistakes. I was dreaming of it before you woke me up. A man and a woman hate cinema. They go around the Hub wrecking projectors, tearing down posters, and roughing up critics. The possibilities for slapstick, for social commentary, for spectacle, are limited only by our imaginations.

Dr. Lisa said, I've never acted.

I said, Anyone who has lived has acted.

That was the genesis of *Rubber Paradise*, our collaboration. Osvald's crippled performance in *A Replicate* proved that I ought to stay behind the camera. I can't act. Millings, unusually photogenic, agreed to play Dr. Lisa's lover.

We filmed for two months during the magic hour, when the buttery light spreads well. Rolf and Dr. Lisa improvised the scenes. I couldn't resist a cameo. The pair flee from the smoking ruins of the Conspicuous to their getaway dinghy. Jogging to their blue doom, they pass a man, no longer young, watching the sun slip under the blushing crepe of the horizon. In his hands, a camera. All that's left to say is he is still dreaming his dream.